The Illustrious Prince

by

E. Phillips Oppenheim

The Illustrious Prince
by E. Phillips Oppenheim

Copyright © 2024

All Rights reserved.
No part of this publication may be reproduced, stored in a retrieval system, or transmitted in any form or by any means, electronic, mechanical, photocopying or Otherwise, without the written permission of the publisher.

The author/editor asserts the moral right to be identified as the author/editor of this work.

ISBN: 978-93-57273-19-0

Published by
DOUBLE 9 BOOKS
2/13-B, Ansari Road
Daryaganj, New Delhi – 110002
info@double9books.com
www.double9books.com
Tel. 011-40042856

This book is under public domain

ABOUT THE AUTHOR

E. Phillips Oppenheim was born on October 22, 1866, in Tohhenham, London, England, to Henrietta Susannah Temperley Budd and Edward John Oppenheim, a leather retailer. After leaving school at age 17, he helped his father in his leather business and used to write in his extra time. His first novel, Expiration (1886), and subsequent thrillers piqued the interest of a wealthy New York businessman who eventually bought out the leather business and made Oppenheim a high-paid director. He is more focused on dedicating most of his time to writing. The novels, volumes of short stories, and plays that followed, numbering more than 150, were about humans with modern heroes, fearless spies, and stylish noblemen. The Long Arm of Mannister (1910), The Moving Finger (1911), and The Great Impersonation (1920) are three of his most famous essays.

CONTENTS

CHAPTER I.
MR. HAMILTON FYNES, URGENT 7

CHAPTER II.
THE END OF THE JOURNEY 13

CHAPTER III.
AN INCIDENT AND AN ACCIDENT 17

CHAPTER IV.
MISS PENELOPE MORSE 25

CHAPTER V.
AN AFFAIR OF STATE 33

CHAPTER VI.
MR. COULSON INTERVIEWED 41

CHAPTER VII.
A FATAL DESPATCH 49

CHAPTER VIII.
AN INTERRUPTED THEATRE PARTY 59

CHAPTER IX.
INSPECTOR JACKS SCORES 71

CHAPTER X.
MR. COULSON OUTMATCHED 79

CHAPTER XI.
A COMMISSION 87

CHAPTER XII.
PENELOPE INTERVENES 95

CHAPTER XIII.
EAST AND WEST 105

CHAPTER XIV.
AN ENGAGEMENT 111

CHAPTER XV.
PENELOPE EXPLAINS 117

CHAPTER XVI.
CONCERNING PRINCE MAIYO 122

CHAPTER XVII.
A GAY NIGHT IN PARIS 128

CHAPTER XVIII.
MR. COULSON IS INDISCREET 134

CHAPTER XIX.
A MOMENTOUS QUESTION 138

CHAPTER XX.
THE ANSWER 145

CHAPTER XXI.
A CLUE 154

CHAPTER XXII.
A BREATH FROM THE EAST 161

CHAPTER XXIII.
ON THE TRAIL 168

CHAPTER XXIV.
PRINCE MAIYO BIDS HIGH 177

CHAPTER XXV.
HOBSON'S CHOICE 185

CHAPTER XXVI.
SOME FAREWELLS 193

CHAPTER XXVII.
A PRISONER 202

CHAPTER XXVIII.
PATRIOTISM 210

CHAPTER XXIX.
A RACE 217

CHAPTER XXX.
INSPECTOR JACKS IMPORTUNATE 226

CHAPTER XXXI.
GOODBYE! 233

CHAPTER XXXII.
PRINCE MAIYO SPEAKS 238

CHAPTER XXXIII.
UNAFRAID 248

CHAPTER XXXIV.
BANZAI! 254

CHAPTER I.
MR. HAMILTON FYNES, URGENT

There was a little murmur of regret amongst the five hundred and eighty-seven saloon passengers on board the steamship Lusitania, mingled, perhaps, with a few expressions of a more violent character. After several hours of doubt, the final verdict had at last been pronounced. They had missed the tide, and no attempt was to be made to land passengers that night. Already the engines had ceased to throb, the period of unnatural quietness had commenced. Slowly, and without noticeable motion, the great liner swung round a little in the river.

A small tug, which had been hovering about for some time, came screaming alongside. There was a hiss from its wave-splashed deck, and a rocket with a blue light flashed up into the sky. A man who had formed one of the long line of passengers, leaning over the rail, watching the tug since it had come into sight, now turned away and walked briskly to the steps leading to the bridge. As it happened, the captain himself was in the act of descending. The passenger accosted him, and held out what seemed to be a letter.

"Captain Goodfellow," he said, "I should be glad if you would glance at the contents of that note."

The captain, who had just finished a long discussion with the pilot and was not in the best of humor, looked a little surprised.

"What, now?" he asked.

"If you please," was the quiet answer. "The matter is urgent."

"Who are you?" the captain asked.

"My name is Hamilton Fynes," the other answered. "I am a saloon passenger on board your ship, although my name does not appear in the list. That note has been in my pocket since we left New York, to deliver to you in the event of a certain contingency happening."

"The contingency being?" the captain asked, tearing open the envelope and moving a little nearer the electric light which shone out from the smoking room.

"That the Lusitania did not land her passengers this evening."

The captain read the note, examined the signature carefully, and whistled softly to himself.

"You know what is inside this?" he asked, looking into his companion's face with some curiosity.

"Certainly," was the brief reply.

"Your name is Mr. Hamilton Fynes, the Mr. Hamilton Fynes mentioned in this letter?"

"That is so," the passenger admitted.

The captain nodded.

"Well," he said, "you had better get down on the lower deck, port side. By the bye, have you any friends with you?"

"I am quite alone," he answered.

"So much the better," the captain declared. "Don't tell any one that you are going ashore if you can help it."

"I certainly will not, sir," the other answered. "Thank you very much."

"Of course, you know that you can't take your luggage with you?" the captain remarked.

"That is of no consequence at all, sir," Mr. Hamilton Fynes answered. "I will leave instructions for my trunk to be sent on after me. I have all that I require, for the moment, in this suitcase."

The captain blew his whistle. Mr. Hamilton Fynes made his way quietly to the lower deck, which was almost deserted. In a very few minutes he was joined by half a dozen sailors, dragging a rope ladder. The little tug came screaming around, and before any of the passengers on the deck above had any idea of what was happening, Mr. Hamilton Fynes was on board the Anna Maria, and on his way down the river, seated in a small, uncomfortable cabin, lit by a single oil lamp.

No one spoke more than a casual word to him from the moment he stepped to the deck until the short journey was at an end. He was shown at once into the cabin, the door of which he closed without a moment's delay. A very brief examination of the interior convinced him that he was indeed alone. Thereupon he seated himself with his back to the wall and his face to the door, and finding an English newspaper on the table, read it until they reached the docks. Arrived there, he exchanged a civil good-night with the captain, and handed a sovereign to the seaman who held his bag while he disembarked.

For several minutes after he had stepped on to the wooden platform, Mr. Hamilton Fynes showed no particular impatience to continue his journey. He stood in the shadow of one of the sheds, looking about him with quick furtive glances, as though anxious to assure himself that there was no one around who was taking a noticeable interest in his movements. Having satisfied himself at length upon this point, he made his way to the London and North Western Railway Station, and knocked at the door of the station-master's office. The station-master was busy, and although Mr. Hamilton Fynes had the appearance of a perfectly respectable transatlantic man of business, there was nothing about his personality remarkably striking,—nothing, at any rate, to inspire an unusual amount of respect.

"You wished to see me, sir?" the official asked, merely glancing up from the desk at which he was sitting with a pile of papers before him.

Mr. Hamilton Fynes leaned over the wooden counter which separated him from the interior of the office. Before he spoke, he glanced around as though to make sure that he had not forgotten to close the door.

"I require a special train to London as quickly as possible," he announced. "I should be glad if you could let me have one within half an hour, at any rate."

The station-master rose to his feet.

"Quite impossible, sir," he declared a little brusquely. "Absolutely out of the question!"

"May I ask why it is out of the question?" Mr. Hamilton Fynes inquired.

"In the first place," the station-master answered, "a special train to London would cost you a hundred and eighty pounds, and in the second place, even if you were willing to pay that sum, it would be at least two hours before I could start you off. We could not possibly disorganize the whole of our fast traffic. The ordinary mail train leaves here at midnight with sleeping-cars."

Mr. Hamilton Fynes held out a letter which he had produced from his breast pocket, and which was, in appearance, very similar to the one which he had presented, a short time ago, to the captain of the Lusitania.

"Perhaps you will kindly read this," he said. "I am perfectly willing to pay the hundred and eighty pounds."

The station-master tore open the envelope and read the few lines contained therein. His manner underwent at once a complete change, very much as the manner of the captain of the Lusitania had done. He took the letter over to his green-shaded writing lamp, and examined the signature carefully. When he returned, he looked at Mr. Hamilton Fynes curiously. There was, however, something more than curiosity in his glance. There was also respect.

"I will give this matter my personal attention at once, Mr. Fynes," he said, lifting the flap of the counter and coming out. "Do you care to come inside and wait in my private office?"

"Thank you," Mr. Hamilton Fynes answered; "I will walk up and down the platform."

"There is a refreshment room just on the left," the station-master remarked, ringing violently at a telephone. "I dare say we shall get you off in less than half an hour. We will do our best, at any rate. It's an awkward time just now to command an absolutely clear line, but if we can once get you past Crewe you'll be all right. Shall we fetch you from the refreshment room when we are ready?"

"If you please," the intending passenger answered.

Mr. Hamilton Fynes discovered that place of entertainment without difficulty, ordered for himself a cup of coffee and a sandwich, and drew a chair close up to the small open fire, taking care, however, to sit almost facing the only entrance to the room. He laid his hat upon the counter, close to which he had taken up his position, and smoothed back with his left hand his somewhat thick black hair. He was a man, apparently of middle age, of middle height, clean-shaven, with good but undistinguished features, dark eyes, very clear and very bright, which showed, indeed, but little need of the pince-nez which hung by a thin black cord from his neck. His hat, low in the crown and of soft gray felt, would alone have betrayed his nationality. His clothes, however, were also American in cut. His boots were narrow and of unmistakable shape. He ate his sandwich with suspicion, and after his first sip of coffee ordered a whiskey and soda. Afterwards he sat leaning back in his chair, glancing every now and then at the clock, but otherwise manifesting no signs of impatience. In less than half an hour an inspector, cap in hand, entered the room and announced that everything was ready. Mr. Hamilton Fynes put on his hat, picked up his suitcase, and followed him on to the platform. A long saloon carriage, with a guard's brake behind and an engine in front, was waiting there.

"We've done our best, sir," the station-master remarked with a note of self-congratulation in his tone. "It's exactly twenty-two minutes since you came into the office, and there she is. Finest engine we've got on the line, and the best driver. You've a clear road ahead too. Wish you a pleasant journey, sir."

"You are very good, sir," Mr. Hamilton Fynes declared. "I am sure that my friends on the other side will appreciate your attention. By what time do you suppose that we shall reach London?"

The station-master glanced at the clock.

"It is now eight o'clock, sir," he announced. "If my orders down the line are properly attended to, you should be there by twenty minutes to twelve."

Mr. Hamilton Fynes nodded gravely and took his seat in the car. He had previously walked its entire length and back again.

"The train consists only of this carriage?" he asked. "There is no other passenger, for instance, travelling in the guard's brake?"

"Certainly not, sir," the station-master declared. "Such a thing would be entirely against the regulations. There are five of you, all told, on board,—driver, stoker, guard, saloon attendant, and yourself."

Mr. Hamilton Fynes nodded, and appeared satisfied.

"No more luggage, sir?" the guard asked.

"I was obliged to leave what I had, excepting this suitcase, upon the steamer," Mr. Hamilton Fynes explained. "I could not very well expect them to get my trunk up from the hold. It will follow me to the hotel tomorrow."

"You will find that the attendant has light refreshments on board, sir, if you should be wanting anything," the station-master announced. "We'll start you off now, then. Good-night, sir!"

Mr. Fynes nodded genially.

"Good-night, Station-master!" he said. "Many thanks to you."

CHAPTER II.
THE END OF THE JOURNEY

Southward, with low funnel belching forth fire and smoke into the blackness of the night, the huge engine, with its solitary saloon carriage and guard's brake, thundered its way through the night towards the great metropolis. Across the desolate plain, stripped bare of all vegetation, and made hideous forever by the growth of a mighty industry, where the furnace fires reddened the sky, and only the unbroken line of ceaseless lights showed where town dwindled into village and suburbs led back again into town. An ugly, thickly populated neighborhood, whose area of twinkling lights seemed to reach almost to the murky skies; hideous, indeed by day, not altogether devoid now of a certain weird attractiveness by reason of low-hung stars. On, through many tunnels into the black country itself, where the furnace fires burned oftener, but the signs of habitation were fewer. Down the great iron way the huge locomotive rushed onward, leaping and bounding across the maze of metals, tearing past the dazzling signal lights, through crowded stations where its passing was like the roar of some earth-shaking monster. The station-master at Crewe unhooked his telephone receiver and rang up Liverpool.

"What about this special?" he demanded.

"Passenger brought off from the Lusitania in a private tug. Orders are to let her through all the way to London."

"I know all about that," the station-master grumbled. "I have three locals on my hands already,—been held up for half an hour. Old Glynn, the director's, in one of them too. Might be General Manager to hear him swear."

"Is she signalled yet?" Liverpool asked.

"Just gone through at sixty miles an hour," was the reply. "She made our old wooden sheds shake, I can tell you. Who's driving her?"

"Jim Poynton," Liverpool answered. "The guvnor took him off the mail specially."

"What's the fellow's name on board, anyhow?" Crewe asked. "Is it a millionaire from the other side, trying to make records, or a member of our bloated aristocracy?"

"The name's Fynes, or something like it," was the reply. "He didn't look much like a millionaire. Came into the office carrying a small handbag and asked for a special to London. Guvnor told him it would take two hours and cost a hundred and eighty pounds. Told him he'd better wait for the mail. He produced a note from some one or other, and you should have seen the old man bustle round. We started him off in twenty minutes."

The station-master at Crewe was interested. He knew very well that it is not the easiest thing in the world to bring influence to bear upon a great railway company.

"Seems as though he was some one out of the common, anyway," he remarked. "The guvnor didn't let on who the note was from, I suppose?"

"Not he," Liverpool answered. "The first thing he did when he came back into the office was to tear it into small pieces and throw them on the fire. Young Jenkins did ask him a question, and he shut him up pretty quick."

"Well, I suppose we shall read all about it in the papers tomorrow," Crewe remarked. "There isn't much that these reporters don't get hold of. He must be some one out of the common—some one with a pull, I mean,—or the captain of the Lusitania would never have let him off before the other passengers. When are the rest of them coming through?"

"Three specials leave here at nine o'clock tomorrow morning," was the reply. "Good night."

The station-master at Crewe hung up his receiver and went about his duties. Twenty miles southward by now, the special was still tearing its way into the darkness. Its solitary passenger had suddenly developed a fit of restlessness. He left his seat and walked once or twice up and down the saloon. Then he opened the rear door, crossed the little open space between, and looked into the guard's brake. The guard was sitting upon a stool, reading a newspaper. He was quite alone, and so absorbed that he did not notice the intruder. Mr. Hamilton Fynes quietly retreated, closing the door behind him. He made his way once more through the saloon, passed the attendant, who was fast asleep in his pantry, and was met by a locked door. He let down the window and looked out. He was within a few feet of the engine, which was obviously attached direct to the saloon. Mr. Hamilton Fynes resumed his seat, having disturbed nobody. He produced some papers from his breast pocket, and spread them out on the table before him. One, a sealed envelope, he immediately returned, slipping it down into a carefully prepared place between the lining and the material of his coat. Of the others he commenced to make a close and minute investigation. It was a curious fact, however, that notwithstanding his recent searching examination, he looked once more nervously around the saloon before he settled down to his task. For some reason or other, there was not the slightest doubt that for the present, at any rate, Mr. Hamilton Fynes was exceedingly anxious to keep his own company. As he drew nearer to his journey's end, indeed, his manner seemed to lose something of that composure of which, during the earlier part of the evening, he had certainly been possessed. Scarcely a minute passed that he did not lean sideways from his seat and look up and down the saloon. He sat like a man who is perpetually on the qui vive. A furtive light shone in his eyes, he was manifestly uncomfortable. Yet how could a man be safer from espionage than he!

Rugby telephoned to Liverpool, and received very much the same answer as Crewe. Euston followed suit.

"Who's this you're sending up tonight?" the station-master asked. "Special's at Willington now, come through without a stop. Is some one trying to make a record round the world?"

Liverpool was a little tired of answering questions, and more than a little tired of this mysterious client. The station-master at Euston, however, was a person to be treated with respect.

"His name is Mr. Hamilton Fynes, sir," was the reply. "That is all we know about him. They have been ringing us up all down the line, ever since the special left."

"Hamilton Fynes," Euston repeated. "Don't know the name. Where did he come from?"

"Off the Lusitania, sir."

"But we had a message three hours ago that the Lusitania was not landing her passengers until tomorrow morning," Euston protested.

"They let our man off in a tug, sir," was the reply.

"It went down the river to fetch him. The guvnor didn't want to give him a special at this time of night, but he just handed him a note, and we made things hum up here. He was on his way in half an hour. We have had to upset the whole of the night traffic to let him through without a stop."

Such a client was, at any rate, worth meeting. The station-master brushed his coat, put on his silk hat, and stepped out on to the platform.

CHAPTER III.
AN INCIDENT AND AN ACCIDENT

Smoothly the huge engine came gliding into the station—a dumb, silent creature now, drawing slowly to a standstill as though exhausted after its great effort. Through the windows of the saloon the station-master could see the train attendant bending over this mysterious passenger, who did not seem, as yet, to have made any preparations for leaving his place. Mr. Hamilton Fynes was seated at a table covered with papers, but he was leaning back as though he had been or was still asleep. The station-master stepped forward, and as he did so the attendant came hurrying out to the platform, and, pushing back the porters, called to him by name.

"Mr. Rice," he said, "If you please, sir, will you come this way?"

The station-master acceded at once to the man's request and entered the saloon. The attendant clutched at his arm nervously. He was a pale, anaemic-looking little person at any time, but his face just now was positively ghastly.

"What on earth is the matter with you?" the station-master asked brusquely.

"There's something wrong with my passenger, sir," the man declared in a shaking voice. "I can't make him answer me. He won't look up, and I don't—I don't think he's asleep. An hour ago I took him some whiskey. He told me not to disturb him again—he had some papers to go through."

The station-master leaned over the table. The eyes of the man who sat there were perfectly wide-open, but there was something unnatural in their fixed stare,—something unnatural, too, in the drawn grayness of his face.

"This is Euston, sir," the station-master began,—"the terminus—"

Then he broke off in the middle of his sentence. A cold shiver was creeping through his veins. He, too, began to stare; he felt the color leaving his own cheeks. With an effort he turned to the attendant.

"Pull down the blinds," he ordered, in a voice which he should never have recognized as his own. "Quick! Now turn out those porters, and tell the inspector to stop anyone from coming into the car."

The attendant, who was shaking like a leaf, obeyed. The station-master turned away and drew a long breath. He himself was conscious of a sense of nausea, a giddiness which was almost overmastering. This was a terrible thing to face without a second's warning. He had not the slightest doubt but that the man who was seated at the table was dead!

At such an hour there were only a few people upon the platform, and two stalwart station policemen easily kept back the loiterers whose curiosity had been excited by the arrival of the special. A third took up his position with his back to the entrance of the saloon, and allowed no one to enter it till the return of the station-master, who had gone for a doctor. The little crowd was completely mystified. No one had the slightest idea of what had happened. The attendant was besieged by questions, but he was sitting on the step of the car, in the shadow of a policeman, with his head buried in his hands, and he did not once look up. Some of the more adventurous tried to peer through the windows at the lower end of the saloon. Others rushed off to interview the guard. In a very few minutes, however, the station-master reappeared upon the scene, accompanied by the doctor. The little crowd stood on one side and the two men stepped into the car.

The doctor proceeded at once with his examination. Mr. Hamilton Fynes, this mysterious person who had succeeded, indeed, in making a record journey, was leaning back in the corner of his seat, his arms folded, his head drooping a little, but his eyes still fixed in that unseeing stare. His body yielded itself unnaturally to the touch. For the main truth the doctor needed scarcely a glance at him.

"Is he dead?" the station-master asked.

"Stone-dead!" was the brief answer.

"Good God!" the station-master muttered. "Good God!"

The doctor had thrown his handkerchief over the dead man's face. He was standing now looking at him thoughtfully.

"Did he die in his sleep, I wonder?" the station-master asked. "It must have been horribly sudden! Was it heart disease?"

The doctor did not reply for a moment. He seemed to be thinking out some problem.

"The body had better be removed to the station mortuary," he said at last. "Then, if I were you, I should have the saloon shunted on to a siding and left absolutely untouched. You had better place two of your station police in charge while you telephone to Scotland Yard."

"To Scotland Yard?" the station-master exclaimed.

The doctor nodded. He looked around as though to be sure that none of that anxious crowd outside could overhear.

"There's no question of heart disease here," he explained. "The man has been murdered!"

The station-master was horrified,—horrified and blankly incredulous.

"Murdered!" he repeated. "Why, it's impossible! There was no one else on the train except the attendant—not a single other person. All my advices said one passenger only."

The doctor touched the man's coat with his finger, and the station-master saw what he had not seen before,—saw what made him turn away, a little sick. He was a strong man, but he was not used to this sort of thing, and he had barely recovered yet from the first shock of finding himself face to face with a dead man. Outside, the crowd upon the platform was growing larger. White faces were being pressed against the windows at the lower end of the saloon.

"There is no question about the man having been murdered," the doctor said, and even his voice shook a little. "His own hand could never have driven that knife home. I can tell you, even, how it was done. The man who stabbed him was in the compartment behind there, leaned over, and drove this thing down, just missing the shoulder. There was no struggle or fight of any sort. It was a diabolical deed!"

"Diabolical indeed!" the station-master echoed hoarsely.

"You had better give orders for us to be shunted down on to a siding just as we are," the doctor continued, "and send one of your men to telephone to Scotland Yard. Perhaps it would be as well, too, not to touch those papers until some one comes. See that the attendant does not go home, or the guard. They will probably be wanted to answer questions."

The station-master stepped out to the platform, summoned an inspector, and gave a few brief orders. Slowly the saloon was backed out of the station again on to a neglected siding, a sort of backwater for spare carriages and empty trucks,—an ignominious resting place, indeed, after its splendid journey through the night. The doors at both ends were closed and two policemen placed on duty to guard them. The doctor and the station-master seated themselves out of sight of their gruesome companion, and the station-master told all that he knew about the despatch of the special and the man who had ordered it. The attendant, who still moved about like a man in a dream, brought them some brandy and soda and served them with shaking hand. They all three talked together in whispers, the attendant telling them the few incidents of the journey down, which, except for the dead man's nervous desire for solitude, seemed to possess very little significance. Then at last there was a sharp tap at the window. A tall, quietly dressed man, with reddish skin and clear gray eyes, was helped up into the car. He saluted the doctor mechanically. His eyes were already travelling around the saloon.

"Inspector Jacks from Scotland Yard, sir," he announced. "I have another man outside. If you don't mind, we'll have him in."

"By all means," the station-master answered. "I am afraid that you will find this rather a serious affair. We have left everything untouched so far as we could."

The second detective was assisted to clamber up into the car. It seemed, however, as though the whole force of Scotland Yard could scarcely do much towards elucidating an affair which, with every question which was asked and answered, grew more mysterious. The papers upon the table before the dead man were simply circulars and prospectuses of no possible importance. His suitcase contained merely a few toilet necessaries and some clean linen. There was not a scrap of paper or even an envelope of any sort in his pockets. In a small leather case they found a thousand dollars in American notes, five ten-pound Bank of England notes, and a single visiting card on which was engraved the name of Mr. Hamilton Fynes. In his trousers pocket was a handful of gold. He had no other personal belongings of any sort. The space between the lining of his coat and the material itself was duly noticed, but it was empty. His watch was a cheap one, his linen unmarked, and his clothes bore only the name of a great New York retail establishment. He had certainly entered the train alone, and both the guard and attendant were ready to declare positively that no person could have been concealed in it. The engine-driver, on his part, was equally ready to swear that not once from the moment when they had steamed out of Liverpool Station until they had arrived within twenty miles of London, had they travelled at less than forty miles an hour. At Willington he had found a signal against him which had brought him nearly to a standstill, and under the regulations he had passed through the station at ten miles an hour. These were the only occasions, however, on which he had slackened speed at all. The train attendant, who was a nervous man, began to shiver again and imagine unmentionable things. The guard, who had never left his own brake, went home and dreamed that his effigy had been added to the collection of Madame Tussaud. The reporters were the only people who were really happy, with the exception, perhaps of Inspector Jacks, who had a weakness for a difficult case.

Fifteen miles north of London, a man lay by the roadside in the shadow of a plantation of pine trees, through which he had staggered only a few minutes ago. His clothes were covered with dust, he had lost his cap, and his trousers were cut about the knee as though from a fall. He was of somewhat less than medium height, dark, slender, with delicate features, and hair almost coal black. His face, as he moved slowly from side to side upon the grass, was livid with pain. Every now and then he raised himself and listened. The long belt of main road, which passed within a few feet of him, seemed almost deserted. Once a cart came lumbering by, and the man who lay there, watching, drew closely back into the shadows. A youth on a bicycle passed, singing to himself. A boy and girl strolled by, arm in arm, happy, apparently, in their profound silence. Only a couple of fields away shone the red and green lights of the railway track. Every few minutes the goods-trains went rumbling over the metals. The man on the ground heard them with a shiver. Resolutely he kept his face turned in the opposite direction. The night mail went thundering northward, and he clutched even at the nettles which grew amongst the grass where he was crouching, as though filled with a sudden terror. Then there was silence once more—silence which became deeper as the hour approached midnight. Passers-by were fewer; the birds and animals came out from their hiding places. A rabbit scurried across the road; a rat darted down the tiny stream. Now and then birds moved in the undergrowth, and the man, who was struggling all the time with a deadly faintness, felt the silence grow more and more oppressive. He began even to wonder where he was. He closed his eyes. Was that really the tinkling of a guitar, the perfume of almond and cherry blossom, floating to him down the warm wind? He began to lose himself in dreams until he realized that actual unconsciousness was close upon him. Then he set his teeth tight and clenched his hands. Away in the distance a faint, long-expected sound came travelling to his ears. At last, then, his long wait was over. Two fiery eyes were stealing along the lonely road. The throb of an engine was plainly audible. He staggered up, swaying a little on his feet, and holding out his hands. The motor car came to a standstill before him, and the man who was driving it sprang to the ground. Words passed between them rapidly,—questions and answers,—the questions of an affectionate servant, and the answers of a man fighting a grim battle for consciousness. But these two spoke in a language of their own, a language which no one who passed along that road was likely to understand.

With a groan of relief the man who had been picked up sank back amongst the cushioned seats, carefully almost tenderly, aided by the chauffeur. Eagerly he thrust his hand into one of the leather pockets and drew out a flask of brandy. The rush of cold air, as the car swung round and started off, was like new life to him. He closed his eyes. When he opened them again, they had come to a standstill underneath a red lamp.

"The doctor's!" he muttered to himself, and, staggering out, rang the bell.

Dr. Spencer Whiles had had a somewhat dreary day, and was thoroughly enjoying a late rubber of bridge with three of his most agreeable neighbors. A summons into the consulting room, however, was so unexpected a thing that he did not hesitate for a moment to obey it, without even waiting to complete a deal. When he entered the apartment, he saw a slim but determined-looking young man, whose clothes were covered with dust, and who, although he sat with folded arms and grim face, was very nearly in a state of collapse.

"You seem to have met with an accident," the doctor remarked. "How did it happen?"

"I have been run over by a motor car," his patient said, speaking slowly and with something singularly agreeable in his voice notwithstanding its slight accent of pain. "Can you patch me up till I get to London?"

The doctor looked him over.

"What were you doing in the road?" he asked.

"I was riding a bicycle," the other answered. "I dare say it was my own fault; I was certainly on the wrong side of the road. You can see what has happened to me. I am bruised and cut; my side is painful, and also my knee. A car is waiting outside now to take me to my home, but I thought that I had better stop and see you."

The doctor was a humane man, with a miserable practice, and he forgot all about his bridge party. For half an hour he worked over his patient. At the end of that time he gave him a brandy and soda and placed a box of cigarettes before him.

"You'll do all right now," he said. "That's a nasty cut on your leg, but you've no broken bones."

"I feel absolutely well again, thank you very much," the young man said. "I will smoke a cigarette, if I may. The brandy, I thank you, no!"

"Just as you like," the doctor answered. "I won't say that you are not better without it. Help yourself to the cigarettes. Are you going back to London in the motor car, then?"

"Yes!" the patient answered. "It is waiting outside for me now, and I must not keep the man any longer. Will you let me know, if you please, how much I owe you?"

The doctor hesitated. Fees were a rare thing with him, and the evidences of his patient's means were somewhat doubtful. The young man put his hand into his pocket.

"I am afraid," he said, "that I am not a very presentable-looking object, but I am glad to assure you that I am not a poor man. I am able to pay your charges and to still feel that the obligation is very much on my side."

The doctor summoned up his courage.

"We will say a guinea, then," he remarked with studied indifference.

"You must allow me to make it a little more than that," the patient answered. "Your treatment was worth it. I feel perfectly recovered already. Good night, sir!"

The doctor's eyes sparkled as he glanced at the gold which his visitor had laid upon the table.

"You are very good, I'm sure," he murmured. "I hope you will have a comfortable journey. With a nerve like yours, you'll be all right in a day or so."

He let his patient out and watched him depart with some curiosity, watched until the great motor-car had swung round the corner of the street and started on its journey to London.

"No bicycle there," he remarked to himself, as he closed the door. "I wonder what they did with it."

CHAPTER IV.
MISS PENELOPE MORSE

It was already a little past the customary luncheon hour at the Carlton, and the restaurant was well filled. The orchestra had played their first selection, and the stream of incoming guests had begun to slacken. A young lady who had been sitting in the palm court for at least half an hour rose to her feet, and, glancing casually at her watch, made her way into the hotel. She entered the office and addressed the chief reception clerk.

"Can you tell me," she asked, "if Mr. Hamilton Fynes is staying here? He should have arrived by the Lusitania last night or early this morning."

It is not the business of a hotel reception clerk to appear surprised at anything. Nevertheless the man looked at her, for a moment, with a curious expression in his eyes.

"Mr. Hamilton Fynes!" he repeated. "Did you say that you were expecting him by the Lusitania, madam?"

"Yes!" the young lady answered. "He asked me to lunch with him here today. Can you tell me whether he has arrived yet? If he is in his room, I should be glad if you would send up to him."

There were several people in the office who were in a position to overhear their conversation. With a word of apology, the man came round from his place behind the mahogany counter. He stood by the side of the young lady, and he seemed to be suffering from some embarrassment.

"Will you pardon my asking, madam, if you have seen the newspapers this morning?" he inquired.

Without a doubt, her first thought was that the question savored of impertinence. She looked at him with slightly upraised eyebrows. She was slim, of medium complexion, with dark brown hair parted in the middle and waving a little about her temples. She was irreproachably dressed, from the tips of her patent shoes to the black feathers in her Paris hat.

"The newspapers!" she repeated. "Why, no, I don't think that I have seen them this morning. What have they to do with Mr. Hamilton Fynes?"

The clerk pointed to the open door of a small private office.

"If you will step this way for one moment, madam," he begged.

She tapped the floor with her foot and looked at him curiously. Certainly the people around seemed to be taking some interest in their conversation.

"Why should I?" she asked. "Cannot you answer my question here?"

"If madam will be so good," he persisted.

She shrugged her shoulders and followed him. Something in the man's earnest tone and almost pleading look convinced her, at least, of his good intentions. Besides, the interest which her question had undoubtedly aroused amongst the bystanders was, to say the least of it, embarrassing. He pulled the door to after them.

"Madam," he said, "there was a Mr. Hamilton Fynes who came over by the Lusitania, and who had certainly engaged rooms in this hotel, but he unfortunately, it seems, met with an accident on his way from Liverpool."

Her manner changed at once. She began to understand what it all meant. Her lips parted, her eyes were wide open.

"An accident?" she faltered.

He gently rolled a chair up to her. She sank obediently into it.

"Madam," he said, "it was a very bad accident indeed. I trust that Mr. Hamilton Fynes was not a very intimate friend or a relative of yours. It would perhaps be better for you to read the account for yourself."

He placed a newspaper in her hands. She read the first few lines and suddenly turned upon him. She was white to the lips now, and there was real terror in her tone. Yet if he had been in a position to have analyzed the emotion she displayed, he might have remarked that there was none of the surprise, the blank, unbelieving amazement which might have been expected from one hearing for the first time of such a calamity.

"Murdered!" she exclaimed. "Is this true?"

"It appears to be perfectly true, madam, I regret to say," the clerk answered. "Even the earlier editions were able to supply the man's name, and I am afraid that there is no doubt about his identity. The captain of the Lusitania confirmed it, and many of the passengers who saw him leave the ship last night have been interviewed."

"Murdered!" she repeated to herself with trembling lips. "It seems such a horrible death! Have they any idea who did it?" she asked. "Has any one been arrested?"

"At present, no, madam," the clerk answered. "The affair, as you will see if you read further, is an exceedingly mysterious one."

She rocked a little in her chair, but she showed no signs of fainting. She picked up the paper and found the place once more. There were two columns filled with particulars of the tragedy.

"Where can I be alone and read this?" she asked.

"Here, if you please, madam," the clerk answered. "I must go back to my desk. There are many arrivals just now. Will you allow me to send you something—a little brandy, perhaps?"

"Nothing, thank you," she answered. "I wish only to be alone while I read this."

He left her with a little sympathetic murmur, and closed the door behind him. The girl raised her veil now and spread the newspaper out on the table before her. There was an account of the tragedy; there were interviews with some of the passengers, a message from the captain. In all, it seemed that wonderfully little was known of Mr. Hamilton Fynes. He had spoken to scarcely a soul on board, and had remained for the greater part of the time in his stateroom. The captain had not even been aware of his existence till the moment when Mr. Hamilton Fynes had sought him out and handed him an order, signed by the head of his company, instructing him to obey in any respect the wishes of this hitherto unknown passenger. The tug which had been hired to meet him had gone down the river, so it was not possible, for the moment, to say by whom it had been chartered. The station-master at Liverpool knew nothing except that the letter presented to him by the dead man was a personal one from a great railway magnate, whose wishes it was impossible to disregard. There had not been a soul, apparently, upon the steamer who had known anything worth mentioning of Mr. Hamilton Fynes or his business. No one in London had made inquiries for him or claimed his few effects. Half a dozen cables to America remained unanswered.

That papers had been stolen from him—papers or money—was evident from the place of concealment in his coat, where the lining had been torn away, but there was not the slightest evidence as to the nature of these documents or the history of the murdered man. All that could be done was to await the news from the other side, which was momentarily expected.

The girl went through it all, line by line, almost word by word. Whatever there might have been of relationship or friendship between her and the dead man, the news of his terrible end left her shaken, indeed, but dry-eyed. She was apparently more terrified than grieved, and now that the first shock had passed away, her mind seemed occupied with thoughts which may indeed have had some connection with this tragedy, but were scarcely wholly concerned with it. She sat for a long while with her hands still resting upon the table but her eyes fixed out of the window. Then at last she rose and made her way outside. Her friend the reception clerk was engaged in conversation with one or two men, a conversation of which she was obviously the subject. As she opened the door, one of them broke off in the midst of what he was saying and would have accosted her. The clerk, however, interposed, and drew her a step or two back into the room.

"Madam," he said, "one of these gentlemen is from Scotland Yard, and the others are reporters. They are all eager to know anything about Mr. Hamilton Fynes. I expect they will want to ask you some questions."

The girl opened her lips and closed them again.

"I regret to say that I have nothing whatever to tell them," she declared. "Will you kindly let them know that?"

The clerk shook his head.

"I am afraid you will find them quite persistent, madam," he said.

"I cannot tell them things which I do not know myself," she answered, frowning.

"Naturally," the clerk admitted; "yet these gentlemen from Scotland Yard have special privileges, of course, and there remains the fact that you were engaged to lunch with Mr. Fynes here."

"If it will help me to get rid of them," she said, "I will speak to the representative of Scotland Yard. I will have nothing whatever to say to the reporters."

The clerk turned round and beckoned to the foremost figure in the little group. Inspector Jacks, tall, lantern-jawed, dressed with the quiet precision of a well-to-do-man of affairs, and with no possible suggestion of his calling in his manner or attire, was by her side almost at once.

"Madam," he said, "I understand that Mr. Hamilton Fynes was a friend of yours?"

"An acquaintance," she corrected him.

"And your name?" he asked.

"I am Miss Morse," she replied,—"Miss Penelope Morse."

"You were to have lunched here with Mr. Hamilton Fynes," the detective continued. "When, may I ask, did the invitation reach you?"

"Yesterday," she told him, "by marconigram from Queenstown."

"You can tell us a few things about the deceased, without doubt," Mr. Jacks said,—"his profession, for instance, or his social standing? Perhaps you know the reason for his coming to Europe?"

The girl shook her head.

"Mr. Fynes and I were not intimately acquainted," she answered. "We met in Paris some years ago, and when he was last in London, during the autumn, I lunched with him twice."

"You had no letter from him, then, previous to the marconigram?" the inspector asked.

"I have scarcely ever received a letter from him in my life," she answered. "He was as bad a correspondent as I am myself."

"You know nothing, then, of the object of his present visit to England?"

"Nothing whatever," she answered.

"When he was over here before," the inspector asked, "do you know what his business was then?"

"Not in the least," she replied.

"You can tell us his address in the States?" Inspector Jacks suggested.

She shook her head.

"I cannot," she answered. "As I told you just now, I have never had a letter from him in my life. We exchanged a few notes, perhaps, when we were in Paris, about trivial matters, but nothing more than that."

"He must at some time, in Paris, for instance, or when you lunched with him last year, have said something about his profession, or how he spent his time?"

"He never alluded to it in any way," the girl answered. "I have not the slightest idea how he passed his time."

The inspector was a little nonplussed. He did not for a moment believe that the girl was telling the truth.

"Perhaps," he said tentatively, "you do not care to have your name come before the public in connection with a case so notorious as this?"

"Naturally," the girl answered. "That, however, would not prevent my telling you anything that I knew. You seem to find it hard to believe, but I can assure you that I know nothing. Mr. Fynes was almost a stranger to me."

The detective was thoughtful.

"So you really cannot help us at all, madam?" he said at length.

"I am afraid not," she answered.

"Perhaps," he suggested, "after you have thought the matter over, something may occur to you. Can I trouble you for your address?"

"I am staying at Devenham House for the moment," she answered.

He wrote it down in his notebook.

"I shall perhaps do myself the honor of waiting upon you a little later on," he said. "You may be able, after reflection, to recall some small details, at any rate, which will be interesting to us. At present we are absurdly ignorant as to the man's affairs."

She turned away from him to the clerk, and pointed to another door.

"Can I go out without seeing those others?" she asked. "I really have nothing to say to them, and this has been quite a shock to me."

"By all means, madam," the clerk answered. "If you will allow me, I will escort you to the entrance."

Two of the more enterprising of the journalists caught them up upon the pavement. Miss Penelope Morse, however, had little to say to them.

"You must not ask me any more questions about Mr. Hamilton Fynes," she declared. "My acquaintance with him was of the slightest. It is true that I came here to lunch today without knowing what had happened. It has been a shock to me, and I do not wish to talk about it, and I will not talk about it, for the present."

She was deaf to their further questions. The hotel clerk handed her into a taximeter cab, and gave the address to the driver. Then he went back to his office, where Inspector Jacks was still sitting.

"This Mr. Hamilton Fynes," he remarked, "seems to have been what you might call a secretive sort of person. Nobody appears to know anything about him. I remember when he was staying here before that he had no callers, and seemed to spend most of his time sitting in the palm court."

The inspector nodded.

"He was certainly a man who knew how to keep his own counsel," he admitted. "Most Americans are ready enough to talk about themselves and their affairs, even to comparative strangers."

The hotel clerk nodded.

"Makes it difficult for you," he remarked.

"It makes the case very interesting," the inspector declared, "especially when we find him engaged to lunch with a young lady of such remarkable discretion as Miss Penelope Morse."

"You know her?" the clerk asked a little eagerly.

The inspector was engaged, apparently, in studying the pattern of the carpet.

"Not exactly," he answered. "No, I have no absolute knowledge of Miss Penelope Morse. By the bye, that was rather an interesting address that she gave."

"Devenham House," the hotel clerk remarked. "Do you know who lives there?"

The inspector nodded.

"The Duke of Devenham," he answered. "A very interesting young lady, I should think, that. I wonder what she and Mr. Hamilton Fynes would have talked about if they had lunched here today."

The hotel clerk looked dubious. He did not grasp the significance of the question.

CHAPTER V.
AN AFFAIR OF STATE

Miss Penelope Morse was perfectly well aware that the taxicab in which she left the Carlton Hotel was closely followed by two others. Through the tube which she found by her side, she altered her first instructions to the driver, and told him to proceed as fast as possible to Harrod's Stores. Then, raising the flap at the rear of the cab, she watched the progress of the chase. Along Pall Mall the taxi in which she was seated gained considerably, but in the Park and along the Bird Cage Walk both the other taxies, risking the police regulations, drew almost alongside. Once past Hyde Park Corner, however, her cab again drew ahead, and when she was deposited in front of Harrod's Stores, her pursuers were out of sight. She paid the driver quickly, a little over double his fare.

"If any one asks you questions," she said, "say that you had instructions to wait here for me. Go on to the rank for a quarter of an hour. Then you can drive away."

"You won't be coming back, then, miss?" the man asked.

"I shall not," she answered, "but I want those men who are following me to think that I am. They may as well lose a little time for their rudeness."

The chauffeur touched his hat and obeyed his instructions. Miss Penelope Morse plunged into the mazes of the Stores with the air of one to whom the place is familiar. She did not pause, however, at any of the counters. In something less than two minutes she had left it again by a back entrance, stepped into another taxicab which was just setting down a passenger, and was well on her way back towards Pall Mall. Her ruse appeared to have been perfectly successful. At any rate, she saw nothing more of the occupants of the two taxicabs.

She stopped in front of one of the big clubs and, scribbling a line on her card, gave it to the door keeper.

"Will you find out if this gentleman is in?" she said. "If he is, will you kindly ask him to step out and speak to me?"

She returned to the cab and waited. In less than five minutes a tall, broad-shouldered young man, clean-shaven, and moving like an athlete, came briskly down the steps. He carried a soft hat in his hand, and directly he spoke his transatlantic origin was apparent.

"Penelope!" he exclaimed. "Why, what on earth—"

"My dear Dicky," she interrupted, laughing at his expression, "you need not look so displeased with me. Of course, I know that I ought not to have come and sent a message into your club. I will admit at once that it was very forward of me. Perhaps when I have told you why I did so, you won't look so shocked."

"I'm glad to see you, anyway," he declared. "There's no bad news, I hope?"

"Nothing that concerns us particularly," she answered. "I simply want to have a little talk with you. Come in here with me, please, at once. We can ride for a short distance anywhere."

"But I am just in the middle of a rubber of bridge," he objected.

"It can't be helped," she declared. "To tell you the truth, the matter I want to talk to you about is of more importance than any game of cards. Don't be foolish, Dicky. You have your hat in your hand. Step in here by my side at once."

He looked a little bewildered, but he obeyed her, as most people did when she was in earnest. She gave the driver an address somewhere in the city. As soon as they were off, she turned towards him.

"Dicky," she said, "do you read the newspapers?"

"Well, I can't say that I do regularly," he answered. "I read the New York Herald, but these London journals are a bit difficult, aren't they? One has to dig the news out,—sort of treasure-hunt all the time."

"You have read this murder case, at any rate," she asked, "about the man who was killed in a special train between Liverpool and London?"

"Of course," he answered, with a sudden awakening of interest. "What about it?"

"A good deal," she answered slowly. "In the first place, the man who was murdered—Mr. Hamilton Fynes—comes from the village where I was brought up in Massachusetts, and I know more about him, I dare say, than any one else in this country. What I know isn't very much, perhaps, but it's interesting. I was to have lunched with him at the Carlton today; in fact, I went there expecting to do so, for I am like you—I scarcely ever look inside these English newspapers. Well, I went to the Carlton and waited and he did not come. At last I went into the office and asked whether he had arrived. Directly I mentioned his name, it was as though I had thrown a bomb shell into the place. The clerk called me on one side, took me into a private office, and showed me a newspaper. As soon as I had read the account, I was interviewed by an inspector from Scotland Yard. Ever since then I have been followed about by reporters."

The young man whistled softly.

"Say, Penelope!" he exclaimed. "Who was this fellow, anyhow, and what were you doing lunching with him?"

"That doesn't matter," she answered. "You don't tell me all your secrets, Mr. Dicky Vanderpole, and it isn't necessary for me to tell you all mine, even if we are both foreigners in a strange country. The poor fellow isn't going to lunch with any one else in this world. I suppose you are thinking what an indiscreet person I am, as usual?"

The young man considered the matter for a moment.

"No," he said; "I didn't understand that he was the sort of person you would have been likely to have taken lunch with. But that isn't my affair. Have you seen the second edition?"

The girl shook her head.

"Haven't I told you that I never read the papers? I only saw what they showed me in at the Carlton."

"The Press Association have cabled to America, but no one seems to be able to make out exactly who the fellow is. His letter to the captain of the steamer was from the chairman of the company, and his introduction to the manager of the London and North Western Railway Company was from the greatest railway man in the world. Mr. Hamilton Fynes must have been a person who had a pretty considerable pull over there. Curiously enough, though, only the name of the man was mentioned in them; nothing about his business, or what he was doing over on this side. He was simply alluded to as

'Mr. Hamilton Fynes—the gentleman bearing this communication.' I expect, after all, that you know more about him than any one."

She shook her head.

"What I know," she said, "or at least most of it, I am going to tell you. A few years ago he was a clerk in a Government office in Washington. He was steady in those days, and was supposed to have a head. He used to write me occasionally. One day he turned up in London quite unexpectedly. He said that he had come on business, and whatever his business was, it took him to St. Petersburg and Berlin, and then back to Berlin again. I saw quite a good deal of him that trip."

"The dickens you did!" he muttered.

Miss Penelope Morse laughed softly.

"Come, Dicky," she said, "don't pretend to be jealous. You're an outrageous flirt, I know, but you and I are never likely to get sentimental about one another."

"Why not?" he grumbled. "We've always been pretty good pals, haven't we?"

"Naturally," she answered, "or I shouldn't be here. Do you want to hear anything more about Mr. Hamilton Fynes?"

"Of course I do," he declared.

"Well, be quiet, then, and don't interrupt," she said. "I knew London well and he didn't. That is why, as I told you before, we saw quite a great deal of one another. He was always very reticent about his affairs, and especially about the business which had taken him on the Continent. Just before he left, however, he gave me—well, a hint."

"What was it?" the young man asked eagerly.

She hesitated.

"He didn't put it into so many words," she said, "and I am not sure, even now, that I ought to tell you, Dicky. Still, you are a fellow countryman and a budding diplomatist. I suppose if I can give you a lift I ought to."

The taxi was on the Embankment now, and they sped along for some time in silence. Mr. Richard Vanderpole was more than a little puzzled.

"Of course, Penelope," he said, "I don't expect you to tell me anything which you feel that you oughtn't to. There is one thing, however, which I must ask you."

She nodded.

"Well?"

"I should like to know what the mischief my being in the diplomatic service has to do with it?"

"If I explained that," she answered, "I should be telling you everything I haven't quite made up my mind to do that yet."

"Tell me this?" he asked. "Would that hint which he dropped when he was here last help you to solve the mystery of his murder?"

"It might," she admitted.

"Then I think," he said, "apart from any other reason, you ought to tell somebody. The police at present don't seem to have the ghost of a clue."

"They are not likely to find one," she answered, "unless I help them."

"Say, Penelope," he exclaimed, "you are not in earnest?"

"I am," she assured him. "It is exactly as I say. I believe I am one of the few people who could put the police upon the right track."

"Is there any reason why you shouldn't?" he asked.

"That's just what I can't make up my mind about," she told him. "However, I have brought you out with me expecting to hear something, and I am going to tell you this. That last time he came to England—the time he went to St. Petersburg and twice to Berlin—he came on government business."

The young man looked, for a moment, incredulous.

"Are you sure of that, Pen?" he asked. "It doesn't sound like our people, you know, does it?"

"I am quite sure," she declared confidently. "You are a very youthful diplomat, Dicky, but even you have probably heard of governments who employ private messengers to carry despatches which for various reasons they don't care to put through their embassies."

"Why, that's so, of course, over on this side," he agreed. "These European nations are up to all manner of tricks. But I tell you frankly, Pen, I never heard of anything of the sort being done from Washington."

"Perhaps not," she answered composedly. "You see, things have developed with us during the last twenty-five years. The old America had only one foreign policy, and that was to hold inviolate the Monroe doctrine. European or Asiatic complications scarcely even interested her. Those times have passed, Dicky. Cuba and the Philippines were the start of other things. We are being drawn into the maelstrom. In another ten years we shall be there, whether we want to be or not."

The young man was deeply interested.

"Well," he admitted, "there's a good deal in what you say, Penelope. You talk about it all as though you were a diplomat yourself."

"Perhaps I am," she answered calmly. "A stray young woman like myself must have something to occupy her thoughts, you know."

He laughed.

"That's not bad," he asserted, "for a girl whom the New York Herald declared, a few weeks ago, to be one of the most brilliant young women in English society."

She shrugged her shoulders scornfully.

"That's just the sort of thing the New York Herald would say," she remarked. "You see, I have to get a reputation for being smart and saying bright things, or nobody would ask me anywhere. Penniless American young women are not too popular over here."

"Marry me, then," he suggested amiably. "I shall have plenty of money some day."

"I'll see about it when you're grown up," she answered. "Just at present, I think we'd better return to the subject of Hamilton Fynes."

Mr. Richard Vanderpole sighed, but seemed not disinclined to follow her suggestion.

"Harvey is a silent man, as you know," he said thoughtfully, "and he keeps everything of importance to himself. At the same time these little matters get about in the shop, of course, and I have never heard of any despatches being brought across from Washington except in the usual way. Presuming that you are right," he added after a moment's pause, "and that this fellow Hamilton Fynes really had something for us, that would account for his being able to get off the boat and securing his special train so easily. No one can imagine where he got the pull."

"It accounts, also," Penelope remarked, "for his murder!"

Her companion started.

"You haven't any idea—" he began.

"Nothing so definite as an idea," she interrupted. "I am not going so far as to say that. I simply know that when a man is practically the secret agent of his government, and is probably carrying despatches of an important nature, that an accident such as he has met with, in a country which is greatly interested in the contents of those despatches, is a somewhat serious thing."

The young man nodded.

"Say," he admitted "you're dead right. The Pacific cruise, and our relations with Japan, seem to have rubbed our friends over here altogether the wrong way. We have irritations enough already to smooth over, without anything of this sort on the carpet."

"I am going to tell you now," she continued, leaning a little towards him, "the real reason why I fetched you out of the club this afternoon and have brought you for this little expedition. The last time I lunched with Mr. Hamilton Fynes was just after his return from Berlin. He intrusted me then with a very important mission. He gave me a letter to deliver to Mr. Blaine Harvey."

"But I don't understand!" he protested. "Why should he give you the letter when he was in London himself?"

"I asked him that question myself, naturally," she answered. "He told me that it was an understood thing that when he was over here on business he was not even to cross the threshold of the Embassy, or hold any direct communication with any person connected with it. Everything had to be done through a third party, and generally in duplicate. There was another man, for instance, who had a copy of the same letter, but I never came across him or even knew his name."

"Gee whiz!" the young man exclaimed. "You're telling me things, and no mistake! Why this fellow Fynes made a secret service messenger of you!"

Penelope nodded.

"It was all very simple," she said. "The first Mrs. Harvey, who was alive then, was my greatest friend, and I was in and out of the place all the time. Now, perhaps, you can understand the significance of that marconigram from Hamilton Fynes asking me to lunch with him at the Carlton today."

Mr. Richard Vanderpole was sitting bolt upright, gazing steadily ahead.

"I wonder," he said slowly, "what has become of the letter which he was going to give you!"

"One thing is certain," she declared. "It is in the hands of those whose interests would have been affected by its delivery."

"How much of this am I to tell the chief?" the young man asked.

"Every word," Penelope answered. "You see, I am trying to give you a start in your career. What bothers me is an entirely different question."

"What is it?" he asked.

She laid her hand upon his arm.

"How much of it I shall tell to a certain gentleman who calls himself Inspector Jacks!"

CHAPTER VI.
MR. COULSON INTERVIEWED

The Lusitania boat specials ran into Euston Station soon after three o'clock in the afternoon. A small company of reporters, and several other men whose profession was not disclosed from their appearance, were on the spot to interview certain of the passengers. A young fellow from the office of the Evening Comet was, perhaps, the most successful, as, from the lengthy description which had been telegraphed to him from Liverpool, he was fortunate enough to accost the only person who had been seen speaking to the murdered man upon the voyage.

"This is Mr. Coulson, I believe?" the young man said with conviction, addressing a somewhat stout, gray-headed American, with white moustache, a Homburg hat, and clothes of distinctly transatlantic cut.

That gentlemen regarded his interlocutor with some surprise but without unfriendliness.

"That happens to be my name, sir," he replied. "You have the advantage of me, though. You are not from my old friends Spencer & Miles, are you?"

"Spencer & Miles," the young man repeated thoughtfully.

"Woollen firm in London Wall," Mr. Coulson added. "I know they wanted to see me directly I arrived, and they did say something about sending to the station."

The young man shook his head, and assumed at the same time his most engaging manner.

"Why, no, sir!" he admitted. "I have no connection with that firm at all. The fact is I am on the staff of an evening paper. A friend of mine in Liverpool—a mutual friend, I believe I may say," he explained—

"wired me your description. I understand that you were acquainted with Mr. Hamilton Fynes?"

Mr. Coulson set down his suitcase for a moment, to light a cigar.

"Well, if I did know the poor fellow just to nod to," he said, "I don't see that's any reason why I should talk about him to you newspaper fellows. You'd better get hold of his relations, if you can find them."

"But, my dear Mr. Coulson," the young man said, "we haven't any idea where they are to be found, and in the meantime you can't imagine what reports are in circulation."

"Guess I can figure them out pretty well," Mr. Coulson remarked with a smile. "We've got an evening press of our own in New York."

The reporter nodded.

"Well," he said, "They'd be able to stretch themselves out a bit on a case like this. You see," he continued confidentially, "we are up against something almost unique. Here is an astounding and absolutely inexplicable murder, committed in a most dastardly fashion by a person who appears to have vanished from the face of the earth. Not a single thing is known about the victim except his name. We do not know whether he came to England on business or pleasure. He may, in short, have been any one from a millionaire to a newspaper man. Judging from his special train," the reporter concluded with a smile, "and the money which was found upon him, I imagine that he was certainly not the latter."

Mr. Coulson went on his way toward the exit from the station, puffing contentedly at his big cigar.

"Well," he said to his companion, who showed not the slightest disposition to leave his side, "it don't seem to me that there's much worth repeating about poor Fynes,—much that I knew, at any rate. Still, if you like to get in a cab with me and ride as far as the Savoy, I'll tell you what I can."

"You are a brick, sir," the young man declared. "Haven't you any luggage, though?"

"I checked what I had through from Liverpool to the hotel," Mr. Coulson answered. "I can't stand being fussed around by all these porters, and having to go and take pot luck amongst a pile of other people's baggage. We'll just take one of these two-wheeled sardine tins that you people call hansoms, and get round to the hotel as quick as we can. There are a few pals of mine generally lunch in the cafe there, and they mayn't all have cleared out if we look alive."

They started a moment or two later. Mr. Coulson leaned forward and, folding his arms upon the apron of the cab, looked about him with interest.

"Say," he remarked, removing his cigar to the corner of his mouth in order to facilitate conversation, "this old city of yours don't change any."

"Not up in this part, perhaps," the reporter agreed. "We've some fine new buildings down toward the Strand."

Mr. Coulson nodded.

"Well," he said, "I guess you don't want to be making conversation. You want to know about Hamilton Fynes. I was just acquainted with him, and that's a fact, but I reckon you'll have to find some one who knows a good deal more than I do before you'll get the stuff you want for your paper."

"The slightest particulars are of interest to us just now," the reporter reminded him.

Mr. Coulson nodded.

"Hamilton Fynes," he said, "so far as I knew him, was a quiet, inoffensive sort of creature, who has been drawing a regular salary from the State for the last fifteen years and saving half of it. He has been coming over to Europe now and then, and though he was a good, steady chap enough, he liked his fling when he was over here, and between you and me, he was the greatest crank I ever struck. I met him in London a matter of three years ago, and he wanted to go to Paris. There were two cars running at the regular time, meeting the boat at Dover. Do you think he would have anything to do with them? Not he! He hired a special train and went down like a prince."

"What did he do that for?" the reporter asked.

"Why, because he was a crank, sir," Mr. Coulson answered confidentially. "There was no other reason at all. Take this last voyage on the Lusitania, now. He spoke to me the first day out because he couldn't help it, but for pretty well the rest of the journey he either kept down in his stateroom or, when he came up on deck, he avoided me and everybody else. When he did talk, his talk was foolish. He was a good chap at his work, I believe, but he was a crank. Seemed to me sometimes as though that humdrum life of his had about turned his brain. The last day out he was fidgeting all the time; kept looking at his watch, studying the chart, and asking the sailors questions. Said he wanted to get up in time to take a girl to lunch on Thursday. It was just for that reason that he scuttled off the boat without a word to any of us, and rushed up to London."

"But he had letters, Mr. Coulson," the reporter reminded him, "from some one in Washington, to the captain of the steamer and to the station-master of the London and North Western Railway. It seems rather odd that he should have provided himself with these, doesn't it?"

"They were easy enough to get," Mr. Coulson answered. "He wasn't a worrying sort of chap, Fynes wasn't. He did his work, year in and year out, and asked no favors. The consequence was that when he asked a queer one he got it all right. It's easier to get a pull over there than it is here, you know."

"This is all very interesting," the reporter said, "and I am sure I'm very much obliged to you, Mr. Coulson. Now can you tell me of anything in the man's life or way of living likely to provoke enmity on the part of any one? This murder was such a cold-blooded affair."

"There I'm stuck," Mr. Coulson admitted. "There's only one thing I can tell you, and that is that I believe he had a lot more money on him than the amount mentioned in your newspapers this morning. My own opinion is that he was murdered for what he'd got. A smart thief would say that a fellow who takes a special tug off the steamer and a special train to town was a man worth robbing. How the thing was done I don't know—that's for your police to find out—but I reckon that whoever killed him did it for his cash."

The reporter sighed. He was, after all, a little disappointed. Mr. Coulson was obviously a man of common sense. His words were clearly pronounced, and his reasoning sound. They had reached the courtyard of the hotel now, and the reporter began to express his gratitude.

"My first drink on English soil," Mr. Coulson said, as he handed his suitcase to the hall-porter, "is always—"

"It's on me," the young man declared quickly. "I owe you a good deal more than drinks, Mr. Coulson."

"Well, come along, anyway," the latter remarked. "I guess my room is all right, porter?"—turning to the man who stood by his side, bag in hand. "I am Mr. James B. Coulson of New York, and I wrote on ahead. I'll come round to the office and register presently."

They made their way to the American bar. The newspaper man and his new friend drank together and, skillfully prompted by the former, the conversation drifted back to the subject of Hamilton Fynes. There was nothing else to be learned, however, in the way of facts. Mr. Coulson admitted that he had been a little nettled by his friend's odd manner during the voyage, and the strange way he had of keeping to himself.

"But, after all," he wound up, "Fynes was a crank, when all's said and done. We are all cranks, more or less,—all got our weak spot, I mean. It was secretiveness with our unfortunate friend. He liked to play at being a big personage in a mysterious sort of way, and the poor chap's paid for it," he added with a sigh.

The reporter left his new-made friend a short time afterwards, and took a hansom to his office. His newspaper at once issued a special edition, giving an interview between their representative and Mr. James B. Coulson, a personal friend of the murdered man. It was, after all, something of a scoop, for not one of the other passengers had been found who was in a position to say anything at all about him. The immediate effect of the interview, however, was to procure for Mr. Coulson a somewhat bewildering succession of callers. The first to arrive was a gentleman who introduced himself as Mr. Jacks, and whose card, sent back at first, was retendered in a sealed envelope with Scotland Yard scrawled across the back of it. Mr. Coulson, who was in the act of changing his clothes, interviewed Mr. Jacks in his chamber.

"Mr. Coulson," the Inspector said, "I am visiting you on behalf of Scotland Yard. We understand that you had some acquaintance with Mr. Hamilton Fynes, and we hope that you will answer a few questions for us."

Mr. Coulson sat down upon a trunk with his hairbrushes in his hand.

"Well," he declared, "you detectives do get to know things, don't you?"

"Nothing so remarkable in that, Mr. Coulson," Inspector Jacks remarked pleasantly. "A newspaper man had been before me, I see."

Mr. Coulson nodded.

"That's so," he admitted. "Seems to me I may have been a bit indiscreet in talking so much to that young reporter. I have just read his account of my interview, and he's got it pat, word by word. Now, Mr. Jacks, if you'll just invest a halfpenny in that newspaper, you don't need to ask me any questions. That young man had a kind of pleasant way with him, and I told him all I knew."

"Just so, Mr. Coulson," the Inspector answered. "At the same time nothing that you told him throws any light at all upon the circumstances which led to the poor fellow's death."

"That," Mr. Coulson declared, "is not my fault. What I don't know I can't tell you."

"You were acquainted with Mr. Fynes some years ago?" the Inspector asked. "Can you tell me what business he was in then?"

"Same as now, for anything I know," Mr. Coulson answered. "He was a clerk in one of the Government offices at Washington."

"Government offices," Inspector Jacks repeated. "Have you any idea what department?"

Mr. Coulson was not sure.

"It may have been the Excise Office," he remarked thoughtfully. "I did hear, but I never took any particular notice."

"Did you ever form any idea as to the nature of his work?" Inspector Jacks asked.

"Bless you, no!" Mr. Coulson replied, brushing his hair vigorously. "It never entered into my head to ask him, and I never heard him mention it. I only know that he was a quiet-living, decent sort of a chap, but, as I put it to our young friend the newspaper man, he was a crank."

The Inspector was disappointed. He began to feel that he was wasting his time.

"Did you know anything of the object of his journey to Europe?" he asked.

"Nary a thing," Mr. Coulson declared. "He only came on deck once or twice, and he had scarcely a civil word even for me. Why, I tell you, sir," Mr. Coulson continued, "if he saw me coming along on the promenade, he'd turn round and go the other way, for fear I'd ask him to come and have a drink. A c-r-a-n-k, sir! You write it down at that, and you won't be far out."

"He certainly seems to have been a queer lot," the Inspector declared. "By the bye," he continued, "you said something, I believe, about his having had more money with him than was found upon his person."

"That's so," Mr. Coulson admitted. "I know he deposited a pocketbook with the purser, and I happened to be standing by when he received it back. I noticed that he had three or four thousand-dollar bills, and there didn't seem to be anything of the sort upon him when he was found."

The Inspector made a note of this.

"You believe yourself, then, Mr. Coulson," he said, closing his pocketbook, "that the murder was committed for the purpose of robbery?"

"Seems to me it's common sense," Mr. Coulson replied. "A man who goes and takes a special train to London from the docks of a city like Liverpool—a city filled with the scum of the world, mind you—kind of gives himself away as a man worth robbing, doesn't he?"

The Inspector nodded.

"That's sensible talk, Mr. Coulson," he acknowledged. "You never heard, I suppose, of his having had a quarrel with any one?"

"Never in my life," Mr. Coulson declared. "He wasn't the sort to make enemies, any more than he was the sort to make friends."

The Inspector took up his hat. His manner now was no longer inquisitorial. With the closing of his notebook a new geniality had taken the place of his official stiffness.

"You are making a long stay here, Mr. Coulson?" he asked.

"A week or so, maybe," that gentleman answered. "I am in the machinery patent line—machinery for the manufacture of woollen goods mostly—and I have a few appointments in London. Afterwards I am going on to Paris. You can hear of me at any time either here or at the Grand Hotel, Paris, but there's nothing further to be got out of me as regards Mr. Hamilton Fynes."

The Inspector was of the same opinion and took his departure. Mr. Coulson waited for some little time, still sitting on his trunk and clasping his hairbrushes. Then he moved over to the table on which stood the telephone instrument and asked for a number. The reply came in a minute or two in the form of a question.

"It's Mr. James B. Coulson from New York, landed this afternoon from the Lusitania," Mr. Coulson said. "I am at the Savoy Hotel, speaking from my room—number 443."

There was a brief silence—then a reply.

"You had better be in the bar smoking-room at seven o'clock. If nothing happens, don't leave the hotel this evening."

Mr. Coulson replaced the receiver and rang off. A page-boy knocked at the door.

"Young lady downstairs wishes to see you, sir," he announced.

Mr. Coulson took up the card from the tray.

"Miss Penelope Morse," he said softly to himself. "Seems to me I'm rather popular this evening. Say I'll be down right away, my boy."

"Very good, sir," the page answered. "There's a gentleman with her, sir. His card's underneath the lady's."

Mr. Coulson examined the tray once more. A gentleman's visiting card informed him that his other caller was Sir Charles Somerfield, Bart.

"Bart," Mr. Coulson remarked thoughtfully. "I'm not quite catching on to that, but I suppose he goes in with the young lady."

"They're both together, sir," the boy announced.

Mr. Coulson completed his toilet and hurried downstairs

CHAPTER VII.
A FATAL DESPATCH

Mr. Coulson found his two visitors in the lounge of the hotel. He had removed all traces of his journey, and was attired in a Tuxedo dinner coat, a soft-fronted shirt, and a neatly arranged black tie. He wore broad-toed patent boots and double lines of braid down the outsides of his trousers. The page boy, who was on the lookout for him, conducted him to the corner where Miss Penelope Morse and her companion were sitting talking together. The latter rose at his approach, and Mr. Coulson summed him up quickly,—a well-bred, pleasant-mannered, exceedingly athletic young Englishman, who was probably not such a fool as he looked,—that is, from Mr. Coulson's standpoint, who was not used to the single eyeglass and somewhat drawling enunciation.

"Mr. Coulson, isn't it?" the young man asked, accepting the other's outstretched hand. "We are awfully sorry to disturb you, so soon after your arrival, too, but the fact is that this young lady, Miss Penelope Morse,"—Mr. Coulson bowed,—"was exceedingly anxious to make your acquaintance. You Americans are such birds of passage that she was afraid you might have moved on if she didn't look you up at once."

Penelope herself intervened.

"I'm afraid you're going to think me a terrible nuisance, Mr. Coulson!" she exclaimed. Mr. Coulson, although he did not call himself a lady's man, was nevertheless human enough to appreciate the fact that the young lady's face was piquant and her smile delightful. She was dressed with quiet but elegant simplicity. The perfume of the violets at her waistband seemed to remind him of his return to civilization.

"Well, I'll take my risks of that, Miss Morse," he declared. "If you'll only let me know what I can do for you—"

"It's about poor Mr. Hamilton Fynes," she explained. "I took up the evening paper only half an hour ago, and read your interview with the reporter. I simply couldn't help stopping to ask whether you could give me any further particulars about that horrible affair. I didn't dare to come here all alone, so I asked Sir Charles to come along with me."

Mr. Coulson, being invited to do so, seated himself on the lounge by the young lady's side. He leaned a little forward with a hand on either knee.

"I don't exactly know what I can tell you," he remarked. "I take it, then, that you were well acquainted with Mr. Fynes?"

"I used to know him quite well," Penelope answered, "and naturally I am very much upset. When I read in the paper an account of your interview with the reporter, I could see at once that you were not telling him everything. Why should you, indeed? A man does not want every detail of his life set out in the newspapers just because he has become connected with a terrible tragedy."

"You're a very sensible young lady, Miss Morse, if you will allow me to say so," Mr. Coulson declared. "You were expecting to see something of Mr. Fynes over here, then?"

"I had an appointment to lunch with him today," she answered. "He sent me a marconigram before he arrived at Queenstown."

"Is that so?" Mr. Coulson exclaimed. "Well, well!"

"I actually went to the restaurant," Penelope continued, "without knowing anything of this. I can't understand it at all, even now. Mr. Fynes always seemed to me such a harmless sort of person, so unlikely to have enemies, or anything of that sort. Don't you think so, Mr. Coulson?"

"Well," that gentleman answered, "to tell you the honest truth, Miss Morse, I'm afraid I am going to disappoint you a little. I wasn't over well acquainted with Mr. Fynes, although a good many people seemed to fancy that we were kind of bosom friends. That newspaper man, for instance, met me at the station and stuck to me like a leech; drove down here with me, and was willing to stand all the liquor I could drink. Then there was a gentleman from Scotland Yard, who was in such a hurry that he came to see me in my bedroom. *He* had a sort of an idea that I had been brought up from infancy with Hamilton

Fynes and could answer a sheaf of questions a yard long. As soon as I got rid of him, up comes that page boy and brings your card."

"It does seem too bad, Mr. Coulson," Penelope declared, raising her wonderful eyes to his and smiling sympathetically. "You have really brought it upon yourself, though, to some extent, haven't you, by answering so many questions for this Comet man?"

"Those newspaper fellows," Mr. Coulson remarked, "are wonders. Before that youngster had finished with me, I began to feel that poor old Fynes and I had been like brothers all our lives. As a matter of fact, Miss Morse, I expect you knew him at least as well as I did."

She nodded her head thoughtfully.

"Hamilton Fynes came from the village in Massachusetts where I was brought up. I've known him all my life."

Mr. Coulson seemed a little startled.

"I didn't understand," he said thoughtfully, "that Fynes had any very intimate friends over this side."

Penelope shook her head.

"I don't mean to imply that we have been intimate lately," she said. "I came to Europe nine years ago, and since then, of course, I have not seen him often. Perhaps it was the fact that he should have thought of me, and that I was actually expecting to have lunch with him today, which made me feel this thing so acutely."

"Why, that's quite natural," Mr. Coulson declared, leaning back a little and crossing his legs. "Somehow we seem to read about these things in the papers and they don't amount to such a lot, but when you know the man and were expecting to see him, as you were, why, then it comes right home to you. There's something about a murder," Mr. Coulson concluded, "which kind of takes hold of you if you've ever even shaken hands with either of the parties concerned in it."

"Did you see much of the poor fellow during the voyage?" Sir Charles asked.

"No, nor any one else," Mr. Coulson replied. "I don't think he was seasick, but he was miserably unsociable, and he seldom left his cabin. I doubt whether there were half a dozen people on board who would have recognized him afterwards as a fellow-passenger."

"He seems to have been a secretive sort of person," Sir Charles remarked.

"He was that," Mr. Coulson admitted. "Never seemed to care to talk about himself or his own business. Not that he had much to talk about," he added reflectively. "Dull sort of life, his. So many hours of work, so many hours of play; so many dollars a month, and after it's all over, so many dollars pension. Wouldn't suit all of us, Sir Charles, eh?"

"I fancy not," Somerfield admitted. "Perhaps he kicked over the traces a bit when he was over this side. You Americans generally seem to find your way about—in Paris, especially."

Mr. Coulson shook his head doubtfully.

"There wasn't much kicking over the traces with poor old Fynes," he said. "He hadn't got it in him."

Somerfield scratched his chin thoughtfully and looked at Penelope.

"Scarcely seems possible, does it," he remarked, "that a man leading such a quiet sort of life should make enemies."

"I don't believe he had any," Mr. Coulson asserted.

"He didn't seem nervous on the way over, did he?" Penelope asked,—"as though he were afraid of something happening?"

Mr. Coulson shook his head.

"No more than usual," he answered. "I guess your police over here aren't quite so smart as ours, or they'd have been on the track of this thing before now. But you can take it from me that when the truth comes out you'll find that our poor friend has paid the penalty of going about the world like a crank."

"A what?" Somerfield asked doubtfully.

"A crank," Mr. Coulson repeated vigorously. "It wasn't much I knew of Hamilton Fynes, but I knew that much. He was one of those nervous, stand-off sort of persons who hated to have people talk to him and yet was always doing things to make them talk about him. I was over in Europe with him not so long ago, and he went on in the same way. Took a special train to Dover when there wasn't any earthly reason for it; travelled with a valet and a courier, when he had no clothes for the valet to look after, and spoke every European language better than his courier. This time the poor fellow's paid for his bit of vanity. Naturally, any one would think he was a millionaire, travelling like that. I guess they boarded the train somehow, or lay hidden in it when it started, and relieved him of a good bit of his savings."

"But his money was found upon him," Somerfield objected.

"Some of it," Mr. Coulson answered,—"some of it. That's just about the only thing that I do know of my own. I happened to see him take his pocketbook back from the purser, and I guess he'd got a sight more money there than was found upon him. I told the smooth-spoken gentleman from Scotland Yard so—Mr. Inspector Jacks he called himself—when he came to see me an hour or so ago."

Penelope sighed gently. She found it hard to make up her mind concerning this quondam acquaintance of her deceased friend.

"Did you see much of Mr. Fynes on the other side, Mr. Coulson?" she asked him.

"Not I," Mr. Coulson answered. "He wasn't particularly anxious to make acquaintances over here, but he was even worse at home. The way he went on, you'd think he'd never had any friends and never wanted any. I met him once in the streets of Washington last year, and had a cocktail with him at the Atlantic House. I had to almost drag him in there. I was pretty well a stranger in Washington, but he didn't do a thing for me. Never asked me to look him up, or introduced me to his club. He just drank his cocktail, mumbled something about being in a hurry, and made off.

"I tell you, sir," Mr. Coulson continued, turning to Somerfield, "that man hadn't a thing to say for himself. I guess his work had something to do with it. You must get kind of out of touch with things, shut up in an office from nine o'clock in the morning till five in the afternoon. Just saving up, he was, for his trip to Europe. Then we happened on the same steamer, but, bless you, he scarcely even shook hands when he saw me. He wouldn't play bridge, didn't care about chess, hadn't even a chair on the deck, and never came in to meals."

Penelope nodded her head thoughtfully.

"You are destroying all my illusions, Mr. Coulson," she said. "Do you know that I was building up quite a romance about poor Mr. Fynes' life? It seemed to me that he must have enemies; that there must have been something in his life, or his manner of living, which accounted for such a terrible crime."

"Why, sure not!" Mr. Coulson declared heartily. "It was a cleverly worked job, but there was no mystery about it. Some chap went for him because he got riding about like a millionaire. A more unromantic figure than Hamilton Fynes never breathed. Call him a crank and you've finished with him."

Penelope sighed once more and looked at the tips of her patent shoes.

"It has been so kind of you," she murmured, "to talk to us. And yet, do you know, I am a little disappointed. I was hoping that you might have been able to tell us something more about the poor fellow."

"He was no talker," Mr. Coulson declared. "It was little enough he had to say to me, and less to any one else."

"It seems strange," she remarked innocently, "that he should have been so shy. He didn't strike me that way when I knew him at home in Massachusetts, you know. He travelled about so much in later years, too, didn't he?"

Penelope's eyes were suddenly upraised. For the first time Mr. Coulson's ready answers failed him. Not a muscle of his face moved under the girl's scrutiny, but he hesitated for a short time before he answered her.

"Not that I know of," he said at length. "No, I shouldn't have called him much of a traveller."

Penelope rose to her feet and held out her hand.

"It has been very nice indeed of you to see us, Mr. Coulson," she said, "especially after all these other people have been bothering you. Of course, I am sorry that you haven't anything more to tell us than we knew already. Still, I felt that I couldn't rest until we had been."

"It's a sad affair, anyhow," Mr. Coulson declared, walking with them to the door. "Don't you get worrying your head, young lady, though, with any notion of his having had enemies, or anything of that sort. The poor fellow was no hero of romance. I don't fancy even your halfpenny papers could drag any out of his life. It was just a commonplace robbery, with a bad ending for poor Fynes. Good evening, miss! Good night, sir! Glad to have met you, Sir Charles."

Mr. Coulson's two visitors left and got into a small electric brougham which was waiting for them. Mr. Coulson himself watched them drive off and glanced at the clock. It was already a quarter past six. He went into the cafe and ordered a light dinner, which he consumed with much obvious enjoyment. Then he lit a cigar and went into the smoking room. Selecting a pile of newspapers, he drew up an easy chair to the fire and made himself comfortable.

"Seems to me I may have a longish wait," he said to himself.

As a matter of fact, he was disappointed. At precisely seven o'clock, Mr. Richard Vanderpole strolled into the room and, after a casual glance around, approached his chair and touched him on the shoulder. In his evening clothes the newcomer was no longer obtrusively American. He was dressed in severely English fashion, from the cut of his white waistcoat to the admirable poise of his white tie. He smiled as he patted Coulson upon the shoulder.

"This is Mr. Coulson, I'm sure," he declared,—"Mr. James B. Coulson from New York?"

"You're dead right," Mr. Coulson admitted, laying down his newspaper and favoring his visitor with a quick upward glance.

"This is great!" the young man continued. "Just off the boat, eh? Well, I am glad to see you,—very glad indeed to make your acquaintance, I should say."

Mr. Coulson replied in similar terms. A waiter who was passing through the room hesitated, for it was a greeting which generally ended in a summons for him.

"What shall it be?" the newcomer asked.

"I've just taken dinner," Mr. Coulson said. "Coffee and cognac'll do me all right."

"And a Martini cocktail for me," the young man ordered. "I am dining down in the restaurant with some friends later on. Come over to this corner, Mr. Coulson. Why, you're looking first-rate. Great boat, the Lusitania, isn't she? What sort of a trip did you have?"

So they talked till the drinks had been brought and paid for, till another little party had quitted the room and they sat in their lonely corner, secure from observation or from any possibility of eavesdropping. Then Mr. Richard Vanderpole leaned forward in his chair and dropped his voice.

"Coulson," he said, "the chief is anxious. We don't understand this affair. Do you know anything?"

"Not a d— —d thing!" Coulson answered.

"Were you shadowed on the boat?" the young man asked.

"Not to my knowledge," Coulson answered. "Fynes was in his stateroom six hours before we started. I can't make head nor tail of it."

"He had the papers, of course?"

"Sewn in the lining of his coat," Coulson muttered. "You read about that in tonight's papers. The lining was torn and the space empty. He had them all right when he left the steamer."

The young man looked around; the room was still empty.

"I'm fresh in this," he said. "I got some information this afternoon, and the chief sent me over to see you on account of it. We had better not discuss possibilities, I suppose? The thing's too big. The chief's almost off his head. Is there any chance, do you think, Coulson, that this was an ordinary robbery? I am not sure that the special train wasn't a mistake."

"None whatever," Coulson declared.

"How do you know?" his companion asked quickly.

"Well, I've lied to those reporters and chaps," Coulson admitted, — "lied with a purpose, of course, as you people can understand. The money found upon Fynes was every penny he had when he left Liverpool."

The young man set his teeth.

"It's something to know this, at any rate," he declared. "You did right, Coulson, to put up that bluff. Now about the duplicates?"

"They are in my suitcase," Coulson answered, "and according to the way things are going, I shan't be over sorry to get rid of them. Will you take them with you?"

"Why, sure!" Vanderpole answered. "That's what I'm here for."

"You had better wait right here, then," Coulson said, "I'll fetch them."

He made his way up to his room, undid his dressing bag, which was fastened only with an ordinary lock, and from between two shirts drew out a small folded packet, no bigger than an ordinary letter. It was a curious circumstance that he used only one hand for the search and with the other gripped the butt of a small revolver. There was no one around, however, nor was he disturbed in any way. In a few minutes he returned to the bar smoking room, where the young man was still waiting, and handed him the letter.

"Tell me," the latter asked, "have you been shadowed at all?"

"Not that I know of," Coulson answered.

"Men with quick instincts," Vanderpole continued, "can always tell when they are being watched. Have you felt anything of the sort?"

Coulson hesitated for one moment.

"No," he said. "I had a caller whose manner I did not quite understand. She seemed to have something at the back of her head about me."

"She! Was it a woman?" the young man asked quickly.

Coulson nodded.

"A young lady," he said,—"Miss Penelope Morse, she called herself."

Mr. Richard Vanderpole stood quite still for a moment.

"Ah!" he said softly. "She might have been interested."

"Does the chief want me at all?" Coulson asked.

"No!" Vanderpole answered. "Go about your business as usual. Leave here for Paris, say, in ten days. There will probably be a letter for you at the Grand Hotel by that time."

They walked together toward the main exit. The young man's face had lost some of its grimness. Once more his features wore that look of pleasant and genial good-fellowship which seems characteristic of his race after business hours.

"Say, Mr. Coulson," he declared, as they passed across the hall, "you and I must have a night together. This isn't New York, by any manner of means, or Paris, but there's some fun to be had here, in a quiet way. I'll phone you tomorrow or the day after."

"Sure!" Mr. Coulson declared. "I'd like it above all things."

"I must find a taxicab," the young man remarked. "I've a busy hour before me. I've got to go down and see the chief, who is dining somewhere in Kensington, and get back again to dine here at half past seven in the restaurant."

"I guess you'll have to look sharp, then." Mr. Coulson remarked. "Do you see the time?"

Vanderpole glanced at the clock and whistled softly to himself.

"Tell you what!" he exclaimed, "I'll write a note to one of the friends I've got to meet, and leave it here. Boy," he added, turning to a page boy, "get me a taxi as quick as you can."

The boy ran out into the Strand, and Vanderpole, sitting down at the table, wrote a few lines, which he sealed and addressed and handed to one of the reception clerks. Then he shook hands with Coulson and threw himself into a corner of the cab which was waiting.

"Drive down the Brompton Road," he said to the man. "I'll direct you later."

It was a quarter past seven when he left the hotel. At half past a policeman held up his hand and stopped the taxi, to the driver's great astonishment, as he was driving slowly across Melbourne Square, Kensington.

"What's the matter?" the man asked. "You can't say I was exceeding my speed limit."

The policeman scarcely noticed him. His head was already through the cab window.

"Where did you take your fare up?" he asked quickly.

"Savoy Hotel," the man answered. "What's wrong with him?"

The policeman opened the door of the cab and stepped in.

"Never you mind about that," he said. "Drive to the South Kensington police station as quick as you can."

CHAPTER VIII.
AN INTERRUPTED THEATRE PARTY

Seated upon a roomy lounge in the foyer of the Savoy were three women who attracted more than an average amount of attention from the passers-by. In the middle was the Duchess of Devenham, erect, stately, and with a figure which was still irreproachable notwithstanding her white hair. On one side sat her daughter, Lady Grace Redford, tall, fair, and comely; on the other, Miss Penelope Morse. The two girls were amusing themselves, watching the people; their chaperon had her eye upon the clock.

"To dine at half-past seven," the Duchess remarked, as she looked around the *entresol* of the great restaurant through her lorgnettes, "is certainly a little trying for one's temper and for one's digestion, but so long as those men accepted, I certainly think they ought to have been here. They know that the play begins at a quarter to nine."

"It isn't like Dicky Vanderpole in the least," Penelope said. "Since he began to tread the devious paths of diplomacy, he has brought exactness in the small things of life down to a fine art."

"He isn't half so much fun as he used to be," Lady Grace declared.

"Fun!" Penelope exclaimed. "Sometimes I think that I never knew a more trying person."

"I have never known the Prince unpunctual," the Duchess murmured. "I consider him absolutely the best-mannered young man I know."

Lady Grace smiled, and glanced at Penelope.

"I don't think you'll get Penelope to agree with you, mother," she said.

"Why not, my dear?" the Duchess asked. "I heard that you were quite rude to him the other evening. We others all find him so charming."

Penelope's lip curled slightly.

"He has so many admirers," she remarked, "that I dare say he will not notice my absence from the ranks. Perhaps I am a little prejudiced. At home, you know, we have rather strong opinions about this fusion of races."

The Duchess raised her eyebrows.

"But a Prince of Japan, my dear Penelope!" she said. "A cousin of the Emperor, and a member of an aristocracy which was old before we were thought of! Surely you cannot class Prince Maiyo amongst those to whom any of your country people could take exception."

Penelope shrugged her shoulders slightly.

"Perhaps," she said, "my feeling is the result of hearing you all praise him so much and so often. Besides, apart from that, you must remember that I am a patriotic daughter of the Stars and Stripes, and there isn't much friendship lost between Washington and Tokio just now."

The Duchess turned away to greet a man who had paused before their couch on his way into the restaurant.

"My dear General," she said, "it seems to me that one meets every one here! Why was not restaurant dining the vogue when I was a girl!"

General Sherrif smiled. He was tall and thin, with grizzled hair and worn features. Notwithstanding his civilian's clothes, there was no possibility of mistaking him anywhere, or under any circumstances, for anything but a soldier.

"It is a delightful custom," he admitted. "It keeps one always on the *qui vive*; one never knows whom one may see. Incidentally, I find it interferes very much with my digestion."

"Digestion!" the Duchess murmured. "But then, you soldiers lead such irregular lives."

"Not always from choice," the General reminded her. "The Russo-Japanese war finished me off. They kept us far enough away from the fighting, when they could, but, by Jove, they did make us move!"

"We are waiting now for Prince Maiyo," the Duchess remarked. "You know him?"

"Know him!" the General answered. "Duchess, if ever I have to write my memoirs, and particularly my reminiscences of this war, I fancy you would find the name of your friend appear there pretty frequently. There wasn't a more brilliant feat of arms in the whole campaign than his flanking movement at Mukden. I met most of the Japanese leaders, and I have always said that I consider him the most wonderful of them all."

The Duchess turned to Penelope.

"Do you hear that?" she asked.

Penelope smiled.

"The Fates are against me," she declared. "If I may not like, I shall at least be driven to admire."

"To talk of bravery when one speaks of that war," the General remarked, "seems invidious, for it is my belief that throughout the whole of the Japanese army such a thing as fear did not exist. They simply did not know what the word meant. But I shall never forget that the only piece of hand-to-hand fighting I saw during the whole time was a cavalry charge led by Prince Maiyo against an immensely superior force of Russians. Duchess," the General declared, "those Japanese on their queer little horses went through the enemy like wind through a cornfield. That young man must have borne a charmed life. I saw him riding and cheering his men on when he must have had at least half a dozen wounds in his body. You will pardon me, Duchess? I see that my party are waiting."

The General hurried away. The Duchess shut up her lorgnettes with a snap, and held out her hand to a newcomer who had come from behind the palms.

"My dear Prince," she exclaimed, "this is charming of you! Some one told me that you were not well,—our wretched climate, of course—and I was so afraid, every moment, that we should receive your excuses."

The newcomer, who was bowing over her hand, was of medium height or a trifle less, dark, and dressed with the quiet exactness of an English gentleman. Only a slight narrowness of the eyes and a greater alertness of movement seemed to distinguish him in any way, as regards nationality, from the men by whom he was surrounded. His voice, when he spoke, contained no trace of accent. It was soft and singularly pleasant. It had, too, one somewhat rare quality—a delightful ring of truth. Perhaps that was one of the reasons why Prince Maiyo was just then, amongst certain circles, one of the most popular persons in Society.

"My dear Duchess," he said, "my indisposition was nothing. And as for your climate, I am beginning to delight in it,—one never knows what to expect, or when one may catch a glimpse of the sun. It is only the grayness which is always the same."

"And even that," the Duchess remarked, smiling, "has been yellow for the last few days. Prince, you know my daughter Grace, and I am sure that you have met Miss Penelope Morse? We are waiting for two other men, Sir Charles Somerfield and Mr. Vanderpole."

The Prince bowed, and began to talk to his hostess' daughter,—a tall, fair girl, as yet only in her second season.

"Here comes Sir Charles, at any rate!" the Duchess exclaimed. "Really, I think we shall have to go in. We can leave a message for Dicky; they all know him at this place. I am afraid he is one of those shocking young men who entertain the theatrical profession here to supper."

A footman at that moment brought a note to the Duchess, which she tore open.

"This is from Dicky!" she exclaimed, glancing it through quickly,— "Savoy notepaper, too, so I suppose he has been here. He says that he may be a few minutes late and that we are not to wait. He will pick us up either here or at the theatre. Prince, shall we let these young people follow us? I haven't heard your excuses yet. Do you know that you were a quarter of an hour late?"

He bent towards her with troubled face.

"Dear Duchess," he said, "believe me, I am conscious of my fault. An unexpected matter, which required my personal attention, presented itself at the last moment. I think I can assure you that nothing of its sort was ever accomplished so quickly. It would only weary you if I tried to explain."

"Please don't," the Duchess begged, "so long as you are here at last. And after all, you see, you are not the worst sinner. Mr. Vanderpole has not yet arrived."

The Prince walked on, for a few steps, in silence.

"Mr. Vanderpole is a great friend of yours, Duchess?" he asked.

The Duchess shook her head.

"I do not know him very well," she said. "I asked him for Penelope."

The Prince looked puzzled.

"But I thought," he said, "that Miss Morse and Sir Charles—"

The Duchess interrupted him with a smile.

"Sir Charles is very much in earnest," she whispered, "but very very slow. Dicky is just the sort of man to spur him on. He admires Penelope, and does not mind showing it. She is such a dear girl that I should love to have her comfortably settled over here."

"She is very intelligent," the Prince said. "She is a young lady, indeed, for whom I have a great admiration. I am only sorry," he concluded, "that I do not seem able to interest her."

"You must not believe that," the Duchess said. "Penelope is a little brusque sometimes, but it is only her manner."

They made their way through the foyer to the round table which had been reserved for them in the centre of the restaurant.

"I suppose I ought to apologize for giving you dinner at such an hour," the Duchess remarked, "but it is our theatrical managers who are to blame. Why they cannot understand that the best play in the world is not worth more than two hours of our undivided attention, and begin everything at nine or a quarter-past, I cannot imagine."

The Prince smiled.

"Dear Duchess," he said, "I think that you are a nation of sybarites. Everything in the world must run for you so smoothly or you are not content. For my part, I like to dine at this hour."

"But then, you take no luncheon, Prince," Lady Grace reminded him.

"I never lunch out," the Prince answered, "but I have always what is sufficient for me."

"Tell me," the Duchess asked, "is it true that you are thinking of settling down amongst us? Your picture is in the new illustrated paper this week, you know, with a little sketch of your career. We are given to understand that you may possibly make your home in this country."

The Prince smiled, and in his smile there seemed to be a certain mysticism. One could not tell, indeed, whether it came from some pleasant thought flitting through his brain, or whether it was that the idea itself was so strange to him.

"I have no plans, Duchess," he said. "Your country is very delightful, and the hospitality of the friends I have made over here is too wonderful a thing to be described; but one never knows."

Lady Grace bent towards Sir Charles, who was sitting by her side.

"I can never understand the Prince," she murmured. "Always he seems as though he took life so earnestly. He has a look upon his face which I never see in the faces of any of you other young men."

"He is a bit on the serious side," Sir Charles admitted.

"It isn't only that," she continued. "He reminds me of that man whom we all used to go and hear preach at the Oratory. He was the same in the pulpit and when one saw him in the street. His eyes seemed to see through one; he seemed to be living in a world of his own."

"He was a religious Johnny, of course," Sir Charles remarked. "They do walk about with their heads in the air."

Lady Grace smiled.

"Perhaps it is religion with the Prince," she said, — "religion of a sort."

"I tell you what I do think," Sir Charles murmured. "I think his pretence at having a good time over here is all a bluff. He doesn't really cotton to us, you know. Don't see how he could. He's never touched a polo stick in his life, knows nothing about cricket, is indifferent to games, and doesn't even understand the meaning of the word 'Sportsman.' There's no place in this country for a man like that."

Lady Grace nodded.

"I think," she said, "that his visit to Europe and his stay amongst us is, after all, in the nature of a pilgrimage. I suppose he wants to carry back some of our civilization to his own people."

Penelope, who overheard, laughed softly and leaned across the table.

"I fancy," she murmured, "that the person you are speaking of would not look at it in quite the same light."

"Has any one seen the evening paper?" the Duchess asked. "It is there any more news about that extraordinary murder?"

"Nothing fresh in the early editions," Sir Charles answered.

"I think," the Duchess declared, "that it is perfectly scandalous. Our police system must be in a disgraceful state. Tell me, Prince,—could anything like that happen in your country?"

"Without doubt," the Prince answered, "life moves very much in the East as with you here. Only with us," he added a little thoughtfully, "there is a difference, a difference of which one is reminded at a time like this, when one reads your newspapers and hears the conversation of one's friends."

"Tell us what you mean?" Penelope asked quickly.

He looked at her as one might have looked at a child,—kindly, even tolerantly. He was scarcely so tall as she was, and Penelope's attitude towards him was marked all the time with a certain frigidity. Yet he spoke to her with the quiet, courteous confidence of the philosopher who unbends to talk to a child.

"In this country," he said, "you place so high a value upon the gift of life. Nothing moves you so greatly as the killing of one man by another, or the death of a person whom you know."

"There is no tragedy in the world so great!" Penelope declared.

The Prince shrugged his shoulders very slightly.

"My dear Miss Morse," he said, "it is so that you think about life and death here. Yet you call yourselves a Christian country—you have a very beautiful faith. With us, perhaps, there is a little more philosophy and something a little less definite in the trend of our religion. Yet we do not dress Death in black clothes or fly from his outstretched hand. We fear him no more that we do the night. It is a thing that comes—a thing that must be."

He spoke so softly, and yet with so much conviction, that it seemed hard to answer him. Penelope, however, was conscious of an almost feverish desire either to contradict him or to prolong the conversation by some means or other.

"Your point of view," she said, "is well enough, Prince, for those who fall in battle, fighting for their country or for a great cause. Don't you think, though, that the horror of death is a more real thing in a case like this, where a man is killed in cold blood for the sake of robbery, or perhaps revenge?"

"One cannot tell," the Prince answered thoughtfully. "The battlefields of life are there for every one to cross. This mysterious gentleman who seems to have met with his death so unexpectedly— he, too, may have been the victim of a cause, knowing his dangers, facing them as a man should face them."

The Duchess sighed.

"I am quite sure, Prince," she said, "that you are a romanticist. But, apart from the sentimental side of it, do things like this happen in your country?"

"Why not?" the Prince answered. "It is as I have been saying: for a worthy cause, or a cause which he believed to be worthy, there is no man of my country worthy of the name who would not accept death with the same resignation that he lays his head upon the pillow and waits for sleep."

Sir Charles raised his glass and bowed across the table.

"To our great allies!" he said, smiling.

The Prince drank his glass of water thoughtfully. He drank wine only on very rare occasions, and then under compulsion. He turned to the Duchess.

"A few days ago," he said, "I heard myself described as being much too serious a person. Tonight I am afraid that I am living up to my reputation. Our conversation seems to have drifted into somewhat gloomy channels. We must ask Miss Morse, I think, to help us to forget. They say," he continued, "that it is the young ladies of your country who hold open the gates of Paradise for their menkind."

He was looking into her eyes. His tone was half bantering, half serious. From across the table Penelope knew that Somerfield was watching her closely. Somehow or other, she was irritated and nervous, and she answered vaguely. Sir Charles intervened with a story about some of their acquaintances, and the conversation drifted into more ordinary channels.

"Some day, I suppose," the Duchess remarked, as the service of dinner drew toward a close, "you will have restaurants like this in Tokio?"

The Prince assented.

"Yes," he said without enthusiasm, "they will come. Our heritage from the West is a sure thing. Not in my days, perhaps, or in the days of those that follow me, but they will come."

"I think that it is absolutely wicked of Dicky," the Duchess declared, as they rose from the table. "I shall never rely upon him again."

"After all, perhaps, it isn't his fault," Penelope said, breathing a little sigh of relief as she rose to her feet. "Mr. Harvey is not always considerate, and I know that several of the staff are away on leave."

"That's right, my dear," the Duchess said, smiling, "stick up for your countrymen. I suppose he'll find us sometime during the evening. We can all go to the theatre together; the omnibus is outside."

The little party passed through the foyer and into the hall of the hotel, where they waited while the Duchess' carriage was called. Mr. Coulson was there in an easy chair, smoking a cigar, and watching the people coming and going. He studied the passers-by with ah air of impersonal but pleased interest. Penelope and Lady Grace were certainly admirable foils. The latter was fair, with beautiful complexion—a trifle sunburnt, blue eyes, good-humored mouth, and features excellent in their way, but a little lacking in expression. Her figure was good; her movements slow but not ungraceful; her dress of white ivory satin a little extravagant for the occasion. She looked exactly what she was,—a well-bred, well-disposed, healthy young Englishwoman, of aristocratic parentage. Penelope, on the other hand, more simply dressed, save for the string of pearls which hung from her neck, had the look of a creature from another world. She had plenty of animation; a certain nervous energy seemed to keep her all the time restless. She talked ceaselessly, sometimes to the Prince, more often to Sir Charles. Her gray-green eyes were bright, her cheeks delicately flushed. She spoke and looked and moved as one on fire with the joy of life. The Prince, noticing that Lady Grace had been left to herself for the last few moments, moved a little towards her and commenced a courteous conversation. Sir Charles took the opportunity to bend over his companion.

"Penelope," he said, "you are queer tonight. Tell me what it is? You don't really dislike the Prince, do you?"

"Why, of course not," she answered, looking back into the restaurant and listening, as though interested in the music. "He is odd, though, isn't he? He is so serious and, in a way, so convincing. He is like a being transplanted into an absolutely alien soil. One would like to laugh at him, and one can't."

"He is rather an anomaly," Sir Charles said, humming lightly to himself. "I suppose, compared with us matter-of-fact people, he must seem to your sex quite a romantic figure."

"He makes no particular appeal to me at all," Penelope declared.

Somerfield was suddenly thoughtful.

"Sometimes, Penelope," he said, "I don't quite understand you, especially when we speak about the Prince. I have come to the conclusion that you either like him very much, or you dislike him very much, or you have some thoughts about him which you tell to no one."

She lifted her skirts. The carriage had been called.

"I like your last suggestion," she declared. "You may believe that that is true."

On their way out, the Prince was accosted by some friends and remained talking for several moments. When he entered the omnibus, there seemed to Penelope, who found herself constantly watching him closely, a certain added gravity in his demeanor. The drive to the theatre was a short one, and conversation consisted only of a few disjointed remarks. In the lobby the Prince laid his hand upon Somerfield's arm.

"Sir Charles," he said, "if I were you, I would keep that evening paper in your pocket. Don't let the ladies see it."

Somerfield looked at him in surprise.

"What do you mean?" he asked.

"To me personally it is of no consequence," the Prince answered, "but your womenfolk feel these things so keenly, and Mr. Vanderpole is of the same nationality, is he not, as Miss Morse? If you take my advice, you will be sure that they do not see the paper until after they get home this evening."

"Has anything happened to Dicky?" Somerfield asked quickly.

The Prince's face was impassive; he seemed not to have heard. Penelope had turned to wait for them.

"The Duchess thinks that we had better all go into the box," she said. "We have two stalls as well, but as Dicky is not here there is really room for five. Will you get some programmes, Sir Charles?"

Somerfield stopped for a minute, under pretence of seeking some change, and tore open his paper. The Prince led Penelope down the carpeted way.

"I heard what you and Sir Charles were saying," she declared quietly. "Please tell me what it is that has happened to Dicky?"

The Prince's face was grave.

"I am sorry," he replied. "I did not know that our voices would travel so far."

"It was not yours," she said. "It was Sir Charles'. Tell me quickly what it is that has happened?"

"Mr. Vanderpole," the Prince answered, "has met with an accident,—a somewhat serious one, I fear. Perhaps," he added, "it would be as well, after all, to break this to the Duchess. I was forgetting the prejudices of your country. She will doubtless wish that our party should be broken up."

Penelope was suddenly very white. He whispered in her ear.

"Be brave," he said. "It is your part."

She stood still for a moment, and then moved on. His words had had a curious effect upon her. The buzzing in her ears had ceased; there was something to be done—she must do it! She passed into the box, the door of which the attendant was holding open.

"Duchess," she said, "I am so sorry, but I am afraid that something has happened to Dicky. If you do not mind, I am going to ask Sir Charles to take me home."

"But my dear child!" the Duchess exclaimed.

"Miss Morse is quite right," the Prince said quietly. "I think it would be better for her to leave at once. If you will allow me, I will explain to you later."

She left the box without another word, and took Somerfield's arm.

"We two are to go," she murmured. "The Prince will explain to the Duchess."

The Prince closed the box door behind them. He placed a chair for the Duchess so that she was not in view of the house.

"A very sad thing has happened," he said quietly. "Mr. Vanderpole met with an accident in a taxicab this evening. From the latest reports, it seems that he is dead!"

CHAPTER IX.
INSPECTOR JACKS SCORES

There followed a few days of pleasurable interest to all Englishmen who travelled in the tube and read their halfpenny papers. A great and enlightened Press had already solved the problem of creating the sensational without the aid of facts. This sudden deluge, therefore, of undoubtedly tragic happenings became almost an embarrassment to them. Black headlines, notes of exclamation, the use of superlative adjectives, scarcely met the case. The murder of Mr. Hamilton Fynes was strange enough. Here was an unknown man, holding a small position in his own country,—a man apparently without friends or social position. He travelled over from America, merely a unit amongst the host of other passengers; yet his first action, on arriving at Liverpool, was to make use of privileges which belonged to an altogether different class of person, and culminated in his arrival at Euston in a special train with a dagger driven through his heart! Here was material enough for a least a fortnight of sensations and countersensations, of rumored arrests and strange theories. Yet within the space of twenty-four hours the affair of Mr. Hamilton Fynes had become a small thing, had shrunk almost into insignificance by the side of the other still more dramatic, still more wonderful happening. Somewhere between the Savoy Hotel and Melbourne Square, Kensington, a young American gentleman of great strength, of undoubted position, the nephew of a Minister, and himself secretary to the Ambassador of his country in London, had met with his death in a still more mysterious, still more amazing fashion. He had left the hotel in an ordinary taxicab, which had stopped on the way to pick up no other passenger. He had left the Savoy alone, and he was discovered in Melbourne Square alone. Yet, somewhere between these two points, notwithstanding the fact that the aggressor must have entered the cab either with or without his consent, Mr. Richard Vanderpole, without a struggle, without any cry sufficiently loud to reach the driver or attract the attention of any passer-by, had been strangled to death by a person who had disappeared as though from the face of the earth. The facts seemed almost unbelievable, and yet they were facts. The driver of the taxi knew only that three times during the course of his drive he had been caught in a block and had had to wait for a few seconds—once at the entrance to Trafalgar Square, again at the junction of Haymarket and Pall Mall, and, for a third time, opposite the Hyde Park Hotel. At neither of these halting places had he heard any one enter or leave the taxi. He had heard no summons from his fare, even though a tube, which was in perfect working order, was fixed close to the back of his head. He had known nothing, in fact, until a policeman had stopped him, having caught a glimpse of the ghastly face inside. There was no evidence which served to throw a single gleam of light upon the affair. Mr. Vanderpole had called at the Savoy Hotel upon a travelling American, who had written to the Embassy asking for some advice as to introducing American patents into Great Britain and France. He left there to meet his chief, who was dining down in Kensington, with the intention of returning at once to join the Duchess of Devenham's theatre party. He was in no manner of trouble. It was not suggested that any one had any cause for enmity against him. Yet this attack upon him must have been carefully planned and carried out by a person of great strength and wonderful nerve. The newspaper-reading public in London love their thrills, and they had one here which needed no artificial embellishments from the pens of those trained in an atmosphere of imagination. The simple truth was, in itself, horrifying. There was scarcely a man or woman who drove in a taxicab about the west end of London during the next few days without a little thrill of emotion.

The murder of Mr. Richard Vanderpole took place on a Thursday night. On Monday morning a gentleman of middle age, fashionably but quietly dressed, wearing a flower in his buttonhole, patent boots, and a silk hat which he had carefully deposited upon the floor, was sitting closeted with Miss Penelope Morse. It was obvious that that young lady did not altogether appreciate the honor done to her by a visit from so distinguished a person as Inspector Jacks!

"I am sorry," he said, "that you should find my visit in the least offensive, Miss Morse. I have approached you, so far as possible, as an ordinary visitor, and no one connected with your household can have any idea as to my identity or the nature of my business. I have done this out of consideration to your feelings. At the same time I have my duty to perform and it must be done."

"What I cannot understand," Penelope said coldly, "is why you should bother me about your duty. When I saw you at the Carlton Hotel, I told you exactly how much I knew of Mr. Hamilton Fynes."

"My dear young lady," Inspector Jacks said, "I will not ask for your sympathy, for I am afraid I should ask in vain; but we are just now, we people at Scotland Yard, up against one of the most extraordinary problems which have ever been put before us. We have had two murders occurring in two days, which have this much, at least, in common — that they have been the work of so accomplished a criminal that at the present moment, although I should not like to tell every one as much, we have not in either case the ghost of a clue."

"That sounds very stupid of you," Penelope remarked, "but I still ask—"

"Don't ask for a minute or two," the Inspector interrupted. "I think I remarked just now that these two crimes had one thing in common, and that was the fact that they had both been perpetrated by a criminal of unusual accomplishments. They also have one other point of similitude."

"What is that?" Penelope asked.

"The victim in both cases was an American," the Inspector said.

Penelope sat very still. She felt the steely eyes of the man who had chosen his seat so carefully, fixed upon her face.

"You do not connect the two affairs in any way?" she asked.

"That is what we are asking ourselves," Mr. Jacks continued. "In the absence of any definite clue, coincidences such as this are always interesting. In this case, as it happens, we can take them even a little further. We find that you, for instance, Miss Penelope Morse, a young American lady, celebrated for her wit and accomplishments, and well known in London society, were to have lunched with Mr. Hamilton Fynes on the day when he made his tragical arrival in London; we find too, curiously enough, that you were one of the party with whom Mr. Richard Vanderpole was to have dined and gone to the theatre on the night of his decease."

Penelope shivered, and half closed her eyes.

"Don't you think," she said, "that the shock of this coincidence, as you call it, has been quite sufficient, without having you come here to remind me of it?"

"Madam," Mr. Jacks said, "I have not come here to gratify any personal curiosity. I have come here in the cause of justice. You should find me a welcome visitor, for both these men who have lost their lives were friends of yours."

"I should be very sorry indeed," Penelope answered, "to stand in the way of justice. No one can hope more fervently than I do that the perpetrator of these deeds will be found and punished. But what I cannot understand is your coming here and reopening the subject with me. I tell you again that I have no possible information for you."

"Perhaps not," the Inspector declared, "but, on the other hand, there are certain questions which you can answer me,—answer them, I mean, not grudgingly and as though in duty bound,—answer them intelligently, and with some apprehension of the things which lie behind."

"And what is the thing that lies behind them?" she asked.

"A theory, madam," the Inspector answered,—"no more. But in this case, unfortunately, we have not passed the stage of theories. My theory, at the present moment, is that the murderer of these two men was the same person."

"You have evidence to that effect," she said, suddenly surprised to find that her voice had sunk to a whisper.

"Very little," Mr. Jacks admitted; "but, you see, in the case of theories one must build them brick by brick. Then if, after all, as we reach the end, the foundation was false, well, we must watch them collapse and start again."

"Supposing we leave these generalities," Penelope remarked, "and get on with those questions which you wish to ask me. My aunt, as you may have heard, is an invalid, and although she seldom leaves her room, this is one of the afternoons when she sometimes sits here for a short time. I should not care to have her find you."

The Inspector leaned back in his chair. It was a very pleasant drawing room, looking out upon the Park. A little French clock, a masterpiece of workmanship, was ticking gayly upon the mantelpiece. Two toy Pomeranians were half hidden in the great rug. The walls were of light blue, soft, yet full of color, and the carpet, of some plain material, was of the same shade. The perfume of flowers—the faint sweetness of mimosa and the sicklier fragrance of hyacinths—seemed almost overwhelming, for the fire was warm and the windows closed. By the side of Penelope's chair were a new novel and a couple of illustrated papers, and Mr. Jacks noticed that although a paper cutter was lying by their side the leaves of all were uncut.

"These questions," he said, "may seem to you irrelevant, yet please answer them if you can. Mr. Hamilton Fynes, for instance,—was he, to your knowledge, acquainted with Mr. Richard Vanderpole?"

"I have never heard them speak of one another," Penelope answered. "I should think it very unlikely."

"You have no knowledge of any common pursuit or interest in life which the two men may have shared?" the Inspector asked. "A hobby, for instance,—a collection of postage stamps, china, any common aim of any sort?"

She shook her head.

"I knew little of Mr. Fynes' tastes. Dicky—I mean Mr. Vanderpole—had none at all except an enthusiasm for his profession and a love of polo."

"His profession," the Inspector repeated. "Mr. Vanderpole was attached to the American Embassy, was he not?"

"I believe so," Penelope answered.

"Mr. Hamilton Fynes," the Inspector continued, "might almost have been said to have followed the same occupation."

"Surely not!" Penelope objected. "I always understood that Mr. Fynes was employed in a Government office at Washington,—something to do with the Customs, I thought, or forest duties."

Mr. Jacks nodded thoughtfully.

"I am not aware, as yet," he said, "of the precise nature of Mr. Fynes' occupation. I only knew that it was, in some shape or form, Government work."

"You know as much about it," she answered, "as I do."

"We have sent," the Inspector continued smoothly, "a special man out to Washington to make all inquiries that are possible on the spot, and incidentally, to go through the effects of the deceased, with a view to tracing any complications in which he may have been involved in this country."

Penelope opened her lips, but closed them again.

"I am not, however," the Inspector continued, "very sanguine of success. In the case of Mr. Vanderpole, for instance, there could have been nothing of the sort. He was too young, altogether too much of a boy, to have had enemies so bitterly disposed towards him. There is another explanation somewhere, I feel convinced, at the root of the matter."

"You do not believe, then," asked Penelope, "that robbery was really the motive?"

"Not ordinary robbery," Mr. Jacks answered. "A man who was capable of these two crimes is capable of easier and greater things. I mean," he explained, "that he could have attempted enterprises of a far more remunerative character, with a prospect of complete success."

"Will you forgive me," she said, "if I ask you to go on with your questions, providing you have any more to ask me? Notwithstanding the excellence of your disguise," she remarked with a faint curl of the lips, "I might find it somewhat difficult to explain your presence if my aunt or any visitors should come in."

"I am sorry, Miss Morse," the Inspector said quietly, "to find you so unsympathetic. Had I found you differently disposed, I was going to ask you to put yourself in my place. I was going to ask you to look at these two tragedies from my point of view and from your own at the same time, and I was going to ask you whether any possible motive suggested itself to you, any possible person or cause, which might be benefited by the removal of these two men."

"If you think, Mr. Jacks," Penelope said, "that I am keeping anything from you, you are very much mistaken. Such sympathy as I have would certainly be with those who are attempting to bring to justice the perpetrator of such unmentionable crimes. What I object to is the unpleasantness of being associated with your inquiries when I am absolutely unable to give you the least help, or to supply you with any information which is not equally attainable to you."

"As, for instance?" the Inspector asked.

"You are a detective," Penelope said coldly. "You do not need me to point out certain things to you. Mr. Hamilton Fynes was robbed and murdered—an American citizen on his way to London. Mr. Richard Vanderpole is also murdered, after a call upon Mr. James B. Coulson, the only acquaintance whom Mr. Fynes is known to have possessed in this country. Did Mr. Fynes share secrets with Mr. Coulson? If so, did Mr. Coulson pass them on to Mr. Vanderpole, and for that reason did Mr. Vanderpole meet with the same death, at the same hands, as had befallen Mr. Fynes?"

Inspector Jacks moved his head thoughtfully.

"It is admirably put," he assented, "and to continue?"

"It is not my place to make suggestions to you," Penelope said. "If you are able to connect Mr. Fynes with the American Government, you arrive at the possibility of these murders having been committed for some political end. I presume you read your newspapers?"

Inspector Jacks smiled, picked up his hat and bowed, while Penelope, with a sigh of relief, moved over to the bell.

"My dear young lady," he said, "you do not understand how important even the point of view of another person is to a man who is struggling to build up a theory. Whether you have helped me as much as you could," he added, looking her in the face, "you only can tell, but you have certainly helped me a little."

The footman had entered. The Inspector turned to follow him. Penelope remained as she had been standing, the hand which had touched the bell fallen to her side, her eyes fixed upon him with a new light stirring their quiet depths.

"One moment, Morton," she said. "Wait outside. Mr. Jacks," she added, as the door closed, "what do you mean? What can I have told you? How can I have helped you?"

The Inspector stood very still for a brief space of time, very still and very silent. His face, too, was quite expressionless. Yet his tone, when he spoke, seemed to have taken to itself a note of sternness.

"If you had chosen," he said slowly, "to have become my ally in this matter, to have ranged yourself altogether on the side of the law, my answer would have been ready enough. What you have told me, however, you have told me against your will and not in actual words. You have told me in such a way, too," he added, "that it is impossible for me to doubt your intention to mislead me. I am forced to conclude that we stand on opposite sides of the way. I shall not trouble you any more, Miss Morse."

He turned to the door. Penelope remained motionless for several moments, listening to his retreating footsteps.

CHAPTER X.
MR. COULSON OUTMATCHED

Mr. James B. Coulson settled down to live what was, to all appearance, a very inoffensive and ordinary life. He rose a little earlier than was customary for an Englishman of business of his own standing, but he made up for this by a somewhat prolonged visit to the barber, a breakfast which bespoke an unimpaired digestion, and a cigar of more than ordinary length over his newspaper. At about eleven o'clock he went down to the city, and returned sometimes to luncheon, sometimes at varying hours, never later, however, than four or five o'clock. From that time until seven, he was generally to be found in the American bar, meeting old friends or making new ones.

On the sixth day of his stay at the Savoy Hotel the waiter who looked after the bar smoking room accosted him as he entered at his usual time, a little after half past four.

"There's a gentleman here, Mr. Coulson, been asking after you," he announced. "I told him that you generally came in about this time. You'll find him sitting over there."

Mr. Coulson glanced in the direction indicated. It was Mr. Jacks who awaited him in the cushioned easy chair. For a single moment, perhaps, his lips tightened and the light of battle flashed in his face. Then he crossed the room apparently himself again,—an undistinguished, perfectly natural figure.

"It's Mr. Jacks, isn't it?" he asked, holding out his hand. "I thought I recognized you."

The Inspector rose to his feet.

"I am sorry to trouble you again, Mr. Coulson," he said, "but if you could spare me just a minute or two, I should be very much obliged."

Mr. Coulson laughed pleasantly.

"You can have all you want of me from now till midnight," he declared. "My business doesn't take very long, and I can only see the people I want to see in the middle of the day. After that, I don't mind telling you that I find time hangs a bit on my hands. Try one of these," he added, producing a cigar case.

The Inspector thanked him and helped himself. Mr. Coulson summoned the waiter.

"Highball for me," he directed. "What's yours, Mr. Jacks?"

"Thank you very much," the Inspector said. "I will take a little Scotch whiskey and soda."

The two men sat down. The corner was a retired one, and there was no one within earshot.

"Say, are you still on this Hamilton Fynes business?" Mr. Coulson asked.

"Partly," the Inspector replied.

"You know, I'm not making reflections," Mr. Coulson said, sticking his cigar in a corner of his mouth and leaning back in a comfortable attitude, "but it does seem to me that you are none too rapid on this side in clearing up these matters. Why, a little affair of that sort wouldn't take the police twenty minutes in New York. We have a big city, full of alien quarters, full of hiding places, and chock full of criminals, but our police catch em, all the same. There's no one going to commit murder in the streets of New York without finding himself in the Tombs before he's a week older. No offence, Mr. Jacks."

"I am not taking any, Mr. Coulson," the Inspector answered. "I must admit that there's a great deal of truth in what you say. It is rather a reflection upon us that we have not as yet even made an arrest, but I think you will also admit that the circumstances of those murders were exceedingly curious."

Mr. Coulson knocked the ash from his cigar.

"Well, as to that," he said, "and if we are to judge only by what we read in the papers, they are curious, without a doubt. But I am not supposing for one moment that you fellows at Scotland Yard don't know more than you've let on to the newspapers. You keep your discoveries out of the Press over here, and a good job, too, but you wouldn't persuade me that you haven't some very distinct theory as to how that crime was worked, and the sort of person who did it. Eh, Mr. Jacks?"

"We are perhaps not quite so ignorant as we seem," the Inspector answered, "and of course you are right when you say that we have a few more facts to go by than have appeared in the newspapers. Still, the affair is an extremely puzzling one,—as puzzling, in its way," Mr. Jacks continued, "as the murder on the very next evening of this young American gentleman."

Mr. Coulson nodded sympathetically. The drinks were brought, and he raised his glass to his guest.

"Here's luck!" he said—"luck to you with your game of human chess, and luck to me with my woollen machinery patents! You were speaking of that second murder," he remarked, setting down his glass. "I haven't noticed the papers much this morning. Has any arrest been made yet?"

"Not yet," the Inspector admitted. "To tell you the truth, we find it almost as puzzling an affair as the one in which Mr. Hamilton Fynes was concerned."

Mr. Coulson nodded. He seemed content, at this stage in their conversation, to assume the role of listener.

"You read the particulars of the murder of Mr. Vanderpole, I suppose?" the Inspector asked.

"Every word," Mr. Coulson answered. "Most interesting thing I've seen in an English newspaper since I landed. Didn't sound like London somehow. Gray old law-abiding place, my partner always calls it."

"I am going to be quite frank with you, Mr. Coulson," the Inspector continued. "I am going to tell you exactly why I have come to see you again tonight."

"Why, that's good," Mr. Coulson declared. "I like to know everything a man's got in his mind."

"I have come to you," the Inspector said, "because, by a somewhat curious coincidence, I find that, besides your slight acquaintance with and knowledge of Mr. Hamilton Fynes, you were also acquainted with this Mr. Richard Vanderpole,—that you were," he continued, knocking the ash off his cigar and speaking a little more slowly, "the last person, except the driver of the taxicab, to have seen him alive."

Mr. Coulson turned slowly around and faced his companion.

"Now, how the devil do you know that?" he asked.

The Inspector smiled tolerantly.

"Well," he said, "that is very simple. The taxicab started from here. Mr. Vanderpole had been visiting some one in the hotel. There was not the slightest difficulty in ascertaining that the person for whom he asked, and with whom he spent some twenty minutes in this very room, was Mr. James B. Coulson of New York."

"Seated on this very couch, sir!" Mr. Coulson declared, striking the arm of it with the flat of his hand,—"seated within a few feet of where you yourself are at this present moment."

The Inspector nodded.

"Naturally," he continued, "when I became aware of so singular an occurrence, I felt that I must lose no time in coming and having a few more words with you."

Mr. Coulson became meditative.

"Upon my word, when you come to think of it," he said, "it is a coincidence, sure! Two men murdered within twenty-four hours, and I seem to have been the last person who knew them, to speak to either. Tell you what, Mr. Jacks, if this goes on I shall get a bit scared. I think I shall let the London business alone and go on over to Paris."

The Inspector smiled.

"I fancy your nerves," he remarked, "are quite strong enough to bear the strain. However, I am sure you will not mind telling me exactly why Mr. Richard Vanderpole, Secretary to the American Embassy here, should have come to see you on Thursday night."

"Why, that's easy," Mr. Coulson replied. "You may have heard of my firm, The Coulson & Bruce Company of Jersey City. I'm at the head of a syndicate that's controlling some very valuable patents which we want to exploit on this side and in Paris. Now my people don't exactly know how we stand under this new patent bill of Mr. Lloyd George's. Accordingly they wrote across to Mr. Blaine-Harvey, putting the matter to him, and asking him to give me his opinion the moment I arrived on this side. You see, it was no use our entering into contracts if we had to build the plant and make the stuff over here. We didn't stand any earthly show of making it pay that way. Well, Mr. Harvey cabled out that I was just to let him know the moment I landed, and before I opened up any business. Sure enough, I called him up on the telephone, an hour or so after I got here, and this young man came round. I can tell you he was all right, too,—a fine, upstanding young fellow, and as bright as they make em. He brought a written opinion with him as to how the law would affect our proceedings. I've got it in my room if you'd care to see it?"

Mr. Jacks listened to his companion's words with unchanged face.

"If it isn't troubling you," he said, "it would be of some interest to me."

Mr. Coulson rose to his feet.

"You sit right here," he declared. "I'll be back in less than five minutes."

Mr. Coulson was as good as his word. In less than the time mentioned he was seated again by his companion's side with a square sheet of foolscap spread out upon the round table. The Inspector ran it through hurriedly. The paper was stamped 'American Embassy,' and it was the digest of several opinions as to the effect of the new patent law upon the import of articles manufactured under processes controlled by the Coulson & Bruce syndicate. At the end there were a few lines in the Ambassador's own handwriting, summing up the situation. Mr. Coulson produced another packet of letters and documents.

"If you've an hour or so to spare, Mr. Jacks," he said, "I'd like to go right into this with you, if it would interest you any. It's my business over here, so naturally I am glad enough of an opportunity to talk it over."

Mr. Jacks passed back the paper promptly.

"I am extremely obliged to you," he said. "I am sure I should find it most interesting. Another time I should be very glad indeed to look through those specifications, but just now I have this affair of my own rather on my mind. About this Mr. Richard Vanderpole, Mr. Coulson, then," he added. "Do I understand that this young man came to you as a complete stranger?"

"Absolutely," Mr. Coulson answered. "I never saw him before in my life. As decent a young chap as ever I met with, all the same," he went on, "and comes of a good American stock, too. They tell me there's going to be an inquest and that I shall be summoned, but I know nothing more than what I've told you. If I did, you'd be welcome to it."

Mr. Jacks leaned back in his chair. Certainly the situation increased in perplexity! The man by his side was talking now of the adaptation of one of his patents to some existing machinery, and Jacks watched him covertly. He considered himself, to some extent, a physiognomist. He told himself it was not possible that this man was playing a part. Mr. James B. Coulson sat there, the absolute incarnation of the genial man of affairs, interested in his business, interested in the great subject of dollar-getting, content with himself and his position,—a person apparently of little imagination, for the shock of this matter concerning which they had been talking had already passed away. He was doing his best to explain with a pencil on the back of an illustrated paper some new system of wool-bleaching.

"Mr. Coulson," the Inspector said suddenly, "do you know a young lady named Miss Penelope Morse?"

It was here, perhaps, that Mr. Coulson sank a little from the heights of complete success. He repeated the name, and obviously took time to think before he answered.

"Miss Penelope Morse," the Inspector continued. "She is a young American lady, who lives with an invalid aunt in Park Lane, and who is taken everywhere by the Duchess of Devenham, another aunt, I believe."

"I suppose I may say that I am acquainted with her," Mr. Coulson admitted. "She came here the other evening with a young man—Sir Charles Somerfield."

"Ah!" the Inspector murmured.

"She'd read that interview of mine with the Comet man," Mr. Coulson said, "and she fancied that perhaps I could tell her something about Hamilton Fynes."

"First time you'd met her, I suppose?" the Inspector remarked.

"Sure!" Mr. Coulson answered. "As a matter of fact, I know very few of my compatriots over here. I am an American citizen myself, and I haven't too much sympathy with any one, man or woman, who doesn't find America good enough for them to live in."

The Inspector nodded.

"Quite so," he agreed. "So you hadn't anything to tell this young lady?"

"Not a thing that she hadn't read in the Comet," Mr. Coulson replied. "What brought her into your mind, anyway?"

"Nothing particular," the Inspector answered carelessly. "Well, Mr. Coulson, I won't take up any more of your time. I am convinced that you have told me all that you know, and I am afraid that I shall have to look elsewhere to find the loose end of this little tangle."

"Stay and have another drink," Mr. Coulson begged. "I've nothing to do. There are one or two boys coming in later who'll like to meet you."

The Inspector shook his head.

"I must be off," he said. "I want to get into my office before six o'clock. I dare say I shall be running across you again before you go back."

He shook hands and turned away. Then Mr. Coulson made what was, perhaps, his second slight mistake.

"Say, Mr. Jacks," he exclaimed, "what made you mention that young lady's name, anyway? I'm curious to know."

The Inspector looked thoughtfully at the end of the fresh cigar which he had just lit.

"Well," he said, "I don't know that there was anything definite in my mind, only it seems a little strange that you and Miss Penelope Morse should both have been acquainted with the murdered man and that you should have come across one another."

"Sort of bond between us, eh?" Mr. Coulson replied. "She seemed a very charming young lady. Cut above Fynes, I should think."

The detective smiled.

"All your American young ladies who come over here are charming," he said. "Goodbye, Mr. Coulson, and many thanks!"

The Inspector passed out, and the man whom he had come to visit, after a moment's hesitation, resumed his seat.

"These aren't American methods," he muttered to himself. "I don't understand them. That man Jacks is either a simpleton or he is too cunning for me."

He crossed to a writing table and scribbled an unnecessary note, addressing it to a firm in the city. Then he rang for a messenger boy and handed it to him for delivery. A few minutes afterwards he strolled out into the hall. The boy was in the act of handing the note to one of the head porters, who carefully copied the address. Mr. Coulson returned to the smoking room, whistling softly to himself.

CHAPTER XI.
A COMMISSION

Mr. Robert Blaine-Harvey, American Ambassador and Plenipotentiary Extraordinary to England, was a man of great culture, surprising personal gifts, and with a diplomatic instinct which amounted almost to genius. And yet there were times when he was puzzled. For at least half an hour he had been sitting in his great library, looking across the Park, and trying to make up his mind on a very important matter. It seemed to him that he was face to face with what amounted almost to a crisis in his career. His two years at the Court of St. James had been pleasant and uneventful enough. The small questions which had presented themselves for adjustment between the two countries were, after all, of no particular importance and were easily arranged. The days seemed to have gone by for that overstrained sensitiveness which was continually giving rise to senseless bickerings, when every trilling breeze seemed to fan the smouldering fires of jealousy. The two great English-speaking nations appeared finally to have realized the absolute folly of continual disputes between countries whose destiny and ideals were so completely in accord and whose interests were, in the main, identical. A period of absolute friendliness had ensued. And now there had come this little cloud. It was small enough at present, but Mr. Harvey was not the one to overlook its sinister possibilities. Two citizens of his country had been barbarously murdered within the space of a few hours, one in the heart of the most thickly populated capital in the world, and there was a certain significance attached to this fact which the Ambassador himself and those others at Washington perfectly well realized. He glanced once more at the most recent letter on the top of this pile of correspondence and away again out into the Park. It was a difficult matter, this. His friends at Washington did not cultivate the art of obscurity in the words which they used, and it had been suggested to him in black and white that the murder of these two men, under the particular circumstances existing, was a matter concerning which he should speak very plainly indeed to certain August personages. Mr. Harvey, who was a born diplomatist, understood the difficulties of such a proceeding a good deal more than those who had propounded it.

There was a knock at the door, and a footman entered, ushering in a visitor.

"The young lady whom you were expecting, sir," he announced discreetly.

Mr. Harvey rose at once to his feet.

"My dear Penelope," he said, shaking hands with her, "this is charming of you."

Penelope smiled.

"It seems quite like old times to feel myself at home here once more," she declared.

Mr. Harvey did not pursue the subject. He was perfectly well aware that Penelope, who had been his first wife's greatest friend, had never altogether forgiven him for his somewhat brief period of mourning. He drew an easy chair up to the side of his desk and placed a footstool for her.

"I should not have sent for you," he said, "but I am really and honestly in a dilemma. Do you know that, apart from endless cables, Washington has favored me with one hundred and forty pages of foolscap all about the events of the week before last?"

Penelope shivered a little.

"Poor Dicky!" she murmured, looking away into the fire. "And to think that it was I who sent him to his death!"

Mr. Harvey shook his head.

"No," he said, "I do not think that you need reproach yourself with that. As a matter of fact, I think that I should have sent Dicky in any case. He is not so well known as the others, or rather he wasn't associated so closely with the Embassy, and he was constantly at the Savoy on his own account. If I had believed that there was any danger in the enterprise," he continued, "I should still have sent him. He was as strong as a young Hercules. The hand which twisted that noose around his neck must have been the hand of a magician with fingers of steel."

Penelope shivered again. Her face showed signs of distress.

"I do not think," she said, "that I am a nervous person, but I cannot bear to think of it even now."

"Naturally," Mr. Harvey answered. "We were all fond of Dicky, and such a thing has never happened, so far as I am aware, in any European country. My own private secretary murdered in broad daylight and with apparent impunity!"

"Murdered—and robbed!" she whispered, looking up at him with a white face.

The frown on the Ambassador's forehead darkened.

"Not only that," he declared, "but the secrets of which he was robbed have gone to the one country interested in the knowledge of them."

"You are sure of that?" she asked hoarsely.

"I am sure of it," Mr. Harvey answered.

Penelope drew a little breath between her teeth. Her thoughts flashed back to a recent dinner party. The Prince was once more at her side. Almost she could hear his voice—low, clear, and yet with that note of inexpressible, convincing finality. She heard him speak of his country reverently, almost prayerfully; of the sacrifices which true patriotism must always demand. What had been in his mind, she wondered, at the back of his inscrutable eyes, gazing, even at that moment, past the banks of flowers, across the crowded room with all its splendor of light and color, through the walls,—whither! She brushed the thought away. It was absurd, incredible! She was allowing herself to be led away by her old distrust of this man.

"I remarked just now," Mr. Harvey continued, "that such a thing had never happened, so far as I was aware, in any European country. My own words seem to suggest something to me. These methods are not European. They savor more of the East."

"I think you had better go on," she said quietly. "There is something in your mind. I can see that. You have told me so much that you had better tell me the rest."

"The contents of those despatches," Mr. Harvey continued, "intrusted in duplicate, as you have doubtless surmised, to Fynes and to Coulson, contained an assurance that the sending of our fleet to the Pacific was in fact, as well as in appearance, an errand of peace. It was a demonstration, pure and simple. Behind it there may have lain, indeed, a masterful purpose, the determination of a great country to affirm her strenuous existence in a manner most likely to impress the nations unused to seeing her in such a role. It became necessary, in view of certain suspicions, for me to be able to prove to the Government here the absolutely pacific nature of our great enterprise. Those despatches contained such proof. And now listen, Penelope. Before the murder of poor Dicky Vanderpole, we know for a fact that a great nation who chooses to consider herself our enemy in Eastern waters was straining every nerve to prepare for war. Today those preparations have slackened. A great loan has been withdrawn in Paris, an invitation cabled to our fleet to visit Yokohama. These things have a plain reading."

"Plain, indeed," Penelope assented, and she spoke in a low tone because there was fear in her heart. "Why have you told me about them? They throw a new light upon everything,—an awful light!"

"I have known you," the Ambassador said quietly, "since you were a baby. Every member of your family has been a friend of mine. You come of a silent race. I know very well that you are a person of discretion. There are certain small ways in which a government can occasionally be served by the help of some one outside its diplomatic service altogether, some one who could not possibly be connected with it. You know this very well, Penelope, because you have already been of service to us on more than one occasion."

"It was a long time ago," she murmured.

"Not so very long," he reminded her. "But for the first of these tragedies, Fynes' despatches would have reached me through you. I am going to ask your help even once more."

In the somewhat cold spring sunlight which came streaming through the large window, Penelope seemed a little pallid, as though, indeed, the fatigue of the season, even in this its earlier stages, were leaving its mark upon her. There were violet rims under her eyes. A certain alertness seemed to have deserted her usually piquant face.

She sat listening with the air of one half afraid, who has no hope of hearing pleasant things.

"It has been remarked," Mr. Harvey continued, "or rather I may say that I myself have noticed, that you are on exceedingly friendly terms with a very distinguished nobleman who is at present visiting this country—I mean, of course, Prince Maiyo."

Her eyebrows were slowly elevated. Was that really the impression people had! Her lips just moved.

"Well?" she asked.

"I have met Prince Maiyo myself," Mr. Harvey continued, "and I have found him a charming representative of his race. I am not going to say a word against him. If he were an American, we should be proud of him. If he belonged to any other country, we should accept him at once for what he appears to be. Unfortunately, however, he belongs to a country which we have some reason to mistrust. He belongs to a country in whose national character we have not absolute confidence. For that reason, my dear Penelope, we mistrust Prince Maiyo."

"I do not know him so well as you seem to imagine," Penelope said slowly. "We are not even friends, in the ordinary acceptation of the word. I am, to some extent, prejudiced against him. Yet I do not believe that he is capable of a dishonorable action."

"Nor do I," the Ambassador declared smoothly. "Yet in every country, almost in every man, the exact standard of dishonor varies. A man will lie for a woman's sake, and even in the law courts, certainly at his clubs and amongst his friends, it will be accounted to his righteousness. A patriot will lie and intrigue for his country's sake. Now I believe that to Prince Maiyo Japan stands far above the whole world of womankind. I believe that for her sake he would go to very great lengths indeed."

"Go on, please," Penelope murmured.

"The Prince is over here on some sort of an errand which it isn't our business to understand," Mr. Harvey said. "I have heard it rumored that it is a special mission entirely concerned with the renewal of the treaty between England and Japan. However that may be, I have sat here, and I have thought, and I have come to this conclusion, ridiculous though it may seem to you at first. I believe that somewhere behind the hand which killed and robbed Hamilton Fynes and poor Dicky stood the benevolent shadow of our friend Prince Maiyo."

"You have no proof?" she asked breathlessly.

"No proof at all," the Ambassador admitted. "I am scarcely in a position to search for any. The conclusion I have come to has been simply arrived at through putting a few facts together and considering them in the light of certain events. In the first place, we cannot doubt that the secret of those despatches reached at once the very people whom we should have preferred to remain in ignorance of them. Haven't I told you of the sudden cessation of the war alarm in Japan, when once she was assured, by means which she could not mistrust, that it was not the intention of the American nation to make war upon her? The subtlety of those murders, and the knowledge by which they were inspired, must have come from some one in an altogether unique position. You may be sure that no one connected with the Japanese Embassy here would be permitted for one single second to take part in any such illegal act. They know better than that, these wily Orientals. They will play the game from Grosvenor Place right enough. But Prince Maiyo is here, and stands apart from any accredited institution, although he has the confidence of his Ambassador and can command the entire devotion of his own secret service. I have not come to this conclusion hastily. I have thought it out, step by step, and in my own mind I am now absolutely convinced that both these murders were inspired by Prince Maiyo."

"Even if this were so," Penelope said, "what can I do? Why have you sent for me? The Prince and I are not on especially friendly terms. It is only just lately that we have been decently civil to one another."

The Ambassador looked at her with some surprise.

"My dear Penelope," he said, "I have seen you together the last three or four evenings. The Prince looks at no one else while you are there. He talks to you, I know, more freely than to any other woman."

"It is by chance," Penelope protested. "I have tried to avoid him."

"Then I cannot congratulate you upon your success," Mr. Harvey said grimly.

"Things have changed a little between us, perhaps," Penelope said. "What is it that you really want?"

"I want to know this," the Ambassador said slowly. "I want to know how Japan became assured that America had no intention of going to war with her. In other words, I want to know whether those papers which were stolen from Fynes and poor Dicky found their way to the Japanese Embassy or into the hands of Prince Maiyo himself."

"Anything else?" she asked with a faint note of sarcasm in her tone.

"Yes," Mr. Harvey replied, "there is something else. I should like to know what attitude Prince Maiyo takes towards the proposed renewal of the treaty between his country and Great Britain."

She shook her head.

"Even if we were friends," she said, "the very closest of friends, he would never tell me. He is far too clever."

"Do not be too sure," Mr. Harvey said. "Sometimes a man, especially an Oriental, who does not understand the significance of your sex in these matters, can be drawn on to speak more freely to a woman than he would ever dream of doing to his best friend. He would not tell you in as many words, of course. On the other hand, he might show you what was in his mind."

"He is going back very shortly," Penelope remarked.

Mr. Harvey nodded.

"That is why I sent for you to come immediately. You will see him tonight at Devenham House."

"With all the rest of the world," she answered, "but a man is not likely to talk confidentially under such conditions."

Mr. Harvey rose to his feet.

"It is only a chance, of course," he admitted, "but remember that you know more than any other person in this country except myself. It would be impossible for the Prince to give you credit for such knowledge. A casual remark, a word, perhaps, may be sufficient."

Penelope held out her hand. The servant for whom the Ambassador had rung was already in the room.

"I will try," she promised. "Ask Mrs. Harvey to excuse my going up to see her this afternoon. I have another call to make, and I want to rest before the function tonight."

The Ambassador bowed, and escorted her to the door.

"I have confidence in you, Penelope," he said. "You will try your best?"

"Oh, yes!" she answered with a queer little laugh, "I shall do that. But I don't think that even you quite understand Prince Maiyo!"

CHAPTER XII.
PENELOPE INTERVENES

The perfume of countless roses, the music of the finest band in Europe, floated through the famous white ballroom of Devenham House. Electric lights sparkled from the ceiling, through the pillared way the ceaseless splashing of water from the fountains in the winter garden seemed like a soft undernote to the murmur of voices, the musical peals of laughter, the swirl of skirts, and the rhythm of flying feet.

Penelope stood upon the edge of the ballroom, her hand resting still upon her partner's arm. She wore a dress of dull rose-color, a soft, clinging silk, which floated about her as she danced, a creation of Paquin's, daring but delightful. Her eyes were very full and soft. She was looking her best, and knew it. Nevertheless, she was just at the moment, a little *distrait*. She was watching the brilliant scene with a certain air of abstraction, as though her interest in it was, after all, an impersonal thing.

"Jolly well every one looks tonight," her partner, who was Sir Charles, remarked. "All the women seem to be wearing smart frocks, and some of those foreign uniforms are gorgeous."

"Even the Prince," Penelope said thoughtfully, "must find some reflection of the philosophy of his own country in such a scene as this. For the last fortnight we have been surfeited with horrors. We have had to go through all sorts of nameless things," she added, shivering slightly, "and tonight we dance at Devenham House. We dance, and drink champagne, and marvel at the flowers, as though we had not a care in the world, as though life moved always to music."

Sir Charles frowned a little.

"The Prince again!" he said, half protesting. "He seems to be a great deal in your thoughts lately, Penelope."

"Why not?" she answered. "It is something to meet a person whom one is able to dislike. Nowadays the whole world is so amiable."

"I wonder how much you really do dislike him," he said.

She looked at him with a mysterious smile.

"Sometimes," she murmured softly, "I wonder that myself."

"Leaving the Prince out of the question," he continued, "what you say is true enough. Only a few days ago, you had to attend that awful inquest, and the last time I saw dear old Dicky Vanderpole, he was looking forward to this very dance."

"It seems callous of us to have come," Penelope declared. "And yet, if we hadn't, what difference would it have made? Every one else would have been here. Our absence would never have been noticed, and we should have sat at home and had the blues. But all the same, life is cruel."

"Can't say I find much to grumble at myself," Sir Charles said cheerfully. "I'm frightfully sorry about poor old Dicky, of course, and every other decent fellow who doesn't get his show. But, after all, it's no good being morbid. Sackcloth and ashes benefit no one. Shall we have another turn?"

"Not yet," Penelope replied. "Wait till the crowd thins a little. Tell me what you have been doing today?"

"Pretty strenuous time," Sir Charles remarked. "Up at nine, played golf at Ranelagh all morning, lunched down there, back to my rooms and changed, called on my tailor, went round to the club, had one game of billiards and four rubbers of bridge."

"Is that all?" Penelope asked.

The faint sarcasm which lurked beneath her question passed unnoticed. Sir Charles smiled good-humoredly.

"Not quite," he answered. "I dined at the Carlton with Bellairs and some men from Woolwich and we had a box at the Empire to see the new ballet. Jolly good it was, too. Will you come one night, if I get up a party?"

"Oh, perhaps!" she answered. "Come and dance."

They passed into the great ballroom, the finest in London, brilliant with its magnificent decorations of real flowers, its crowd of uniformed men and beautiful women, its soft yet ever-present throbbing of wonderful music. At the further end of the room, on a slightly raised dais, still receiving her guests, stood the Duchess of Devenham. Penelope gave a little start as they saw who was bowing over her hand.

"The Prince!" she exclaimed.

Sir Charles whispered something a little under his breath.

"I wonder," she remarked with apparent irrelevance, "whether he dances."

"Shall I go and find out for you?" Sir Charles asked.

She had suddenly grown absent. She had the air of scarcely hearing what he said.

"Let us stop," she said. "I am out of breath."

He led her toward the winter garden. They sat by a fountain, listening to the cool play of the water.

"Penelope," Somerfield said a little awkwardly, "I don't want to presume, you know, nor to have you think that I am foolishly jealous, but you have changed towards me the last few weeks, haven't you?"

"The last few weeks," she answered, "have been enough to change me toward any one. All the same, I wasn't conscious of anything particular so far as you are concerned."

"I always thought," he continued after a moment's hesitation, "that there was so much prejudice in your country against—against all Asiatic races."

She looked at him steadfastly for a minute.

"So there is," she answered. "What of it?"

"Nothing, except that it is a prejudice which you do not seem to share," he remarked.

"In a way I do share it," she declared, "but there are exceptions, sometimes very wonderful exceptions."

"Prince Maiyo, for instance," he said bitterly. "Yet a fortnight ago I could have sworn that you hated him."

"I think that I do hate him," Penelope affirmed. "I try to. I want to. I honestly believe that he deserves my hatred. I have more reason for feeling this way than you know of, Sir Charles."

"If he has dared—" Somerfield began.

"He has dared nothing that he ought not to," Penelope interrupted. "His manners are altogether too perfect. It is the chill faultlessness of the man which is so depressing. Can't you understand," she added, speaking in a tone of greater intensity, "that that is why I hate him? Hush!"

She gripped his sleeve warningly. There was suddenly the murmur of voices and the trailing of skirts. A little party seemed to have invaded the winter garden—a little party of the principal guests. The Duchess herself came first, and her fingers were resting upon the arm of Prince Maiyo. She stopped to speak to Penelope, and turned afterwards to Somerfield. Prince Maiyo held out his hand for Penelope's programme.

"You will spare me some dances?" he pleaded. "I come late, but it is not my fault."

She yielded the programme to him without a word.

"Those with an X,'" she said, "are free. One has to protect oneself."

He smiled as he wrote his own name, unrebuked, in four places.

"Our first dance, then, is number 10," he said. "It is the next but one. I shall find you here, perhaps?"

"Here or amongst the chaperons," she answered, as they passed on.

"You admire Miss Morse?" the Duchess asked him.

"Greatly," the Prince answered. "She is natural, she has grace, and she has what I do not find so much in this country—would you say charm?"

"It is an excellent word," the Duchess answered. "I am inclined to agree with you. Her aunt, with whom she lives, is a confirmed invalid, so she is a good deal with me. Her mother was my half-sister."

The Prince bowed.

"She will marry, I suppose?" he said.

"Naturally," the Duchess answered. "Sir Charles, poor fellow, is a hopeless victim. I should not be surprised if she married him, some day or other."

The Prince looked behind for a moment; then he stopped to admire a magnificent orchid.

"It will be great good fortune for Sir Charles Somerfield," he said.

Somerfield scarcely waited until the little party were out of sight.

"Penelope," he exclaimed, "you've given that man four dances!"

"I am afraid," she answered, "that I should have given him eight if he had asked for them."

He rose to his feet.

"Will you allow me to take you back to your aunt?" he asked.

"No!" she answered. "My aunt is quite happy without me, and I should prefer to remain here."

He sat down, fuming.

"Penelope, what do you mean by it?" he demanded.

"And what do you mean by asking me what I mean by it?" she replied. "You haven't any especial right that I know of."

"I wish to Heaven I had!" he answered with a noticeable break in his voice.

There was a short silence. She turned away; she felt that she was suddenly surrounded by a cloud of passion.

"Penelope," he pleaded,—

She stopped him.

"You must not say another word," she declared. "I mean it,—you must not."

"I have waited for some time," he reminded her.

"All the more reason why you should wait until the right time," she insisted. "Be patient for a little longer, do. Just now I feel that I need a friend more than I have ever needed one before. Don't let me lose the one I value most. In a few weeks' time you shall say whatever you like, and, at any rate, I will listen to you. Will you be content with that?"

"Yes!" he answered.

She laid her fingers upon his arm.

"I am dancing this with Captain Wilmot," she said. "Will you come and bring me back here afterwards, unless you are engaged?"

The Prince found her alone in the winter garden, for Somerfield, when he had seen him coming, had stolen away. He came towards her quickly, with the smooth yet impetuous step which singled him out at once as un-English. He had the whole room to cross to come to her, and she watched him all the way. The corners of his lips were already curved in a slight smile. His eyes were bright, as one who looks upon something which he greatly desires. Slender though his figure was, his frame was splendidly knit, and he carried himself as one of the aristocrats of the world. As he approached, she scanned his face curiously. She became critical, anxiously but ineffectively. There was not a feature in his face with which a physiognomist could have found fault.

"Dear young lady," he said, bowing low, "I come to you very humbly, for I am afraid that I am a deceiver. I shall rob you of your pleasure, I fear. I have put my name down for four dances, and, alas! I do not dance."

She made room for him by her side.

"And I," she said, "am weary of dancing. One does nothing else, night after night. We will talk."

"Talk or be silent," he answered softly. "Myself I believe that you are in need of silence. To be silent together is a proof of great friendship, is it not?"

She nodded.

"It seems to me that I have been through so much the last fortnight." she said.

"You have suffered where you should not have suffered," he assented gravely. "I do not like your laws at all. At what they called the inquest your presence was surely not necessary! You were a woman and had no place there. You had," he added calmly, "so little to tell."

"Nothing," she murmured.

"Life to me just now," he continued, "is so much a matter of comparison. It is for that, indeed, that I am here. You see, I have lived nearly all my life in my own country and only a very short time in Europe. Then my mother was an English lady, and my father a Japanese nobleman. Always I seem to be pulled two different ways, to be struggling to see things from two different points of view. But there is one subject in which I think I am wholly with my own country."

"And that?" she asked.

"I do not think," he said, "that the rougher and more strenuous paths of life were meant to be trodden by your sex. Please do not misunderstand me," he went on earnestly. "I am not thinking of the paths of literature and of art, for there the perceptions of your sex are so marvellously acute that you indeed may often lead where we must follow. I am speaking of the more material things of life."

She was suddenly conscious of a shiver which seemed to spread from her heart throughout her limbs. She sat quite still, gripping her little lace handkerchief in her fingers.

"I mean," he continued, "the paths which a man must tread who seeks to serve his country or his household,—the every-day life in which sometimes intrigue or force is necessary. Do you agree with me, Miss Morse?"

"I suppose so," she faltered.

"That is why," he added, "it was painful to me to see you stand there before those men, answering their questions,—men whose walk in life was different, of an order removed from yours, who should not even have been permitted to approach you upon bended knees. Do not think that I am suggesting any fault to you—do not think that I am forcing your confidence in any way. But these are the thoughts which came to me only a little time ago."

She was silent. They listened together to the splashing of the water. What was the special gift, she wondered, which gave this man such insight? She felt her heart beating; she was conscious that he was looking at her. He knew already that it was through her medium that those despatches which never reached London were to have been handed on to their destination! He must know that she was to some extent in the confidence of her country's Ambassador! Perhaps he knew, too, those other thoughts which were in her mind,—knew that it had been her deliberate intent to deceive him, to pluck those secrets which he carried with him, even from his heart! What a fool she had been to dream, for a moment, of measuring her wits against his!

He began to speak again, and his voice seemed pitched in lighter key.

"After all," he said, "you must think it strange of me to be so egotistical—to speak all the time so much of my likes and dislikes. To you I have been a little more outspoken than to others."

"You have found me an interesting subject for investigation perhaps?" she asked, looking up suddenly.

"You possess gifts," he admitted calmly, "which one does not find amongst the womenfolk of my country, nor can I say that I have found them to any extent amongst the ladies of the English Court."

"Gifts of which you do not approve when possessed by my sex," she suggested.

"You are a law to yourself, Miss Morse," he said. "What one would not admire in others seems natural enough in you. You have brains and you have insight. For that reason I have been with you a little outspoken,—for that reason and another which I think you know of. You see, my time over here grows nearer to an end with every day. Soon I must carry away with me, over the seas, all the delightful memories, the friendships, the affections, which have made this country such a pleasant place for me."

"You are going soon?" she asked quickly.

"Very soon," he answered. "My work is nearly finished, if indeed I may dignify it by the name of work. Then I must go back."

She shrank a little away from him, as though the word were distasteful to her.

"Do you mean that you will go back for always?" she asked.

"There are many chances in life," he answered. "I am the servant of the Emperor and my country."

"There is no hope, then," she continued, "of your settling down here altogether?"

For once the marble immobility of his features seemed disturbed. He looked at her in honest amazement.

"Here!" he exclaimed. "But I am a son of Japan!"

"There are many of your race who do live here," she reminded him.

He smiled with the air of one who is forced to humor a person of limited vision.

"With them it is, alas! a matter of necessity," he said. "It is very hard indeed to make you understand over here how we feel about such things,—there seems to be a different spirit amongst you

Western races, a different spirit or a lack of spirit—I do not know which I should say. But in Japan the love of our country is a passion which seems to throb with every beat of our hearts. If we leave her, it is for her good. When we go back, it is our reward."

"Then you are here now for her good?" she asked.

"Assuredly," he answered.

"Tell me in what way?" she begged. "You have been studying English customs, their methods of education, their political life, perhaps?"

He turned his head slowly and looked into her eyes. She bore the ordeal well, but she never forgot it. It seemed to her afterwards that he must have read every thought which had flashed through her brain. She felt like a little child in the presence of some mysterious being, thoughts of whom had haunted her dreams, now visible in bodily shape for the first time.

"My dear young lady," he said, "please do not ask me too much, for I love to speak the truth, and there are many things which I may not tell. Only you must understand that the country I love—my own country—must enter soon upon a new phase of her history. We who look into the future can see the great clouds gathering. Some of us must needs be pioneers, must go forward a little to learn our safest, and best course. May I tell you that much?"

"Of course," she answered softly.

"And now," he added, leaving his seat as though with reluctance, "the Duchess reminded me, above all things, that directly I found you I was to take you to supper. One of your royal princes has been good enough to signify his desire that we should sit at the same table."

She rose at once.

"Does the Duchess know that you are taking me?" she asked.

"I arranged it with her," he answered. "My time draws soon to an end and I am to be spoilt a little."

They crossed the ballroom together and mounted the great stairs. Something—she never knew quite what it was—prompted her to detain him as they paused on the threshold of the supper room.

"You do not often read the papers, Prince," she said. "Perhaps you have not seen that, after all, the police have discovered a clue to the Hamilton Fynes murder."

The Prince looked down upon her for a moment without reply.

"Yes?" he murmured softly.

She understood that she was to go on—that he was anxious for her to go on.

"Some little doctor in a village near Willington, where the line passes, has come forward with a story about attending to a wounded man on the night of the murder," she said.

He was very silent. It seemed to her that there was something strange about the immovability of his features. She looked at him wonderingly. Then it suddenly flashed upon her that this was his way of showing emotion. Her lips parted. The color seemed drawn from her cheeks. The majordomo of the Duchess stood before them with a bow.

"Her Grace desires me to show your Highness to your seats," he announced.

Prince Maiyo turned to his companion.

"Will you allow me to precede you through the crush?" he said. "We are to go this way."

CHAPTER XIII.
EAST AND WEST

After the supper there were obligations which the Prince, whose sense of etiquette was always strong, could not avoid. He took Penelope back to her aunt, reminding her that the next dance but one belonged to him. Miss Morse, who was an invalid and was making one of her very rare appearances in Society, watched him curiously as he disappeared.

"I wonder what they'd think of your new admirer in New York, Penelope," she remarked.

"I imagine," Penelope answered, "that they would envy me very much."

Miss Morse, who was a New Englander of the old-fashioned type, opened her lips, but something in her niece's face restrained her.

"Well, at any rate," she said, "I hope we don't go to war with them. The Admiral wrote me, a few weeks ago, that he saw no hope for anything else."

"It would be a terrible complication," the Duchess sighed, "especially considering our own alliance with Japan. I don't think we need consider it seriously, however. Over in America you people have too much common sense."

"The Government have, very likely," Miss Morse admitted, "but it isn't always the Government who decide things or who even rule the country. We have an omnipotent Press, you know. All that's wanted is a weak President, and Heaven knows where we should be!"

"Of course," the Duchess remarked, "Prince Maiyo is half an Englishman. His mother was a Stretton-Wynne. One of the first intermarriages, I should think. Lord Stretton-Wynne was Ambassador to Japan."

"I think," said Penelope, "that if you could look into Prince Maiyo's heart you would not find him half an Englishman. I think that he is more than seven-eighths a Japanese."

"I have heard it whispered," the Duchess remarked, leaning forward, "that he is over here on an exceedingly serious mission. One thing is quite certain. No one from his country, or from any other country, for that matter, has ever been so entirely popular amongst us. He has the most delightful manners of any man I ever knew of any race."

Sir Charles came up, with gloomy face, to claim a dance. After it was over, he led Penelope back to her aunt almost in silence.

"You are dancing again with the Prince?" he asked.

"Certainly," she answered. "Here he comes."

The Prince smiled pleasantly at the young man, who towered like a giant above him, and noticed at once his lack of cordiality.

"I am selfish!" he exclaimed, pausing with Penelope's hand upon his coat sleeve. "I am taking you too much away from your friends, and spoiling your pleasure, perhaps, because I do not dance. Is it not so? It is your kindness to a stranger, and they do not all appreciate it."

"We will go into the winter garden and talk it over," she answered, smiling.

They found their old seats unoccupied. Once more they sat and listened to the fall of the water.

"Prince," said Penelope, "there is one thing I have learned about you this evening, and that is that you do not love questions. And yet there is one other which I should like to ask you."

"If you please," the Prince murmured.

"You spoke, a little time ago," she continued, "of some great crisis with which your country might soon come face to face. Might I ask you this: were you thinking of war with the United States?"

He looked at her in silence for several moments.

"Dear Miss Penelope," he said,—"may I call you that? Forgive me if I am too forward, but I hear so many of our friends—"

"You may call me that," she interrupted softly.

"Let me remind you, then, of what we were saying a little time ago," he went on. "You will not take offence? You will understand,

I am sure. Those things that lie nearest to my heart concerning my country are the things of which I cannot speak."

"Not even to me?" she pleaded. "I am so insignificant. Surely I do not count?"

"Miss Penelope," he said, "you yourself are a daughter of that country of which we have been speaking."

She was silent.

"You think, then," she asked, "that I put my country before everything else in the world?"

"I believe," he answered, "that you would. Your country is too young to be wholly degenerate. It is true that you are a nation of fused races—a strange medley of people, but still you are a nation. I believe that in time of stress you would place your country before everything else."

"And therefore?" she murmured.

"And therefore," he continued with a delightful smile, "I shall not discuss my hopes or fears with you. Or if we do discuss them," he went on, "let us weave them into a fairy tale. Let us say that you are indeed the Daughter of All America and that I am the Son of All Japan. You know what happens in fairyland when two great nations rise up to fight?"

"Tell me," she begged.

"Why, the Daughter of All America and the Son of All Japan stand hand in hand before their people, and as they plight their troth, all bitter feelings pass away, the shouts of anger cease, and there is no more talk of war."

She sighed, and leaned a little towards him. Her eyes were soft and dusky, her red lips a little parted.

"But I," she whispered, "am not the Daughter of All America."

"Nor am I," he answered with a sigh, "the Son of all Japan."

There was a breathless silence. The water splashed into the basin, the music came throbbing in through the flower-hung doorways. It seemed to Penelope that she could almost hear her heart beat. The blood in her veins was dancing to the one perfect waltz. The moments passed. She drew a little breath and ventured to look at him. His face was still and white, as though, indeed, it had been carved out of marble, but the fire in his eyes was a living thing.

"We have actually been talking nonsense," she said, "and I thought that you, Prince, were far too serious."

"We were talking fairy tales," he answered, "and they are not nonsense. Do not you ever read the history of your country as it was many hundreds of years ago, before this ugly thing they call civilization weakened the sinews of our race and besmirched the very face of duty? Do you not like to read of the times when life was simpler and more natural, and there was space for every man to live and grow and stretch out his hands to the skies, — every man and every woman? They call them, in your literature, the days of romance. They existed, too, in my country. It is not nonsense to imagine for a little time that the ages between have rolled away and that those days are with us?"

"No," she answered, "it is not nonsense. But if they were?"

He raised her fingers to his lips and kissed them. The touch of his hand, the absolute delicacy of the salute itself, made it unlike any other caress she had ever known or imagined.

"The world might have been happier for both of us," he whispered.

Somerfield, sullen and discontented, came and looked at them, moved away, and then hesitatingly returned.

"Willmott is waiting for you," he said. "The last was my dance, and this is his."

She rose at once and turned to the Prince.

"I think that we should go back," she said. "Will you take me to my aunt?"

"If it must be so," he answered. "Tell me, Miss Penelope," he added, "may I ask your aunt or the Duchess to bring you one day to my house to see my treasures? I cannot say how long I shall remain in this country. I would like you so much to come before I break up my little home."

"Of course we will," she answered. "My aunt goes nowhere, but the Duchess will bring me, I am sure. Ask her when I am there, and we can agree about the day."

He leaned a little towards her.

"Tomorrow?" he whispered.

She nodded. There were three engagements for the next day of which she took no heed.

"Tomorrow," she said. "Come and let us arrange it with the Duchess."

Prince Maiyo left Devenham House to find the stars paling in the sky, and the light of an April dawn breaking through the black clouds eastwards. He dismissed his electric brougham with a little wave of the hand, and turned to walk to his house in St. James's Square. As he walked, he bared his head. After the long hours of artificially heated rooms, there was something particularly soothing about the fresh sweetness of the early spring morning. There was something, it seemed to him, which reminded him, however faintly, of the mornings in his own land,—the perfume of the flowers from the window-boxes, perhaps, the absence of that hideous roar of traffic, or the faint aromatic scent from the lime trees in the Park, heavy from recent rain. It was the quietest hour of the twenty-four,—the hour almost of dawn. The night wayfarers had passed away, the great army of toilers as yet slumbered. One sad-eyed woman stumbled against him as he walked slowly up Piccadilly. He lifted his hat with an involuntary gesture, and her laugh changed into a sob. He turned round, and emptied his pockets of silver into her hand, hurrying away quickly that his eyes might not dwell upon her face.

"A coward always," he murmured to himself, a little wearily, for he knew where his weakness lay,—an invincible repugnance to the ugly things of life. As he passed on, however, his spirits rose again. He caught a breath of lilac scent from a closed florist's shop. He looked up to the skies, over the housetops, faintly blue, growing clearer every moment. Almost he fancied that he looked again into the eyes of this strange girl, recalled her unexpected yet delightful frankness, which to him, with his love of abstract truth, was, after all, so fascinating. Oh, there was much to be said for this Western world!—much to be said for those whose part it was to live in it! Yet, never so much as during that brief night walk through the silent streets, did he realize how absolutely unfitted he was to be even a temporary sojourner in this vast city. What would they say of him if they knew,—of him, a breaker of their laws, a guest, and yet a sinner against all their conventions; a guest, and yet one whose hand it was which would strike them, some day or other, the great blow! What would she think of him? He wondered whether she would realize the truth, whether she would understand. Almost as he asked himself the question, he smiled. To him it seemed a strange proof of the danger in which a weaker man would stand of passing under the yoke of this hateful Western civilization. To dream of her—yes! To see her face shining upon him from every beautiful place, to feel the delight of her presence with every delicious sensation,—the warmth of the sunlight, the perfume of the blossoms he loved! There was joy in this, the joy of the artist and the lover. But to find her in his life, a real person, a daughter of this new world, whose every instinct would be at war with his—that way lay slavery! He brushed the very thought from him.

As he reached the door of his house in St. James' Square, it opened slowly before him. He had brought his own servants from his own country, and in their master's absence sleep was not for them. His butler spoke to him in his own language. The Prince nodded and passed on. On his study table—a curious note of modernism where everything seemed to belong to a bygone world—was a cablegram. He tore it open. It consisted of one word only. He let the thin paper fall fluttering from his fingers. So the time was fixed!

Then Soto came gliding noiselessly into the room, fully dressed, with tireless eyes but wan face,—Soto, the prototype of his master, the most perfect secretary and servant evolved through all the years.

"Master," he said, "there has been trouble here. An Englishman came with this card."

The Prince took it, and read the name of Inspector Jacks.

"Well?" he murmured.

"The man asked questions," Soto continued. "We spoke English so badly that he was puzzled. He went away, but he will come again."

The Prince smiled, and laid his hand almost caressingly upon the other's shoulder.

"It is of no consequence, Soto," he said,—"no consequence whatever."

CHAPTER XIV.
AN ENGAGEMENT

"Your rooms, Prince, are wonderful," Penelope said to him. "I knew that you were a man of taste, but I did not know that you were also a millionaire."

He laughed softly.

"In my country," he answered, "there are no millionaires. The money which we have, however, we spend, perhaps a little differently. But, indeed, none of my treasures here have cost me anything. They have come to me through more generations than I should care to reckon up. The bronze idol, for instance, upon my writing case is four hundred years old, to my certain knowledge, and my tapestries were woven when in this country your walls went bare."

"What I admire more than anything," the Duchess declared, "is your beautiful violet tone."

"I am glad," he answered, "that you like my coloring. Some people have thought it sombre. To me dark colors indoors are restful."

"Everything about the whole place is restful," Penelope said,— "your servants with their quaint dresses and slippered feet, your thick carpets, the smell of those strange burning leaves, and, forgive me if I say so, your closed windows. I suppose in time I should have a headache. For a little while it is delicious."

The Prince sighed.

"Fresh air is good," he said, "but the air that comes from your streets does not seem to me to be fresh, nor do I like the roar of your great city always in my ears. Here I cut myself off, and I feel that I can think. Duchess, you must try those preserved fruits. They come to me from my own land. I think that the secret of preserving them is not known here. You see, they are packed with rose leaves and lemon plant. There is a golden fig, Miss Penelope,—the fruit of great knowledge, the magical fruit, too, they say. Eat that and close your eyes and you can look back and tell us all the wonders of the past. That is to say," he added with a faint smile, "if the magic works."

"But the magic never does work," she protested with a little sigh, "and I am not in the least interested in the past. Tell me something about the future?"

"Surely that is easier," he answered. "Over the past we have lost our control,—what has been must remain to the end of time. The future is ours to do what we will with."

"That sounds so reasonable," the Duchess declared, "and it is so absolutely false. No one can do what they will with the future. It is the future which does what it will with us."

The Prince smiled tolerantly.

"It depends a good deal, does it not," he said, "upon ourselves? Miss Penelope is the daughter of a country which is still young, which has all its future before it, and which, has proclaimed to the world its fixed intention of controlling its own destinies. She, at any rate, should have imbibed the national spirit. You are looking at my curtains," he added, turning to Penelope. "Let me show you the figures upon them, and I will tell you the allegory."

He led her to the window, and explained to her for some moments the story of the faded images which represented one chapter out of the mythology of his country. And then she stopped him.

"Always," she said, "you and I seem to be talking of things that are dead and past, or of a future which is out of our reach. Isn't it possible to speak now and then of the present?"

"Of the actual present?" he asked softly. "Of this very moment?"

"Of this very moment, if you will," she answered. "Your fairy tale the other night was wonderful, but it was a long way off."

The Prince was summoned away somewhat abruptly to bid farewell to a little stream of departing guests. Today, more than ever, he seemed to belong, indeed to the world of real and actual things, for a cousin of his mother's, a Lady Stretton-Wynne, was helping him receive his guests—his own aunt, as Penelope told herself more than once, struggling all the time with a vague incredulity. When he was able to rejoin her, she was examining a curious little coffer which stood upon an ivory table.

"Show me the mystery of this lock," she begged. "I have been trying to open it ever since you went away. One could imagine that the secrets of a nation might be hidden here."

He smiled, and taking the box from her hands, touched a little spring. Almost at once the lid flew open.

"I am afraid," he said, "that it is empty."

She peered in.

"No," she exclaimed, "there is something there! See!" She thrust in her hand and drew out a small, curiously shaped dagger of fine blue steel and a roll of silken cord. She held them up to him.

"What are these?" she asked. "Are they symbols—the cord and the knife of destiny?"

He took them gently from her hand and replaced them in the box. She heard the lock go with a little click, and looked into his face, surprised at his silence.

"Is there anything the matter?" she asked. "Ought I not to have taken them up?"

Almost as the words left her lips, she understood. His face was inscrutable, but his very silence was ominous. She remembered a drawing in one of the halfpenny papers, the drawing of a dagger found in a horrible place. She remembered the description of that thin silken cord, and she began to tremble.

"I did not know that anything was in the box," he said calmly. "I am sorry if its contents have alarmed you."

She scarcely heard his words. The room seemed wheeling round with her, the floor unsteady beneath her feet. The atmosphere of the place had suddenly become horrible,—the faint odor of burning leaves, the pictures, almost like caricatures, which mocked her from the walls, the grinning idols, the strangely shaped weapons in their cases of black oak. She faltered as she crossed the room, but recovered herself.

"Aunt," she said, "if you are ready, I think that we ought to go."

The Duchess was more than ready. She rose promptly. The Prince walked with them to the door and handed them over to his majordomo.

"It has been so nice of you," he said to the Duchess, "to honor my bachelor abode. I shall often think of your visit."

"My dear Prince," the Duchess declared, "it has been most interesting. Really, I found it hard to believe, in that charming room of yours, that we had not actually been transported to your wonderful country."

"You are very gracious," the Prince answered, bowing low.

Penelope's hands were within her muff. She was talking some nonsense—she scarcely knew what, but her eyes rested everywhere save on the face of her host. Somehow or other she reached the door, ran down the steps and threw herself into a corner of the brougham. Then, for the first time, she allowed herself to look behind. The door was already closed, but between the curtains which his hands had drawn apart, Prince Maiyo was standing in the room which they had just quitted, and there was something in the calm impassivity of his white, stern face which seemed to madden her. She clenched her hands and looked away.

"Really, I was not so much bored as I had feared," the Duchess remarked composedly. "That Stretton-Wynne woman generally gets on my nerves, but her nephew seemed to have a restraining effect upon her. She didn't tell me more than once about her husband's bad luck in not getting Canada, and she never even mentioned her girls. But I do think, Penelope," she continued, "that I shall have to talk to you a little seriously. There's the best-looking and richest young bachelor in London dying to marry you, and you won't have a word to say to him. On the other hand, after starting by disliking him heartily, you are making yourself almost conspicuous with this fascinating young Oriental. I admit that he is delightful, my dear Penelope, but I think you should ask yourself whether it is quite worth while. Prince Maiyo may take home with him many Western treasures, but I do not think that he will take home a wife."

"If you say another word to me, aunt," Penelope exclaimed, "I shall shriek!"

The Duchess, being a woman of tact, laughed the subject away and pretended not to notice Penelope's real distress. But when they had reached Devenham House, she went to the telephone and called up Somerfield.

"Charlie," she said,—

"Right o'!" he interrupted. "Who is it?"

"Be careful what you are saying," she continued, "because it isn't any one who wants you to take them out to supper."

"I only wish you did," he answered. "It's the Duchess, isn't it?"

"The worst of having a distinctive voice," she sighed. "Listen. I want to speak to you."

"I am listening hard," Somerfield answered. "Hold the instrument a little further away from you,—that's better."

"We have been to the Prince's for tea this afternoon—Penelope and I," she said.

"I know," he assented. "I was asked, but I didn't see the fun of it. It puts my back up to see Penelope monopolized by that fellow," he added gloomily.

"Well, listen to what I have to say," the Duchess went on. "Something happened there—I don't know what—to upset Penelope very much. She never spoke a word coming home, and she has gone straight up to her room and locked herself in. Somehow or other the Prince managed to offend her. I am sure of that, Charlie!"

"I'm beastly sorry," Somerfield answered. "I meant to say that I was jolly glad to hear it."

The Duchess coughed.

"I didn't quite hear what you said before," she said severely. "Perhaps it is just as well. I rang up to say that you had better come round and dine with us tonight. You will probably find Penelope in a more reasonable frame of mind."

"Awfully good of you," Somerfield declared heartily. "I'll come with pleasure."

Dinner at Devenham House that evening was certainly a domestic meal. Even the Duke was away, attending a political gathering. Penelope was pale, but otherwise entirely her accustomed self. She talked even more than usual, and though she spoke of a headache, she declined all remedies. To Somerfield's surprise, she made not the slightest objection when he followed her into the library after dinner.

"Penelope," he said, "something has gone wrong. Won't you tell me what it is? You look worried."

She returned his anxious gaze, dry-eyed but speechless.

"Has that fellow, Prince Maiyo, done or said anything—"

She interrupted him.

"No!" she cried. "No! don't mention his name, please! I don't want to hear his name again just now."

"For my part," Somerfield said bitterly, "I never want to hear it again as long as I live!"

There was a short silence. Suddenly she turned towards him.

"Charlie," she said, "you have asked me to marry you six times."

"Seven," he corrected. "I ask you again now—that makes eight."

"Very well," she answered, "I accept—on one condition."

"On any," he exclaimed, his voice trembling with joy. "Penelope, it sounds too good to be true. You can't be in earnest."

"I am," she declared. "I will marry you if you will see that our engagement is announced everywhere tomorrow, and that you do not ask me for anything at all, mind, not even—not anything—for three months' time, at least. Promise that until then you will not let me hear the sound of the word marriage?"

"I promise," he said firmly. "Penelope, you mean it? You mean this seriously?"

She gave him her hands and a very sad little smile.

"I mean it, Charlie," she answered. "I will keep my word."

CHAPTER XV.
PENELOPE EXPLAINS

Once more Penelope found herself in the library of the great house in Park Lane, where Mr. Blaine-Harvey presided over the interests of his country. This time she came as an uninvited, even an unexpected guest. The Ambassador, indeed, had been fetched away by her urgent message from the reception rooms, where his wife was entertaining a stream of callers. Penelope refused to sit down.

"I have not much to say to you, Mr. Harvey," she said. "There is just something which I have discovered and which you ought to know. I want to tell it you as quickly as possible and get away."

"A propos of our last conversation?" he asked eagerly.

She bowed her head.

"It concerns Prince Maiyo," she admitted.

"You are sure that you will not sit down?" he persisted. "You know how interesting this is to me."

She smiled faintly.

"To me," she said, "it is terrible. My only desire is to tell you and have finished with it. You remember, when I was here last, you told me that it was your firm belief that somewhere behind the hand which murdered Hamilton Fynes and poor Dicky stood the shadow of Prince Maiyo."

"I remember it perfectly," he answered.

"You were right," Penelope said.

The Ambassador drew a little breath. It was staggering, this, even if expected.

"I have talked with the Prince several times since our conversation," Penelope continued. "So far as any information which he gave me or seemed likely to give me, I might as well have talked in a foreign language. But in his house, the day before yesterday, in his own library, hidden in a casket which opened only with a secret lock, I found two things."

"What were they?" the Ambassador asked quickly.

"A roll of silken cord," Penelope said, "such as was used to strangle poor Dicky, and a strangely shaped dagger exactly like the picture of the one with which Hamilton Fynes was stabbed."

"Did he know that you found them?" Mr. Blaine-Harvey asked.

"He was with me," Penelope answered. "He even, at my request, opened the casket. He must have forgotten that they were there."

"Perhaps," the Ambassador said thoughtfully, "he never knew."

"One cannot tell," Penelope answered.

"Did he say anything when you discovered them?" the Ambassador asked.

"Nothing," Penelope declared. "It was not necessary. I saw his face. He knows that I understand. It may have been some one else connected with the house, of course, but the main fact is beyond all doubt. Those murders were instigated, if they were not committed, by the Prince."

The Ambassador walked to the window and back again.

"Penelope," he said, "you have only confirmed what I felt must be so, but even then the certainty of it is rather a shock."

She gave him her hand.

"I have told you the truth," she said. "Make what use of it you will. There is one other thing, perhaps, which I ought to tell you. The Prince is going back to his own country very shortly."

Mr. Harvey nodded.

"I have just been given to understand as much," he said. "At present he is to be met with every day. I believe that he is even now in my drawing rooms."

"Where I ought to be," Penelope said, turning toward the door, "only I felt that I must see you first."

"I will not come with you," Mr. Harvey said. "There is no need for our little conference to become the subject of comment. By the bye," he added, "let me take this opportunity of wishing you every happiness. I haven't seen Somerfield yet, but he is a lucky fellow. As an American, however, I cannot help grudging another of our most popular daughters to even the best of Englishmen."

Penelope's smile was a little forced.

"Thank you very much," she said. "It is all rather in the air, at present, you know. We are not going to be married for some time."

"When it comes off," the Ambassador said, "I am going to talk to the Duchess and Miss Morse. I think that I ought to give you away."

Penelope made her way into Mrs. Blaine-Harvey's reception rooms, crowded with a stream of guests, who were sitting about, drinking tea and listening to the music, passing in and out all the time. Curiously enough, almost the first person whom she saw was the Prince. He detached himself from a little group and came at once towards her. He took her hand in his and for a moment said nothing. Notwithstanding the hours of strenuous consideration, the hours which she had devoted to anticipating and preparing for this meeting, she felt her courage suddenly leaving her, a sinking at the knees, a wild desire to escape, at any cost. The color which had been so long denied her streamed into her cheeks. There was something baffling, yet curiously disturbing, in the manner of his greeting.

"Is it true?" he asked.

She did not pretend to misunderstand him. It was amazing that he should ignore that other tragical incident, that he should think of nothing but this! Yet, in a way, she accepted it as a natural thing.

"It is true that I am engaged to Sir Charles Somerfield," she answered.

"I must wish you every happiness," he said slowly. "Indeed, that wish comes from my heart, and I think that you know it. As for Sir Charles Somerfield, I cannot imagine that he has anything left in the world to wish for."

"You are a born courtier, Prince," she murmured. "Please remember that in my democratic country one has never had a chance of getting used to such speeches."

"Your country," he remarked, "prides itself upon being the country where truth prevails. If so, you should have become accustomed by now to hearing pleasant things about yourself. So you are going to marry Sir Charles Somerfield!"

"Why do you say that over to yourself so doubtfully?" she asked. "You know who he is, do you not? He is rich, of old family, popular with everybody, a great sportsman, a mighty hunter. These are the things which go to the making of a man, are they not?"

"Beyond a doubt," the Prince answered gravely. "They go to the making of a man. It is as you say."

"You like him personally, don't you?" she asked.

"Sir Charles Somerfield and I are almost strangers," the Prince replied. "I have not seen much of him, and he has so many tastes which I cannot share that it is hard for us to come very near together. But if you have chosen him, it is sufficient. I am quite sure that he is all that a man should be."

"Tell me in what respect your tastes are so far apart?" she asked. "You say that as though there were something in the manner of his life of which you disapproved."

"We are sons of different countries, Miss Penelope," the Prince said. "We look out upon life differently, and the things which seem good to him may well seem idle to me. Before I go," he added a little hesitatingly, "we may speak of this again. But not now."

"I shall remind you of that promise, Prince," she declared.

"I will not fail to keep it," he replied. "You have, at least," he added after a moment's pause, "one great claim upon happiness. You are the son and the daughter of kindred races."

She looked at him as though not quite understanding.

"I was thinking," he continued simply, "of my own father and mother. My father was a Japanese nobleman, with the home call of all the centuries strong in his blood. He was an enlightened man, but he saw nothing in the manner of living or the ideals of other countries to compare with those of the country of his own birth. I sometimes think that my mother and father might have been happier had one of them been a little more disposed to yield to the other I think, perhaps, that their union would have been a more successful one. They were married, and they lived together, but they lived apart."

"It was not well for you, this," she remarked.

He shrugged his shoulders.

"Do not mistake me," he begged. "So far as I am concerned, I am content. I am Japanese. The English blood that is in my veins is but as a drop of water compared to the call of my own country. And yet there are some things which have come to me from my mother—things which come most to the surface when I am in this, her own country—which make life at times a little sad. Forgive me if I have been led on to speak too much of myself. Today one should think of nothing but of you and of your happiness."

He turned to accept the greeting of an older woman who had lingered for a moment, in passing, evidently anxious to speak to him. Penelope watched his kindly air, listened to the courteous words which flowed from his lips, the interest in his manner, which his whole bearing denoted, notwithstanding the fact that the woman was elderly and plain, and had outlived the friends of her day and received but scanty consideration from the present generation. It was typical of him, too, she realized. It was never to the great women of the world that he unbent most thoroughly. Gray hairs seemed to inspire his respect, to command his attentions in a way that youth and beauty utterly failed to do. These things seemed suddenly clear to Penelope as she stood there watching him. A hundred little acts of graceful kindness, which she had noticed and admired, returned to her memory. It was this man whom she had lifted her hand to betray! It was this man who was to be accounted guilty, even of crime! There came a sudden revulsion of feeling. The whole mechanical outlook upon life, as she had known it, seemed, even in those few seconds, to become a false and meretricious thing. Whatever he had done or countenanced was right. She had betrayed his hospitality. She had committed an infamous breach of trust. An overwhelming desire came over her to tell him everything. She took a quick step forward and found herself face to face with Somerfield. The Prince was buttonholed by some friends and led away. The moment had passed.

"Come and talk to the Duchess," Somerfield said. "She has something delightful to propose."

CHAPTER XVI.
CONCERNING PRINCE MAIYO

The Duchess looked up from her writing table and nodded to her husband, who had just entered.

"Good morning, Ambrose!" she said. "Do you want to talk to me?"

"If you can spare me five minutes," the Duke suggested. "I don't think that I need keep you longer."

The Duchess handed her notebook to her secretary, who hastened from the room. The Duke seated himself in her vacant chair.

"About our little party down in Hampshire next week," he began.

"I am waiting to hear from you before I send out any invitations," the Duchess answered.

"Quite so," the Duke assented. "To tell you the truth, I don't want anything in the nature of a house party. What I should really like would be to get Maiyo there almost to ourselves."

His wife looked at him in some surprise.

"You seem particularly anxious to make things pleasant for this young man," she remarked. "If he were the son of the Emperor himself, no one could do more for him than you people have been doing these last few weeks."

The Duke of Devenham, Chancellor of the Duchy of Lancaster, whose wife entertained for his party, and whose immense income, derived mostly from her American relations, was always at its disposal, was a person almost as important in the councils of his country as the Prime Minister himself. It sometimes occurred to him that the person who most signally failed to realize this fact was the lady who did him the honor to preside over his household.

"My dear Margaret," he said, "you can take my word for it that we know what we are about. It is very important indeed that we should keep on friendly terms with this young man,—I don't mean as a personal matter. It's a matter of politics—perhaps of something greater, even, than that."

The Duchess liked to understand everything, and her husband's reticence annoyed her.

"But we have the Japanese Ambassador always with us," she remarked. "A most delightful person I call the Baron Hesho, and I am sure he loves us all."

"That is not exactly the point, my dear," the Duke explained. "Prince Maiyo is over here on a special mission. We ourselves have only been able to surmise its object with the aid of our secret service in Tokio. You can rest assured of one thing, however. It is of vast importance to the interests of this country that we secure his goodwill."

The Duchess smiled good humoredly.

"Well, my dear Ambrose," she said, "I don't know what more we can do than feed him properly and give him pleasant people to talk to. He doesn't go in for sports, does he? All I can promise is that we will do our best to be agreeable to him."

"I am sure of it, my dear," the Duke said. "You haven't committed yourself to asking any one, by the bye?"

"Not a soul," his wife answered, "except Sir Charles. I had to ask him, of course, for Penelope."

"Naturally," the Duke assented. "I am glad Penelope will be there. I only wish that she were English instead of American, and that Maiyo would take a serious fancy to her."

"Perhaps," the Duchess said dryly, "you would like him to take a fancy to Grace?"

"I shouldn't mind in the least," her husband declared. "I never met a young man whom I respected and admired more."

"Nor I, for that matter," the Duchess agreed. "And yet, somehow or other—"

"Somehow or other?" the Duke repeated courteously.

"Well, I never altogether trust these paragons," his wife said. "In all the ordinary affairs of life the Prince seems to reach an almost perfect standard. I sometimes wonder whether he would be as trustworthy in the big things. Nothing else you want to talk about, Ambrose?"

"Nothing at all," the Duke said, rising to his feet. "I only wanted to make it plain that we don't require a house party next week."

"I shan't ask a soul," the Duchess answered. "Do you mind ringing the bell as you pass? I'll have Miss Smith back again and send these letters off."

"Good!" the Duke declared. "I'm going down to the House, but I don't suppose there'll be anything doing. By the bye, we shall have to be a little feudal next week. Japan is a country of many ceremonies, and, after all, Maiyo is one of the Royal Family. I have written Perkins, to stir him up a little."

The Duke drove down to the House, but called first in Downing Street. He found the Prime Minister anxious to see him.

"You've arranged about Maiyo coming down to you next week?" he asked.

"That's all right," the Duke answered. "He is coming, for certain. One good thing about that young man—he never breaks an engagement."

The Prime Minister consulted a calendar which lay open before him.

"Do you mind," he asked, "if I come, too, and Bransome?"

"Why, of course not," the Duke replied. "We shall be delighted. We have seventy bedrooms, and only half a dozen or so of us. But tell me—is this young man as important as all that?"

"We shall have to have a serious talk," the Prime Minister said, "in a few days' time. I don't think that even you grasp the exact position of affairs as they stand today. Just now I am bothered to death about other things. Heseltine has just been in from the Home Office. He is simply inundated with correspondence from America about those two murders."

The Duke nodded.

"It's an odd thing," he remarked, "that they should both have been Americans."

"Heseltine thinks there's something behind this correspondence," the Prime Minister said slowly. "Washington was very secretive about the man Fynes' identity. I found that out from Scotland Yard. Do you know, I'm half inclined to think, although I can't get a word out of Harvey, that this man Fynes—"

The Prime Minister hesitated.

"Well?" the Duke asked a little impatiently.

"I don't want to go too far," his chief said. "I am making some fresh inquiries, and I am hoping to get at the bottom of the matter very shortly. One thing is very certain, though, and that is that no two murders have ever been committed in this city with more cold-blooded deliberation, and with more of what I should call diabolical cleverness. Take the affair of poor young Vanderpole, for instance. The person who entered his taxi and killed him must have done so while the vehicle was standing in the middle of the road at one of the three blocks. Not only that, but he must have been a friend, or some one posing as a friend—some one, at any rate, of his own order. Vanderpole was over six feet high, and as muscular as a young bull. He could have thrown any one out into the street who had attempted to assault him openly."

"It is the most remarkable case I ever heard of in my life," the Duke admitted, helping himself to a cigarette from a box which he had just discovered.

"There is another point," the Prime Minister continued. "There are features in common about both these murders. Not only were they both the work of a most accomplished criminal, but he must have been possessed of an iron nerve and amazing strength. The dagger by which Hamilton Fynes was stabbed was driven through the middle of his heart. The cord with which Vanderpole was strangled must have been turned by a wrist of steel. No time for a word afterwards, mind, or before. It was a wonderful feat. I am not surprised that the Americans can't understand it."

"They don't suggest, I suppose," the Duke asked, "that we are not trying to clear the matter up?"

"They don't suggest it," his chief answered, "but I can't quite make out what's at the back of their heads. However, I won't bother you about that now. If I were to propound Heseltine's theory to you, you would think that he had been reading the works of some of our enterprising young novelists. Things will have cleared up, I dare say, by next week. I am coming round to the House for a moment if you're not in a hurry."

The Duke assented, and waited while the secretary locked up the papers which the Prime Minister had been examining, and prepared others to be carried into the House. The two men left the place together, and the Duke pointed toward his brougham.

"Do you mind walking?" the Prime Minister said. "There is another matter I'd like to talk to you about, and there's nowhere better than the streets for a little conversation. Besides, I need the air."

"With pleasure," the Duke answered, who loathed walking.

He directed his coachman to precede them, and they started off, arm in arm.

"Devenham," the Prime Minister said, "we were speaking, a few minutes ago, of Prince Maiyo. I want you to understand this, that upon that young man depends entirely the success or failure of my administration."

"You are serious?" the Duke exclaimed.

"Absolutely," the Prime Minister answered. "I know quite well what he is here for. He is here to make up his mind whether it will pay Japan to renew her treaty with us, or whether it would be more to her advantage to enter into an alliance with any other European power. He has been to most of the capitals in Europe. He has been here with us. By this time he has made up his mind. He knows quite well what his report will be. Yet you can't get a word out of him. He is a delightful young fellow, I know, but he is as clever as any trained diplomatist I have ever come across. I've had him to dine with me alone, and I've done all that I could to make him talk. When he went away, I knew just exactly as much as I did before he came."

"He seems pleased enough with us," the Duke remarked.

"I am not so sure," the Prime Minister answered. "He has travelled about a good deal in England. I heard of him in Manchester and Sheffield, Newcastle and Leicester, absolutely unattended. I wonder what he was doing there."

"From my experience of him," the Duke said, "I don't think we shall know until he chooses to tell us."

"I am afraid you are right," the Prime Minister declared. "At the same time you might just drop a hint to your wife, and to that remarkably clever young niece of hers, Miss Penelope Morse. Of course, I don't expect that he would unbosom himself to any one, but, to tell you the truth, as we are situated now, the faintest hint as regards his inclinations, or lack of inclinations, towards certain things would be of immense service. If he criticised any of our institutions, for instance, his remarks would be most interesting. Then he has been spending several months in various capitals. He would not be likely to tell any one his whole impressions of those few months, but a phrase, a word, even a gesture, to a clever woman might mean a great deal. It might also mean a great deal to us."

"I'll mention it," the Duke promised, "but I am afraid my womenfolk are scarcely up to this sort of thing. The best plan would be to tackle him ourselves down at Devenham."

"I thought of that," the Prime Minister assented. "That is why I am coming down myself and bringing Bransome. If he will have nothing to say to us within a week or so of his departure, we shall know what to think. Remember my words, Devenham,—when our chronicler dips his pen into the ink and writes of our government, our foreign policy, at least, will be judged by our position in the far East. Exactly what that will be depends upon Prince Maiyo. With a renewal of our treaty we could go to the country tomorrow. Without it, especially if the refusal should come from them, there will be some very ugly writing across the page."

The Duke threw away his cigarette.

"Well," he said, "we can only do our best. The young man seems friendly enough."

The Prime Minister nodded.

"It is precisely his friendliness which I fear," he said.

CHAPTER XVII.
A GAY NIGHT IN PARIS

Mr. James B. Coulson was almost as much at home at the Grand Hotel, Paris, as he had been at the Savoy in London. His headquarters were at the American Bar, where he approved of the cocktails, patronized the highballs, and continually met fellow-countrymen with whom he gossiped and visited various places of amusement. His business during the daytime he kept to himself, but he certainly was possessed of a bagful of documents and drawings relating to sundry patents connected with the manufacture of woollen goods, the praises of which he was always ready to sing in a most enthusiastic fashion.

Mr. Coulson was not a man whose acquaintance it was difficult to make. From five to seven every afternoon, scorning the attractions of the band outside and the generally festive air which pervaded the great tea rooms, he sat at the corner of the bar upon an article of furniture which resembled more than anything else an office stool, dividing his attention between desultory conversation with any other gentleman who might be indulging in a drink, and watching the billiards in which some of his compatriots were usually competing. It was not, so far as one might judge, a strenuous life which Mr. Coulson was leading. He had been known once or twice to yawn, and he had somewhat the appearance of a man engaged in an earnest but at times not altogether successful attempt to kill time. Perhaps for that reason he made acquaintances with a little more than his customary freedom. There was a young Englishman, for instance, whose name, it appeared, was Gaynsforth, with whom, after a drink or two at the bar, he speedily became on almost intimate terms.

Mr. Gaynsforth was a young man, apparently of good breeding and some means. He was well dressed, of cheerful disposition, knew something about the woollen trade, and appeared to take a distinct liking to his new friend. The two men, after having talked business together for some time, arranged to dine together and have what they called a gay evening. They retired to their various apartments to change, Mr. Gaynsforth perfectly well satisfied with his progress, Mr. James B. Coulson with a broad grin upon his face.

After a very excellent dinner, for which Mr. Gaynsforth insisted upon paying, they went to the Folies Bergeres, where the Englishman developed a thirst which, considering the coolness of the evening, was nothing short of amazing. Mr. Coulson, however, kept pace with him steadily, and toward midnight their acquaintance had steadily progressed until they were certainly on friendly if not affectionate terms. A round of the supper places, proposed by the Englishman, was assented to by Mr. Coulson with enthusiasm. About three o'clock in the morning Mr. Coulson had the appearance of a man for whom the troubles of this world are over, and who was realizing the ecstatic bliss of a temporary Nirvana. Mr. Gaynsforth, on the other hand, although half an hour ago he had been boisterous and unsteady, seemed suddenly to have become once more the quiet, discreet-looking young Englishman who had first bowed to Mr. Coulson in the bar of the Grand Hotel and accepted with some diffidence his offer of a drink. To prevent his friend being jostled by the somewhat mixed crowd in which they then were, Mr. Gaynsforth drew nearer and nearer to him. He even let his hand stray over his person, as though to be sure that he was not carrying too much in his pockets.

"Say, old man," he whispered in his ear,—they were sitting side by side now in the Bal Tabarin,—"if you are going on like this, Heaven knows where you'll land at the end of it all! I'll look after you as well as I can,—where you go, I'll go—but we can't be together every second of the time. Don't you think you'd be safer if you handed over your pocketbook to me?"

"Right you are!" Mr. Coulson declared, falling a little over on one side. "Take it out of my pocket. Be careful of it now. There's five hundred francs there, and the plans of a loom which I wouldn't sell for a good many thousands."

Mr. Gaynsforth possessed himself quickly of the pocketbook, and satisfied himself that his friend's description of its contents was fairly correct.

"You've nothing else upon you worth taking care of?" he whispered. "You can trust me, you know. You haven't any papers, or anything of that sort?"

Then Mr. James B. Coulson, who was getting tired of his part, suddenly sat up, and a soberer man had never occupied that particular chair in the Bal Tabarin.

"And if I have, my young friend," he said calmly, "what the devil business is it of yours?"

Mr. Gaynsforth was taken aback and showed it. He recovered himself as quickly as possible, and realized that he had been living in a fool's paradise so far as the condition of his companion was concerned. He realized, also, that the first move in the game between them had been made and that he had lost.

"You are too good an actor for me, Mr. Coulson," he said. "Suppose we get to business."

"That's all right," Mr. Coulson answered. "Let's go somewhere where we can get some supper. We'll go to the Abbaye Theleme, and you shall have the pleasure of entertaining me."

Mr. Gaynsforth handed back the pocketbook and led the way out of the place without a word. It was only a few steps up the hill, and they found themselves then in a supper place of a very different class. Here Mr. Coulson, after a brief visit to the lavatory, during which he obliterated all traces of his recent condition, seated himself at one of the small flower-decked tables and offered the menu to his new friend.

"It's up to you to pay," he said, "so you shall choose the supper. Personally, I'm for a few oysters, a hot bird, and a cold bottle."

Mr. Gaynsforth, who was still somewhat subdued, commanded the best supper procurable on these lines. Mr. Coulson, having waved his hand to a few acquaintances and chaffed the Spanish dancing girls in their own language,—not a little to his companion's astonishment,—at last turned to business.

"Come," he said, "you and I ought to understand one another. You are over here from London either to pump me or to rob me. You are either a detective or a political spy or a secret service agent of some sort, or you are on a lay of your own. Now, put it in a business form, what can I do for you? Make your offer, and let's see where we are."

Mr. Gaynsforth began to recover himself. It did not follow, because he had made one mistake, that he was to lose the game.

"I am neither a detective, Mr. Coulson," he said, "nor a secret service agent,—in fact, I am nothing of that sort at all. I have a friend, however, who for certain reasons does not care to approach you himself, but who is nevertheless very much interested in a particular event, or rather incident, in which you are concerned."

"Good!" Mr. Coulson declared. "Get right on."

"That friend," Mr. Gaynsforth continued calmly, "is prepared to pay a thousand pounds for full information and proof as to the nature of those papers which were stolen from Mr. Hamilton Fynes on the night of March 22nd."

"A thousand pounds," Mr. Coulson repeated. "Gee whiz!"

"He is also," the Englishman continued, "prepared to pay another thousand for a satisfactory explanation of the murder of Mr. Richard Vanderpole on the following day."

"Say, your friend's got the stuff!" Mr. Coulson remarked admiringly.

"My friend is not a poor man," Mr. Gaynsforth admitted. "You see, there's a sort of feeling abroad that these two things are connected. I am not working on behalf of the police. I am not working on behalf of any one who desires the least publicity. But I am working for some one who wants to know and is prepared to pay."

"That's a very interesting job you're on, and no mistake," Mr. Coulson declared. "I wonder you waste time coming over here on the spree when you've got a piece of business like that to look after."

"I came over here," Mr. Gaynsforth replied, "entirely on the matter I have mentioned to you."

"What, over here to Paris?" Mr. Coulson exclaimed.

"Not only to Paris," the other replied dryly, "but to discover one Mr. James B. Coulson, whose health I now have the pleasure of drinking."

Mr. Coulson drained the glass which the waiter had just filled.

"Well, this licks me!" he exclaimed. "How any one in their senses could believe that there was any connection between me and Hamilton Fynes or that other young swell, I can't imagine."

"You knew Hamilton Fynes," Mr. Gaynsforth remarked. "That fact came out at the inquest. You appeared to have known him better than most men. Mr. Vanderpole had just left you when he was murdered,—that also came out at the inquest."

"Kind of queer, wasn't it," Mr. Coulson remarked meditatively, "how I seemed to get hung up with both of them? You may also remember that at the inquest Mr. Vanderpole's business with me was testified to by the chief of his department."

"Certainly," Mr. Gaynsforth answered. "However, that's neither here nor there. Everything was properly arranged, so far as you were concerned, of course. That doesn't alter my friend's convictions. This is a business matter with me, and if the two thousand pounds don't sound attractive enough, well, the amount must be revised, that's all. But I want you to understand this, Mr. Coulson, I represent a man or a syndicate, or call it what you will."

"Call it a Government," Mr. Coulson muttered under his breath.

"Call it what you will," Mr. Gaynsforth continued, with an air of not having heard the interruption, "we have the money and we want the information. You can give it to us if you like. We don't ask for too much. We don't even ask for the name of the man who committed these crimes. But we do want to know the nature of those papers, exactly what position Mr. Hamilton Fynes occupied in the Stamp and Excise Duty department at Washington, and, finally, what the mischief you are doing over here in Paris."

"Have you ordered the supper?" Mr. Coulson inquired anxiously.

"I have ordered everything you suggested," Mr. Gaynsforth answered,—"some oysters, a chicken en casserole, lettuce salad, some cheese, and a magnum of Pommery."

"It is understood that you are my host?" Mr. Coulson insisted.

"Absolutely," his companion declared. "I consider it an honor."

"Then," Mr. Coulson said, pointing out his empty glass to the *sommelier*, "we may as well understand one another. To you I am Mr. James B. Coulson, travelling in patents for woollen machinery. If you put a quarter of a million of francs upon that table, I am still Mr. James B. Coulson, travelling in woollen machinery. And if you add a million to that, and pile up the notes so high that they touch the ceiling, I remain Mr. James B. Coulson, travelling in patents for woollen machinery. Now, if you'll get that firmly into your head and stick to it and believe it, there's no reason why you and I shouldn't have a pleasant evening."

Mr. Gaynsforth, although he was an Englishman and young, showed himself to be possessed of a sense of humor. He leaned back in his seat and roared with laughter.

"Mr. Coulson," he said, "I congratulate you and your employers. To the lower regions with business! Help yourself to the oysters and pass the wine."

CHAPTER XVIII.
MR. COULSON IS INDISCREET

On the following morning Mr. Coulson received what he termed his mail from America. Locked in his room on the fifth floor of the hotel, he carefully perused the contents of several letters. A little later he rang and ordered his bill. At four o'clock he left the Gare du Nord for London.

Like many other great men, Mr. Coulson was not without his weakness. He was brave, shrewd, and far-seeing. He enjoyed excellent health, and he scarcely knew the meaning of the word nerves. Nevertheless he suffered from seasickness. The first thing he did, therefore, when aboard the boat at Boulogne, was to bespeak a private cabin. The steward to whom he made his application shook his head with regret. The last two had just been engaged. Mr. Coulson tried a tip, and then a larger tip, with equal lack of success. He was about to abandon the effort and retire gloomily to the saloon, when a man who had been standing by, wrapped in a heavy fur overcoat, intervened.

"I am afraid, sir," he said, "that it is I who have just secured the last cabin. If you care to share it with me, however, I shall be delighted. As a matter of fact, I use it very little myself. The night has turned out so fine that I shall probably promenade all the time."

"If you will allow me to divide the expense," Mr. Coulson replied, "I shall be exceedingly obliged to you, and will accept your offer. I am, unfortunately, a bad sailor."

"That is as you will, sir," the gentleman answered. "The amount is only trifling."

The night was a bright one, but there was a heavy sea running, and even in the harbor the boat was rocking. Mr. Coulson groaned as he made his way across the threshold of the cabin.

"I am going to have a horrible time," he said frankly. "I am afraid you'll repent your offer before you've done with me."

His new friend smiled.

"I have never been seasick in my life," he said, "and I only engage a cabin for fear of wet weather. A fine night like this I shall not trouble you, so pray be as ill as you like."

"It's nothing to laugh at," Mr. Coulson remarked gloomily.

"Let me give you a little advice," his friend said, "and I can assure you that I know something of these matters, for I have been on the sea a great deal. Let me mix you a stiff brandy and soda. Drink it down and eat only a dry biscuit. I have some brandy of my own here."

"Nothing does me any good," Mr. Coulson groaned.

"This," the stranger remarked, producing a flask from his case and dividing the liquor into equal parts, "may send you to sleep. If so, you'll be across before you wake up. Here's luck!"

Mr. Coulson drained his glass. His companion was in the act of raising his to his lips when the ship gave a roll, his elbow caught the back of a chair, and the tumbler slipped from his fingers.

"It's of no consequence," he declared, ringing for the steward. "I'll go into the smoking room and get a drink. I was only going to have some to keep you company. As a matter of fact, I prefer whiskey."

Mr. Coulson sat down upon the berth. He seemed indisposed for speech.

"I'll leave you now, then," his friend said, buttoning his coat around him. "You lie flat down on your back, and I think you'll find yourself all right."

"That brandy," Mr. Coulson muttered, "was infernally — - strong."

His companion smiled and went out. In a quarter of an hour he returned and locked the door. They were out in the Channel now, and the boat was pitching heavily. Mr. James B. Coulson, however, knew nothing of it. He was sleeping like one who wakes only for the Judgment Day. Over his coat and waistcoat the other man's fingers travelled with curious dexterity. The oilskin case in which Mr. Coulson was in the habit of keeping his private correspondence was reached in a very few minutes. The stranger turned out the letters and read them, one by one, until he came to the one he sought. He held it for a short time in his hand, looked at the address with a faint smile, and slipped his fingers lightly along the gummed edge of the envelope.

"No seal," he said softly to himself. "My friend Mr. Coulson plays the game of travelling agent to perfection."

He glided out of the cabin with the letter in his hand. In about ten minutes he returned. Mr. Coulson was still sleeping. He replaced the letter, pressing down the envelope carefully.

"My friend," he whispered, looking down upon Mr. Coulson's uneasy figure, "on the whole, I have been perhaps a little premature. I think you had better deliver this document to its proper destination. If only there was to have been a written answer, we might have met again! It would have been most interesting."

He slipped the oilskin case back into the exact position in which he had found it, and watched his companion for several minutes in silence. Then he went to his dressing bag and from a phial mixed a little draught. Lifting the sleeping man's head, he forced it down his throat.

"I think," he said, "I think, Mr. Coulson, that you had better wake up."

He unlocked the door and resumed his promenade of the deck. In the bows he stood for some time, leaning with folded arms against a pillar, his eyes fixed upon the line of lights ahead. The great waves now leaped into the moonlight, the wind sang in the rigging and came booming across the waters, the salt spray stung his cheeks. High above his head, the slender mast, with its Marconi attachment, swang and dived, reached out for the stars, and fell away with a shudder. The man who watched, stood and dreamed until the voyage was almost over. Then he turned on his heel and went back to see how his cabin companion was faring.

Mr. Coulson was sitting on the edge of his bunk. He had awakened with a terrible headache and a sense of some hideous indiscretion. It was not until he had examined every paper in his pocket and all his money that he had begun to feel more comfortable. And in the meantime he had forgotten altogether to be seasick.

"Well, how has the remedy worked?" the stranger inquired.

Mr. Coulson looked him in the face. Then he drew a short breath of relief. He had been indiscreet, but he had alarmed himself unnecessarily. There was nothing about the appearance of the quiet, dark little man, with the amiable eyes and slightly foreign manner, in the least suspicious.

"It's given me a brute of a headache," he declared, "but I certainly haven't been seasick up till now, and I must say I've never crossed before without being ill."

The stranger laughed soothingly.

"That brandy and soda would keep you right." He said. "When we get to Folkestone, you'll be wanting a supper basket. Make yourself at home. I don't need the cabin. It's a glorious night outside. I shouldn't have come in at all except to see how you were getting on."

"How long before we are in?" Mr. Coulson asked.

"About a quarter of an hour," was the answer. "I'll come for you, if you like. Have a few minute's nap if you feel sleepy."

Mr. Coulson got up.

"Not I!" he said. "I am going to douse my head in some cold water. That must have been the strongest brandy and soda that was ever brewed, to send me off like that."

His friend laughed as he helped him out on to the deck.

"I shouldn't grumble at it, if I were you," he said carelessly. "It saved you from a bad crossing."

Mr. Coulson washed his face and hands in the smoking room lavatory, and was so far recovered, even, as to be able to drink a cup of coffee before they reached the harbor. At Folkestone he looked everywhere for his friend, but in vain. At Charing Cross he searched once more. The little dark gentleman, with the distinguished air and the easy, correct speech, who had mixed his brandy and soda, had disappeared.

"And I owe the little beggar for half that cabin," Mr. Coulson thought with a sensation of annoyance. "I wonder where he's hidden himself!"

CHAPTER XIX.
A MOMENTOUS QUESTION

The Duke paused, in his way across the crowded reception rooms, to speak to his host, Sir Edward Bransome, Secretary of State for Foreign Affairs.

"I have just written you a line, Bransome," he said, as they shook hands. "The chief tells me that he is going to honor us down at Devenham for a few days, and that we may expect you also."

"You are very kind, Duke," Bransome answered. "I suppose Haviland explained the matter to you."

The Duke nodded.

"You are going to help me entertain my other distinguished visitor," he remarked. "I fancy we shall be quite an interesting party."

Bransome glanced around.

"I hope most earnestly," he said, "that we shall induce our young friend to be a little more candid with us than he has been. One can't get a word out of Hesho, but I'm bound to say that I don't altogether like the look of things. The Press are beginning to smell a rat. Two leading articles this morning, I see, upon our Eastern relations."

The Duke nodded.

"I read them," he said. "We are informed that the prestige and success of our ministry will entirely depend upon whether or not we are able to arrange for the renewal of our treaty with Japan. I remember the same papers shrieking themselves hoarse with indignation when we first joined hands with our little friends across the sea!"

His secretary approached Bransome and touched him on the shoulder.

"There is a person in the anteroom, sir," he said, "whom I think that you ought to see."

The Duke nodded and passed on. The Secretary drew his chief on one side.

"This man has just arrived from Paris, sir," he continued, "and is the bearer of a letter which he is instructed to deliver into your hands only."

Bransome nodded.

"Is he known to us at all?" he asked. "From whom does the letter come?"

The young man hesitated.

"The letter itself, sir, has nothing to do with France, I imagine," he said. "The person I refer to is an American, and although I have no positive information, I believe that he is sometimes intrusted with the carrying of despatches from Washington to his Embassy. Once or twice lately I have had it reported to me that communications from the other side to Mr. Harvey have been sent by hand. It seems as though they had some objection to committing important documents to the post."

Bransome walked through the crowded rooms by the side of his secretary, stopping for a moment to exchange greetings here and there with his friends. His wife was giving her third reception of the session to the diplomatic world.

"Washington has certainly shown signs of mistrust lately," he remarked, "but if communications from them are ever tampered with, it is more likely to be on their side than ours. They have a particularly unscrupulous Press to deal with, besides political intriguers. If this person you speak of is really the bearer of a letter from there," he added, "I think we can both guess what it is about."

The secretary nodded.

"Shall I ring up Mr. Haviland, sir?" he asked.

"Not yet," Bransome answered. "It is just possible that this person requires an immediate reply, in which case it may be convenient for me not to be able to get at the Prime Minister. Bring him along into my private room, Sidney."

Sir Edward Bransome made his way to his study, opened the door with a Yale key, turned on the electric lights, and crossed slowly to the hearthrug. He stood there, for several moments, with his elbow upon the mantelpiece, looking down into the fire. A darker shadow had stolen across his face as soon as he was alone. In his court dress and brilliant array of orders, he was certainly a very distinguished-looking figure. Yet the last few years had branded lines into his face which it was doubtful if he would ever lose. To be Secretary of State for Foreign Affairs to the greatest power which the world had as yet known must certainly seem, on paper, to be as brilliant a post as a man's ambition could covet. Many years ago it had seemed so to Bransome himself. It was a post which he had deliberately coveted, worked for, and strived for. And now, when in sight of the end, with two years of office only to run, he was appalled at the ever-growing responsibilities thrust upon his shoulders. There was never, perhaps, a time when, on paper, things had seemed smoother, when the distant mutterings of disaster were less audible. It was only those who were behind the curtain who realized how deceptive appearances were.

In a few minutes his secretary reappeared, ushering in Mr. James B. Coulson. Mr. Coulson was still a little pale from the effects of his crossing, and he wore a long, thick ulster to conceal the deficiencies of his attire. Nevertheless his usual breeziness of manner had not altogether deserted him. Sir Edward looked him up and down, and finding him look exactly as Mr. James B. Coulson of the Coulson & Bruce Syndicate should look, was inclined to wonder whether his secretary had made a mistake.

"I was told that you wished to see me," he said. "I am Sir Edward Bransome."

Mr. James B. Coulson nodded appreciatively.

"Very good of you, Sir Edward," he said, "to put yourself out at this time of night to have a word or two with me. I am sorry to have troubled you, anyway, but the matter was sort of urgent."

Sir Edward bent his head.

"I understand, Mr. Coulson," he said, "that you come from the United States."

"That is so, sir," Mr. Coulson replied. "I am at the head of a syndicate, the Coulson & Bruce Syndicate, which in course of time hope to revolutionize the machinery used for spinning wool all over the world. Likewise we have patents for other machinery connected with the manufacture of all varieties of woollen goods. I am over here on a business trip, which I have just concluded."

"Satisfactorily, I trust?" Sir Edward remarked.

"Well, I'm not grumbling, sir," Mr. Coulson assented. "Here and there I may have missed a thing, and the old fashioned way of doing business on this side bothers me a bit, but on the whole I'm not grumbling."

Bransome bowed. Perhaps, after all, the man was not a fool!

"I have a good many friends round about Washington," Mr. Coulson continued, "and sometimes, when they know I am coming across, one or the other of them finds it convenient to hand me a letter. It isn't the postage stamp that worries them," he added with a little laugh, "but they sort of feel that anything committed to me is fairly safe to reach its right destination."

"Without disputing that fact for one moment, Mr. Coulson," Sir Edward remarked, "I might also suggest that the ordinary mail service between our countries has reached a marvellous degree of perfection."

"The Post Office," Mr. Coulson continued meditatively, "is a great institution, both on your side and ours, but a letter posted in Washington has to go through a good many hands before it is delivered in London."

Sir Edward smiled.

"It is a fact, sir," he said, "which the various Governments of Europe have realized for many years, in connection with the exchange of communications one with the other. Your own great country, as it grows and expands, becomes, of necessity, more in touch with our methods. Did I understand that you have a letter for me, Mr. Coulson?"

Mr. Coulson produced it.

"Friend of mine you may have heard of," he said, "asked me to leave this with you. I am catching the Princess Cecilia from Southampton tomorrow. I thought, perhaps, if I waited an hour or so, I might take the answer back with me."

"It is getting late, Mr. Coulson," Sir Edward reminded him, glancing at the clock.

Mr. Coulson smiled.

"I think, Sir Edward," he said, "that in your line of business time counts for little."

Sir Edward motioned his visitor to a chair and touched the bell.

"I shall require the A3X cipher, Sidney," he said to his secretary.

Mr. Coulson looked up.

"Why," he said, "I don't think you'll need that. The letter you've got in your hand is just a personal one, and what my friend has to say to you is written out there in black and white."

Sir Edward withdrew the enclosure from its envelope and raised his eyebrows.

"Isn't this a trifle indiscreet?" he asked.

"Why, I should say not," Mr. Coulson answered. "My friend—Mr. Jones we'll call him—knew me and, I presume, knew what he was about. Besides, that is a plain letter from the head of a business firm to—shall we say a client? There's nothing in it to conceal."

"At the same time," Sir Edward remarked, "it might have been as well to have fastened the flap of the envelope."

Mr. Coulson held out his hand.

"Let me look," he said.

Sir Edward gave it into his hands. Mr. Coulson held it under the electric light. There was no indication in his face of any surprise or disturbance.

"Bit short of gum in our stationery office," he remarked.

Sir Edward was looking at him steadily.

"My impressions were," he said, "when I opened this letter, that I was not the first person who had done so. The envelope flew apart in my fingers."

Mr. Coulson shook his head.

"The document has never been out of my possession, sir," he said. "It has not even left my person. My friend Mr. Jones does not believe in too much secrecy in matters of this sort. I have had a good deal of experience now and am inclined to agree with him. A letter in a double-ended envelope, stuck all over with sealing wax, is pretty certain to be opened in case of any accident to the bearer. This one, as you may not have noticed, is written in the same handwriting and addressed in the same manner as the remainder of my letters of introduction to various London and Paris houses of business."

Sir Edward said no more. He read the few lines written on a single sheet of notepaper, starting a little at the signature. Then he read them again and placed the document beneath a paper weight in front of him. When he leaned across the table, his folded arms formed a semicircle around it.

"This letter, Mr. Coulson," he said, "is not an official communication."

"It is not," Mr. Coulson admitted. "I fancy it occurred to my friend Jones that anything official would be hardly in place and might be easier to evade. The matter has already cropped up in negotiations between Mr. Harvey and your Cabinet, but so far we are without any definite pronouncement,—at least, that is how my friend Mr. Jones looks at it."

Sir Edward smiled.

"The only answer your friend asks for is a verbal one," he remarked.

"A verbal one," Mr. Coulson assented, "delivered to me in the presence of one other person, whose name you will find mentioned in that letter."

Sir Edward bowed his head. When he spoke again, his manner had somehow changed. It had become at once more official,—a trifle more stilted.

"This is a great subject, Mr. Coulson," he said. "It is a subject which has occupied the attention of His Majesty's Ministers for many months. I shall take the opinion of the other person whose name is mentioned in this letter, as to whether we can grant Mr. Jones' request. If we should do so, it will not, I am sure, be necessary to say to you that any communication we may make on the subject tonight will be from men to a man of honor, and must be accepted as such. It will be our honest and sincere conviction, but it must also be understood that it does not bind the Government of this country to any course of action."

Mr. Coulson smiled and nodded his head.

"That is what I call diplomacy, Sir Edward," he remarked. "I always tell our people that they are too bullheaded. They don't use enough words. What about that other friend of yours?"

Sir Edward glanced at his watch.

"It is possible," he said, "that by this time Mr. —--- Mr. Smith, shall we call him, to match your Mr. Jones?—is attending my wife's reception, from which your message called me. If he has not yet arrived, my secretary shall telephone for him."

Mr. Coulson indicated his approval.

"Seems to me," he remarked, "that I have struck a fortunate evening for my visit."

Sir Edward touched the bell and his secretary appeared.

"Sidney," he said, "I want you to find the gentleman whose name I am writing upon this piece of paper. If he is not in the reception rooms and has not arrived, telephone for him. Say that I shall be glad if he would come this way at once. He will understand that it is a matter of some importance."

The secretary bowed and withdrew, after a glance at the piece of paper which he held in his hand. Sir Edward turned toward his visitor.

"Mr. Coulson," he said, "will you allow me the privilege of offering you some refreshment?"

"I thank you, sir," Mr. Coulson answered. "I am in want of nothing but a smoke."

Sir Edward turned to the bell, but his visitor promptly stopped him.

"If you will allow me, sir," he said, "I will smoke one of my own. Home-made article, five dollars a hundred, but I can't stand these strong Havanas. Try one."

Sir Edward waved them away.

"If you will excuse me," he said, "I will smoke a cigarette. Since you are here, Mr. Coulson, I may say that I am very glad to meet you. I am very glad, also, of this opportunity for a few minutes' conversation upon another matter."

Mr. Coulson showed some signs of surprise.

"How's that?" he asked.

"There is another subject," Sir Edward said, "which I should like to discuss with you while we are waiting for Mr. Smith."

CHAPTER XX.
THE ANSWER

Mr. Coulson moved his cigar into a corner of his mouth, as though to obtain a clear view of his questioner's face. His expression was one of bland interest.

"Well, I guess you've got me puzzled, Sir Edward," he said. "You aren't thinking of doing anything in woollen machinery, are you?"

Sir Edward smiled.

"I think not, Mr. Coulson," he answered. "At any rate, my question had nothing to do with your other very interesting avocation. What I wanted to ask you was whether you could tell me anything about a compatriot of yours—a Mr. Hamilton Fynes?"

"Hamilton Fynes!" Mr. Coulson repeated thoughtfully. "Why, that's the man who got murdered on the cars, going from Liverpool to London."

"That is so," Sir Edward admitted.

Mr. Coulson shook his head.

"I told that reporter fellow all I knew about him," he said. "He was an unsociable sort of chap, you know, Sir Edward, and he wasn't in any line of business."

"H'm! I thought he might have been," the Minister answered, glancing keenly for a moment at his visitor. "To tell you the truth, Mr. Coulson, we have been a great deal bothered about that unfortunate incident, and by the subsequent murder of the young man who was attached to your Embassy here. Scotland Yard has strained every nerve to bring the guilty people to justice, but so far unsuccessfully. It seems to me that your friends on the other side scarcely seem to give us credit for our exertions. They do not help us in the least. They assure us that they had no knowledge of Mr. Fynes other than has appeared in the papers. They recognize him only as an American citizen going about his legitimate business. A little more confidence on their part would, I think, render our task easier."

Mr. Coulson scratched his chin for a moment thoughtfully.

"Well," he said, "I can understand their feeling a bit sore about it. I'm not exactly given to brag when I'm away from my own country—one hears too much of that all the time—but between you and me, I shouldn't say that it was possible for two crimes like that to be committed in New York City and for the murderer to get off scot free in either case."

"The matter," Sir Edward declared, "has given us a great deal of anxiety, and I can assure you that the Home Secretary himself has taken a strong personal interest in it, but at the same time, as I have just pointed out to you, our investigations are rendered the more difficult from the fact that we cannot learn anything definite concerning this Mr. Hamilton Fynes or his visit to this country. Now, if we knew, for instance," Sir Edward continued, "that he was carrying documents, or even a letter, similar to the one you have just handed to me, we might at once discover a motive to the crime, and work backwards until we reached the perpetrator."

Mr. Coulson knocked the ash from his cigar.

"I see what you are driving at," he said. "I am sorry I can be of no assistance to you, Sir Edward."

"Neither in the case of Mr. Hamilton Fynes or in the case of Mr. Richard Vanderpole?" Sir Edward asked.

Mr. Coulson shook his head.

"Quite out of my line," he declared.

"Notwithstanding the fact," Sir Edward reminded him quietly, "that you were probably the last person to see Vanderpole alive? He came to the Savoy to call upon you before he got into the taxicab where he was murdered. That is so, isn't it?"

"Sure!" Mr. Coulson answered. "A nice young fellow he was, too. Well set up, and real American manners,—'Hail, fellow, well met!' with you right away."

"I suppose, Mr. Coulson," the Minister suggested smoothly, "it wouldn't answer your purpose to put aside that bluff about patents for the development of the woollen trade for a few moments, and tell me exactly what passed between you and Mr. Vanderpole at the Savoy Hotel, and the object of his calling upon you? Whether, for instance, he took away with him documents or papers intended for the Embassy and which you yourself had brought from America?"

"You do think of things!" Mr. Coulson remarked admiringly. "You're on the wrong track this time, though, sure. Still, supposing I were able to tell you that Mr. Vanderpole was carrying papers of importance to my country, and that Mr. Hamilton Fynes was also in possession of the same class of document, how would it help you? In what fresh direction should you look then for the murderers of these two men?"

"Mr. Coulson," Sir Edward said, "we should consider the nature of those documents, and we should see to whose advantage it was that they were suppressed."

Mr. Coulson's face seemed suddenly old and lined. He spoke with a new vigor, and his eyes were very keen and bright under his bushy eyebrows.

"And supposing it was your country's?" he asked. "Supposing they contained instructions to our Ambassador which you might consider inimical to your interests? Do you mean that you would look at home for the murderer? You mean that you have men so devoted to their native land that they were willing to run the risk of death by the hangman to aid her? You mean that your Secret Service is perfected to that extent, and that the scales of justice are held blindfolded? Or do you mean that Scotland Yard would have its orders, and that these men would go free?"

"I was not thinking of my own country," Sir Edward admitted. "I must confess that my thoughts had turned elsewhere."

"Let me tell you this, sir," Mr. Coulson continued. "I should imagine that the trouble with Washington, if there is any, is simply that they will not believe that your police have a free hand. They will not believe that you are honestly and genuinely anxious for the discovery of the perpetrator of these crimes. I speak without authority, you understand? I am no more in a position to discuss this affair than any other tourist from my country who might happen to come along."

Sir Edward shrugged his shoulders.

"Can you suggest any method," he asked a little dryly, "by means of which we might remove this unfortunate impression?"

Mr. Coulson flicked the ash once more from the end of his cigar and looked at it thoughtfully.

"This isn't my show," he said, "and, you understand, I am giving the views of Mr. James B. Coulson, and nobody but Mr. James B. Coulson, but if I were in your position, and knew that a friendly country was feeling a little bit sore at having two of her citizens disposed of so unceremoniously, I'd do my best to prove, by the only possible means, that I was taking the matter seriously."

"The only possible means being?" Sir Edward asked.

"I guess I'd offer a reward," Mr. Coulson admitted.

Sir Edward did not hesitate for a moment.

"Your idea is an excellent one, Mr. Coulson," he said. "It has already been mooted, but we will give it a little emphasis. Tomorrow we will offer a reward of one thousand pounds for any information leading to the apprehension of either murderer."

"That sounds bully," Mr. Coulson declared.

"You think that it will have a good effect upon your friends in Washington?"

"Me?" Mr. Coulson asked. "I know nothing about it. I've given you my personal opinion only. Seems to me, though, it's the best way of showing that you're in earnest."

"Before we quit this subject finally, Mr. Coulson," Sir Edward said, "I am going to ask you a question which you have been asked before."

"Referring to Hamilton Fynes?" Mr. Coulson asked.

"Yes!"

"Get your young man to lay his hand on that copy of the Comet," Mr. Coulson begged earnestly. "I told that pushing young journalist all I knew and a bit more. I assure you, my information isn't worth anything."

"Was it meant to be worth anything?" Sir Edward asked.

Mr. Coulson remained imperturbable.

"If you don't mind, Sir Edward," he said, "I guess we'll drop the subject of Mr. Hamilton Fynes. We can't get any forwarder. Let it go at that."

There was a knock at the door. Sir Edward's secretary ushered in a tall, plainly dressed gentleman, who had the slightly aggrieved air of a man who has been kept out of his bed beyond the usual time.

"My dear Bransome," he said, shaking hands, "isn't this a little unreasonable of you? Business at this hour of the night! I was in the midst of a most amusing conversation with a delightful acquaintance of your wife's, a young lady who turned up her nose at Hegel and had developed a philosophy of her own. I was just beginning to grasp its first principles. Nothing else, I am quite sure, would have kept me awake."

Sir Edward leaned across the table towards Mr. Coulson. Mr. Coulson had risen to his feet.

"This gentleman," he said, "is Mr. Smith."

The newcomer opened his lips to protest, but Sir Edward held out his hand.

"One moment," he begged. "Our friend here—Mr. J. B. Coulson from New York—has brought a letter from America. He is sailing tomorrow,—leaving London somewhere about eight o'clock in the morning, I imagine. He wishes to take back a verbal reply. The letter, you will understand, comes from a Mr. Jones, and the reply is delivered in the presence of—Mr. Smith. Our friend here is not personally concerned in these affairs. As a matter of fact, I believe he has been on the Continent exploiting some patents of his own invention."

The newcomer accepted the burden of his altered nomenclature and took up the letter. He glanced at the signature, and his manner became at once more interested. He accepted the chair which Sir Edward had placed by his side, and, drawing the electric light a little nearer, read the document through, word by word. Then he folded it up, and glanced first at his colleague and afterwards at Mr. Coulson.

"I understand," he said, "that this is a private inquiry from a private gentleman, who is entitled, however, to as much courtesy as it is possible for us to show him."

"That is exactly the position, sir," Mr. Coulson replied. "Negotiations of a more formal character are naturally conducted between your Foreign Office and the Foreign Office of my country. These few lines come from man to man. I think that it occurred to my friend that it might save a great deal of trouble, a great deal of specious diplomacy, and a great many hundred pages of labored despatches, if, at the bottom of it all, he knew your true feelings concerning this question. It is, after all, a simple matter," Mr. Coulson continued, "and yet it is a matter with so many ramifications that after much discussion it might become a veritable chaos."

Mr. Smith inclined his head gently.

"I appreciate the situation," he said. "My friend here—Sir Edward Bransome—and I have already discussed the matter at great length. We have also had the benefit of the advice and help of a greater Foreign Minister than either of us could ever hope to become. I see no objection to giving you the verbal reply you ask for. Do you, Bransome?"

"None whatever, sir."

"I leave it to you to put it in your own words," Mr. Smith continued. "The affair is within your province, and the policy of His Majesty's Ministers is absolutely fixed."

Sir Edward turned toward their visitor.

"Mr. Coulson," he said, "we are asked by your friend, in a few plain words, what the attitude of Great Britain would be in the event of a war between Japan and America. My answer—our answer—to you is this,—no war between Japan and America is likely to take place unless your Cabinet should go to unreasonable and uncalled-for extremes. We have ascertained, beyond any measure of doubt, the sincere feeling of our ally in this matter. Japan does not desire war, is not preparing for it, is unwilling even to entertain the possibility of it. At the same time she feels that her sons should receive the same consideration from every nation in the world as the sons of other people. Personally it is our profound conviction that the good sense, the fairness, and the generous instincts of your great country will recognize this and act accordingly. War between your country and Japan is an impossible thing. The thought of it exists only in the frothy vaporings of cheap newspapers, and the sensational utterances of the catch politician who must find an audience and a hearing by any methods. The sober possibility of such a conflict does not exist."

Mr. Coulson listened attentively to every word. When Sir Edward had finished, he withdrew his cigar from his mouth and knocked the ash on to a corner of the writing table.

"That's all very interesting indeed, Sir Edward," he declared. "I am very pleased to have heard what you have said, and I shall repeat it to my friend on the other side, who, I am sure, will be exceedingly obliged to you for such a frank exposition of your views. And now," he continued, "I don't want to keep you gentlemen up too late, so perhaps you will be coming to the answer of my question."

"The answer!" Sir Edward exclaimed. "Surely I made myself clear?"

"All that you have said," Mr. Coulson admitted, "has been remarkably clear, but the question I asked you was this,—what is to be the position of your country in the event of war between Japan and America?"

"And I have told you," Sir Edward declared, "that war between Japan and America is not a subject within the scope of practical politics."

"We may consider ourselves—my friend Mr. Jones would certainly consider himself," Mr. Coulson affirmed, — "as good a judge as you, Sir Edward, so far as regards that matter. I am not asking you whether it is probable or improbable. You may know the feelings of your ally. You do not know ours. We may look into the future, and we may see that, sooner or later, war between our country and Japan is a necessity. We may decide that it is better for us to fight now than later. These things are in the clouds. They only enter into the present discussion to this extent, but it is not for you to sit here and say whether war between the United States and Japan is possible or impossible. What Mr. Jones asks you is—what would be your position if it should take place? The little diatribe with which you have just favored me is exactly the reply we should have expected to receive formally from Downing Street. It isn't that sort of reply I want to take back to Mr. Jones."

Mr. Smith and his colleague exchanged glances, and the latter drew his chief on one side.

"You will excuse me for a moment, I know, Mr. Coulson," he said.

"Why, by all means," Mr. Coulson declared. "My time is my own, and it is entirely at your service. If you say the word, I'll go outside and wait."

"It is not necessary," Sir Edward answered.

The room was a large one, and the two men walked slowly up and down, Mr. Smith leaning all the time upon his colleague's shoulder. They spoke in an undertone, and what they said was inaudible to Mr. Coulson. During his period of waiting he drew another cigar from his pocket, and lit it from the stump of the old one. Then he made himself a little more comfortable in his chair, and looked around at the walls of the handsomely furnished but rather sombre apartment with an air of pleased curiosity. It was scarcely, perhaps, what he should have expected from a man in a similar position in his own country, but it was, at any rate, impressive. Presently they came back to him. This time it was Mr. Smith who spoke.

"Mr. Coulson," he said, "we need not beat about the bush. You ask us a plain question and you want a plain answer. Then I must tell you this. The matter is not one concerning which I can give you any definite information. I appreciate the position of your friend Mr. Jones, and I should like to have met him in the same spirit as he has shown in his inquiry, but I may tell you that, being utterly convinced that Japan does not seek war with you, and that therefore no war is likely, my Government is not prepared to answer a question which they consider based upon an impossibility. If this war should come, the position of our country would depend entirely upon the rights of the dispute. As a corollary to that, I would mention two things. You read your newspapers, Mr. Coulson?"

"Sure!" that gentleman answered.

"You are aware, then," Mr. Smith continued, "of the present position of your fleet. You know how many months must pass before it can reach Eastern waters. It is not within the traditions of this country to evade fulfillment of its obligations, however severe and unnatural they may seem, but in three months' time, Mr. Coulson, our treaty with Japan will have expired."

"You are seeking to renew it!" Mr. Coulson declared quickly.

Mr. Smith raised his eyebrows.

"The renewal of that treaty," he said, "is on the knees of the gods. One cannot tell. I go so far only as to tell you that in three months the present treaty will have expired."

Mr. Coulson rose slowly to his feet and took up his hat.

"Gentlemen both," he said, "that's what I call plain speaking. I suppose it's up to us to read between the lines. I can assure you that my friend Mr. Jones will appreciate it. It isn't my place to say a word outside the letter which I have handed to you. I am a plain business man, and these things don't come in my way. That is why I feel I can criticize,—I am unprejudiced. You are Britishers, and you've got one eternal fault. You seem to think the whole world must see a matter as you see it. If Japan has convinced you that she doesn't seek a war with us, it doesn't follow that she's convinced us. As to the rights of our dispute, don't rely so much upon hearing one side only. Don't be dogmatic about it, and say this thing is and that thing isn't. You may bet your last dollar that America isn't going to war about trifles. We are the same flesh and blood, you know. We have the same traditions to uphold. What we do is what we should expect you to do if you were in our place. That's all, gentlemen. Now I wish you both good night! Mr. Smith, I am proud to shake hands with you. Sir Edward, I say the same to you."

Bransome touched the bell and summoned his secretary.

"Sidney, will you see this gentleman out?" he said. "You are quite sure there is nothing further we can do for you, Mr. Coulson?"

"Nothing at all, I thank you, sir," that gentleman answered. "I have only got to thank you once more for the pleasure of this brief interview. Good night!"

"Good night, and bon voyage!" Sir Edward answered.

The door was closed. The two men looked at one another for a moment. Mr. Smith shrugged his shoulders and helped himself to a cigarette.

"I wonder," he remarked thoughtfully, "how our friends in Japan convinced themselves so thoroughly that Mr. Jones was only playing ships!"

Sir Edward shook his head.

"It makes one wonder," he said.

CHAPTER XXI.
A CLUE

By midday on the following morning London was placarded with notices, the heading of which was sensational enough to attract observation from every passer-by, young or old, rich or poor. One thousand pounds' reward for the apprehension of the murderer of either Hamilton Fynes or Richard Vanderpole! Inspector Jacks, who was amongst the first to hear the news, after a brief interview with his chief put on his hat and walked round to the Home Office. He sought out one of the underlings with whom he had some acquaintance, and whom he found ready enough, even eager, to discuss the matter.

"There wasn't a word about any reward," Inspector Jacks was told, "until this morning. We had a telephone message from the chief's bedroom and phoned you up at once. It's a pretty stiff amount, isn't it?"

"It is," the Inspector admitted. "Our chief seems to be taking quite a personal interest in the matter all at once."

"I'll lay two to one that some one was on to him at Sir Edward Bransome's reception last night," the other remarked. "I know very well that there was no idea of offering a reward yesterday afternoon. We might have come out with a hundred pounds or so, a little later on, perhaps, but there was nothing of this sort in the air. I've no desire to seem censorious, you know, Jacks," the young man went on, leaning back in his chair and lighting a cigarette, "but it does seem a dashed queer thing that you can't put your finger upon either of these fellows."

Inspector Jacks nodded gloomily.

"No doubt it seems so to you," he admitted. "You forget that we have to have a reasonable amount of proof before we can tap a man on the shoulder and ask him to come with us. It isn't so abroad or in America. There they can hand a man up with less than half the evidence we have to be prepared with, and, of course, they get the reputation of being smarter on the job. We may learn enough to satisfy ourselves easily, but to get up a case which we can put before a magistrate and be sure of not losing our man, takes time."

"So you've got your eye on some one?" The young man asked curiously.

"I did not say so," the Inspector answered warily. "By the bye, do you think there would be any chance of five minutes' interview with your chief?"

The young man shook his head slowly.

"What a cheek you've got, Jacks!" he declared. "You're not serious, are you?"

"Perfectly," Inspector Jacks answered. "And to tell you the truth, my young friend, I am half inclined to think that when he is given to understand, as he will be by you, if he doesn't know it already, that I am in charge of the investigations concerning these two murders, he will see me."

The young man was disposed to consider the point.

"Well," he remarked, "the chief does seem plaguy interested, all of a sudden. I'll pass your name in. If you take a seat, it's just possible that he may spare you a minute or two in about an hour's time. He won't be able to before then, I'm sure. There's a deputation almost due, and two other appointments before luncheon time."

The Inspector accepted a newspaper and an easy chair. His young friend disappeared and returned almost immediately, looking a little surprised.

"I've managed it for you," he explained. "The chief is going to spare you five minutes at once. Come along and I'll show you in."

Inspector Jacks took up his hat and followed his acquaintance to the private room of the Home Secretary. That personage nodded to him upon his entrance and continued to dictate a letter. When he had finished, he sent his clerk out of the room and, motioning Mr. Jacks to take a seat by his side, leaned back in his own chair with the air of one prepared to relax for a moment. He was a man of somewhat insignificant presence, but he had keen gray eyes, half the time concealed under thick eyebrows, and flashing out upon you now and then at least expected moments.

"From Scotland Yard, I understand, Mr. Jacks?" he remarked.

"At your service, sir," the Inspector answered. "I am in charge of the investigations concerning these two recent murders."

"Quite so," the Home Secretary remarked. "I am very glad to meet you, Mr. Jacks. So far, I suppose, you are willing to admit that you gentlemen down at Scotland Yard have not exactly distinguished yourselves."

"We are willing to admit that," Inspector Jacks said.

"I do not know whether the reward will help you very much," the Home Secretary continued. "So far as you people personally are concerned, I imagine that it will make no difference. The only point seems to be that it may bring you outside help which at the present time is being withheld."

"The offering of the reward, sir," Inspector Jacks said, "can do no harm, and it may possibly assist us very materially."

"I am glad to have your opinion, Mr. Jacks," the Home Secretary said.

There was a moment's pause. The Minister trifled with some papers lying on the desk before him. Then he turned to his visitor and continued,—

"You will forgive my reminding you, Mr. Jacks, that I am a busy man and that this is a busy morning. You had some reason, I presume, for wishing to see me?"

"I had, sir," the Inspector answered. "I took the liberty of waiting upon you, sir, to ask whether the idea of a reward for so large a sum came spontaneously from your department?"

The Home Secretary raised his eyebrows.

"Really, Mr. Jacks," he began,—

"I hope, sir," the Inspector protested, "that you will not think I am asking this question through any irrelevant curiosity. I am beginning to form a theory of my own as to these two murders, but it needs building up. The offering of a reward like this, if it emanates from the source which I suspect that it does, gives a solid foundation to my theories. I am here, sir, in the interests of justice only, and I should be exceedingly obliged to you if you would tell me whether the suggestion of this large reward did not come from the Foreign Office?"

The Minister considered for several moments, and then slowly inclined his head.

"Mr. Jacks," he said, "your question appears to me to be a pertinent one. I see not the slightest reason to conceal from you the fact that your surmise is perfectly accurate."

A flash of satisfaction illuminated for a moment the detective's inexpressive features. He rose and took up his hat.

"I am very much obliged to you, sir," he said. "The information which you have given me is extremely valuable."

"I am glad to hear you say so," the Home Secretary declared. "You understand, of course, that it is within the province of my department to assist at all times and in any possible way the course of justice. Is there anything more I can do for you?"

Inspector Jacks hesitated.

"If you would not think it a liberty, sir," he said, "I should be very glad indeed if you would give me a note which would insure me an interview with Sir Edward Bransome."

"I will give it you with pleasure," the Secretary answered, "although I imagine that he would be quite willing to see you on your own request."

He wrote a few lines and passed them over. Inspector Jacks saluted, and turned towards the door.

"You'll let me know if anything turns up?" the Home Secretary said.

"You shall be informed at once, sir," the Inspector assured him, a as he left the room.

Sir Edward Bransome was just leaving his house when Inspector Jacks entered the gate. The latter, who knew him by sight, saluted and hesitated for a moment.

"Did you wish to speak to me?" Sir Edward asked, drawing back from the step of his electric brougham.

The Inspector held out his letter. Sir Edward tore it open and glanced through the few lines which it contained. Then he looked keenly for a moment at the man who stood respectfully by his side.

"So you are Inspector Jacks from Scotland Yard," he remarked.

"At your service, sir," the detective answered.

"You can get in with me, if you like," Sir Edward continued, motioning toward the interior of his brougham. "I am due in Downing Street now, but I dare say you could say what you wish to on the way there."

"Certainly, sir," Inspector Jacks answered. "It will be very good of you indeed if you can spare me those few minutes."

The brougham glided away.

"Now, Mr. Jacks," Sir Edward said, "what can I do for you? If you want to arrest me, I shall claim privilege."

The Inspector smiled.

"I am in charge, sir," he said, "of the investigations concerning the murder of Mr. Hamilton Fynes and Mr. Richard Vanderpole. The news of the reward came to us at Scotland Yard this morning. Its unusual amount led me to make some injuries at the Home Office. I found that what I partly expected was true. I found, sir, that your department has shown some interest in the apprehension of these two men."

Sir Edward inclined his head slowly.

"Well?" he said.

"Sir Edward Bransome," the Inspector continued, "I have a theory of my own as to these murders, and though it may take me some time to work it out, I feel myself day by day growing nearer the truth. These were not ordinary crimes. Any one can see that. They were not even crimes for the purpose of robbery—not, that is to say, for robbery in the ordinary sense of the word. That is apparent even to those who write for the Press. It has been apparent to us from the first. It is beginning to dawn upon me now what the nature of the motive must be which was responsible for them. I have in my possession a slight, a very slight clue. The beginning of it is there, and the end. It is the way between which is tangled."

Sir Edward lit a cigarette and leaned back amongst the cushions. With a little gesture he indicated his desire that Inspector Jacks should proceed.

"My object in seeking for a personal interview with you, sir," Inspector Jacks continued, "is to ask you a somewhat peculiar question. If I find that my investigations lead me in the direction which at present seems probable, it is no ordinary person whom I shall have to arrest when the time comes. The reward which has been offered is a large one, and it is not for me to question the bona fide nature of it. I would not presume, sir, even to ask you whether it was offered by reason of any outside pressure, but there is one question which I must ask. Do you really wish, sir, that the murderer or murderers of these two men shall be brought to justice?"

Sir Edward looked at his companion in steadfast amazement.

"My dear Inspector," he said, "what is this that you have in your mind? I hold no brief for any man capable of such crimes as these. Representations have been made to us by the American Government that the murder of two of her citizens within the course of twenty-four hours, and the absence of any arrest, is somewhat of a reflection upon our police service. It is for your assistance, and in compliment to our friends across the Atlantic, that the reward was offered."

Inspector Jacks seemed a little at a loss.

"It is your wish, then, sir," he said slowly, "that the guilty person or persons be arrested without warning, whoever they may be?"

"By all means," Sir Edward affirmed. "I cannot conceive, Inspector, what you have in your mind which could have led you for a moment to suspect the contrary."

The brougham had come to a standstill in front of a house in Downing Street. Inspector Jacks descended slowly. It was hard for him to decide on the spot how far to take into his confidence a person whose attitude was so unsympathetic.

"I am exceedingly obliged to you for your answer to my question, sir," he said, saluting. "I hope that in a few days we shall have some news for you."

Sir Edward watched him disappear as he mounted the steps of the Prime Minister's house.

"I wonder," he said to himself thoughtfully, "what that fellow can have in his mind!"

Inspector Jacks did not at once return to Scotland Yard. On his way there he turned into St. James' Square, and stood for several moments looking at the corner house on the far side. Finally, after a hesitation which seldom characterized his movements, he crossed the road and rang the bell. The door was opened almost at once by a Japanese butler.

"Is your master at home?" the Inspector asked.

"His Highness does not see strangers," the man replied coldly.

"Will you take him my card?" the Inspector asked.

The man bowed, and showed him into an apartment on the ground floor. Then with the card in his hand, he turned reluctantly away.

"His Highness shall be informed that you are here," he said. "I fear, however, that you waste your time. I go to see."

Inspector Jacks subsided into a bamboo chair and looked out of the window with a frown upon his forehead. It was certain that he was not proceeding with altogether his usual caution. As a matter of tactics, this visit of his might very well be fatal!

CHAPTER XXII.
A BREATH FROM THE EAST

Inspector Jacks was a man who had succeeded in his profession chiefly on account of an average amount of natural astuteness, and also because he was one of those favored persons whose nervous system was a whole and perfect thing. Yet, curiously enough, as he sat in this large, gloomy apartment into which he had been shown, a room filled with art treasures whose appearance and significance were entirely strange to him, he felt a certain uneasiness which he was absolutely unable to understand. He was somewhat instinctive in his likes and dislikes, and from the first he most heartily disliked the room itself,—its vague perfumes, its subdued violet coloring, the faces of the grinning idols, which seemed to meet his gaze in every direction, the pictures of those fierce-looking warriors who brandished two-edged swords at him from the walls. They belonged to the period when Japanese art was perhaps in its crudest state, and yet in this uncertain atmosphere they seemed to possess an extraordinary vitality, as though indeed they were prepared at a moment's notice to leap from their frames and annihilate this mysterious product of modern days, who in black clothes and silk hat, unarmed and without physical strength, yet wielded the powers of life and death as surely as they in their time had done.

The detective rose from his seat and walked around the room. He made a show of examining the arms against the walls, the brocaded hangings with their wonderful design of faded gold, the ivory statuettes, the black god who sat on his haunches and into whose face seemed carved some dumb but eternal power. Movement was in some respects a solace, but the sound of a hansom bell tinkling outside was a much greater relief. He crossed to the windows and looked out over the somewhat silent square. A hurdy-gurdy was playing in the corner opposite the club, just visible from where he stood. The members were passing in and out. The commissionaire stood stolidly in his place, raising every now and then his cab whistle to his lips. A flickering sunlight fell upon the wind-shaken lilac trees in the square enclosure. Inspector Jacks found himself wishing that the perfume of those lilacs might reach even to where he stood, and help him to forget for a moment that subtler and to him curiously unpleasant odor which all the time became more and more apparent. So overpowering did he feel it that he tried even to open the window, but found it an impossible task. The atmosphere seemed to him to be becoming absolutely stifling.

He turned around and walked uneasily toward the door. He decided then that this was some sort of gruesome nightmare with which he was afflicted. He was quite certain that in a few minutes he would wake in his little iron bedstead with the sweat upon his forehead and a reproachful consciousness of having eaten an indiscreet supper. It could not possibly be a happening in real life! It could not be true that his knees were sinking beneath the weight of his body, that the clanging of iron hammers was really smiting the drums of his ears, that the purple of the room was growing red, and that his veins were strained to bursting! He threw out his arms in a momentary instinct of fiercely struggling consciousness. The idols on the walls jeered at him. Those strangely clad warriors seemed to him now to be looking down upon his discomfiture with a satanic smile, mocking the pygmy who had dared to raise his hand against one so jealously guarded. Clang once more went the blacksmith's hammers, and then chaos!...

The end of the nightmare was not altogether according to Inspector Jacks' expectations. He found himself in a small back room, stretched upon a sofa before the open French-windows, through which came a pleasant vision of waving green trees and a pleasanter stream of fresh air. His first instinct was to sniff, and a sense of relief crept through him when he realized that this room, at any rate, was free from abnormal odors. He sat up on the couch. A pale-faced Japanese servant stood by his side with a glass in his hand. A few feet away, the man whom he had come to visit was looking down upon him with an expression of grave concern in his kindly face.

"You are better, I trust, sir?" Prince Maiyo said.

"I am better," Inspector Jacks muttered. "I don't know—I can't imagine what happened to me."

"You were not feeling quite well, perhaps, this morning," the Prince said soothingly. "A little run down, no doubt. Your profession—I gather from your card that you come from Scotland Yard—is an arduous one. I came into the room and found you lying upon your back, gasping for breath."

Inspector Jacks was making a swift recovery. He noticed that the glass which the man-servant was holding was empty. He had a dim recollection of something having been forced through his lips. Already he was beginning to feel himself again.

"I was absolutely and entirely well," he declared stoutly, "both when I left home this morning and when I entered that room to wait for you. I don't know what it was that came over me," he continued doubtfully, "but the atmosphere seemed suddenly to become unbearable."

Prince Maiyo nodded understandingly.

"People often complain," he admitted. "So many of my hangings in the room have been wrapped in spices to preserve them, and my people burn dead blossoms there occasionally. Some of us, too," he concluded, "are very susceptible to strange odors. I should imagine, perhaps, that you are one of them."

Inspector Jacks shook his head.

"I call myself a strong man," he said, "and I couldn't have believed that anything of the sort would have happened to me."

"I shouldn't worry about it," the Prince said gently. "Go and see your doctor, if you like, but I have known many people, perfectly healthy, affected in the same way. I understood that you wished to have a word with me. Do you feel well enough to enter upon your business now, or would you prefer to make another appointment?"

"I am feeling quite well again, thank you," the Inspector said slowly. "If you could spare me a few minutes, I should be glad to explain the matter which brought me here."

The Prince merely glanced at his servant, who bowed and glided noiselessly from the room. Then he drew an easy chair to the side of the couch where Mr. Jacks was still sitting.

"I am very much interested to meet you, Mr. Inspector Jacks," he remarked, with a glance at the card which he was still holding in his fingers. "I have studied very many of your English institutions during my stay over here with much interest, but it has not been my good fortune to have come into touch at all with your police system. Sir Goreham Briggs—your chief, I believe—has invited me several times to Scotland Yard, and I have always meant to avail myself of his kindness. You come to me, perhaps, from him?"

The Inspector shook his head.

"My business, Prince," he said, "is a little more personal."

Prince Maiyo raised his eyebrows.

"Indeed?" he said. "Well, whatever it is, let us hear it. I trust that I have not unconsciously transgressed against your laws?"

Inspector Jacks hesitated. After all, his was not so easy a task.

"Prince," he said, "my errand is not in any way a pleasant one, and I should be very sorry indeed to find myself in the position of bringing any annoyance upon a stranger and a gentleman who is so highly esteemed. At the same time there are certain duties in connection with my every-day life which I cannot ignore. In England, as I dare say you know, sir, the law is a great leveller. I have heard that it is not quite so in your country, but over here we all stand equal in its sight."

"That is excellent," the Prince said. "Please believe, Mr. Inspector Jacks, that I do not wish to stand for a single moment between you and your duty, whatever it may be. Let me hear just what you have to say, as though I were an ordinary dweller here. While I am in England, at any rate," he added with a smile, "I am subject to your laws, and I do my best to obey them."

"It has fallen to my lot," Inspector Jacks said, "to take charge of the investigations following upon the murder of a man named Hamilton Fynes, who was killed on his way from Liverpool to London about a fortnight ago."

The Prince inclined his head.

"I believe," he said amiably, "that I remember hearing the matter spoken of. It was the foundation of a debate, I recollect, at a recent dinner party, as to the extraordinarily exaggerated value people in your country seem to claim for human life, as compared to us Orientals. But pray proceed, Mr. Inspector Jacks," the Prince continued courteously. "The investigation, I am sure, is in most able hands."

"You are very kind, sir," said the Inspector. "I do my best, but I might admit to you that I have never found a case so difficult to grasp. Our methods perhaps are slow, but they are, in a sense, sure. We are building up our case, and we hope before long to secure the criminal, but it is not an easy task."

The Prince bowed. This time he made no remark.

"The evidence which I have collected from various sources," Inspector Jacks continued, "leads me to believe that the person who committed this murder was a foreigner."

"What you call an alien," the Prince suggested. "There is much discussion, I gather, concerning their presence in this country nowadays."

"The evidence which I possess," the detective proceeded, "points to the murderer belonging to the same nationality as Your Highness."

The Prince raised his eyebrows.

"A Japanese?" he asked.

The Inspector assented.

"I am sorry," the Prince said, with a touch of added gravity in his manner, "that one of my race should have committed a misdemeanor in this country, but if that is so, your way, of course, is clear. You must arrest him and deal with him as an ordinary English criminal. He is here to live your life, and he must obey your laws."

"In time, sir," Inspector Jacks said slowly, "we hope to do so, but over here we may not arrest upon suspicion. We have to collect evidence, and build and build until we can satisfy any reasonable individual that the accused person is guilty."

The Prince sighed sympathetically.

"It is not for me," he said, "to criticize your methods."

"I come now," Inspector Jacks said slowly, "to the object of my call upon Your Highness. Following upon what I have just told you, certain other information has come into my possession to this effect—that not only was this murderer a Japanese, but we have evidence which seems to suggest that he was attached in some way to your household."

"To my household!" the Prince repeated.

"To this household, Your Highness," the detective repeated.

The Prince shook his head slowly.

"Mr. Jacks," he said, "you are, I am sure, a very clever man. Let me ask you one question. Has it ever fallen to your lot to make a mistake?"

"Very often indeed," the Inspector admitted frankly.

"Then I am afraid," the Prince said, "that you are once more in that position. I have attached to my household fourteen Japanese servants, a secretary, a majordomo, and a butler. It may interest you, perhaps, to know that during my residence in this country not one of my retinue, with the exception of my secretary, who has been in Paris for some weeks, has left this house."

The Inspector stared at the Prince incredulously.

"Never left the house?" he repeated. "Do you mean, sir, that they do not go out for holidays, for exercise, to the theatre?"

The Prince shook his head.

"Such things are not the custom with us," he said. "They are my servants. The duty of their life is service. London is a world unknown to them—London and all these Western cities. They have no desire to be made mock of in your streets. Their life is given to my interests. They do not need distractions."

Inspector Jacks was dumfounded. Such a state of affairs seemed to him impossible.

"Do you mean that they do not take exercise," he asked, "that they never breathe the fresh air?"

The Prince smiled.

"Such fresh air as your city can afford them," he said, "is to be found in the garden there, into which I never penetrate and which is for their use. I see that you look amazed, Mr. Inspector Jacks. This thing which I have told you seems strange, no doubt, but you must not confuse the servants of my country with the servants of yours. I make no comment upon the latter. You know quite well what they are; so do I. With us, service is a religion,—service to country and service to master. These men who perform the duties of my household would give their lives for me as cheerfully as they would for their country, should the occasion arise."

"But their health?" the Inspector protested. "It is not, surely, well for them to be herded together like this?"

The Prince smiled.

"I am not what is called a sportsman in this country, Mr. Inspector Jacks," he said, "but you shall go to the house of any nobleman you choose, and if you will bring me an equal number of your valets or footmen or chefs, who can compete with mine in running or jumping or wrestling, then I will give you a prize what you will—a hundred pounds, or more. You see, my servants have learned the secret of diet. They drink nothing save water. Sickness is unknown to them."

The Inspector was silent for some time. Then he rose to his feet.

"Prince," he said, "what should you declare, then, if I told you that a man of obvious Japanese extraction was seen to enter your house on the morning after the murder, and that he was a person to whom certain circumstances pointed as being concerned in that deed?"

"Mr. Inspector Jacks," the Prince said calmly, "I was the only person of my race who entered my house that morning."

The Inspector moved toward the door.

"Your Highness," he said gravely, "I am exceedingly obliged to you for your courteous attention, and for your kindness after my unfortunate indisposition."

The Prince smiled graciously.

"Mr. Inspector Jacks," he said, "your visit has been of great interest to me. If I can be of any further assistance, pray do not hesitate to call upon me."

CHAPTER XXIII.
ON THE TRAIL

Inspector Jacks studied the brass plate for a moment, and then rang the patients' bell. The former, he noticed was very much in want of cleaning, and for a doctor's residence there was a certain lack of smartness about the house and its appointments which betokened a limited practice. The railing in front was broken, and no pretence had been made at keeping the garden in order. Inspector Jacks had time to notice these things, for it was not until after his second summons that the door was opened by Dr. Whiles himself.

"Good morning!" the latter said tentatively. Then, with a slight air of disappointment, he recognized his visitor.

"Good morning, doctor!" Inspector Jacks replied. "You haven't forgotten me, I hope? I came down to see you a short time ago, respecting the man who was knocked down by a motor car and treated by you on a certain evening."

The doctor nodded.

"Will you come in?" he asked.

He led the way into a somewhat dingy waiting room. A copy of *The Field*, a month old, a dog-eared magazine, and a bound volume of *Good Words* were spread upon the table. The room itself, except for a few chairs, was practically bare.

"I do not wish to take up too much of your time, Dr. Whiles," the Inspector began,—

The doctor laughed shortly.

"You needn't bother about that," he said. "I'm tired of making a bluff. My time isn't any too well occupied."

The Inspector glanced at his watch,—it was a few minutes past twelve.

"If you are really not busy," he said, "I was about to suggest to you that you should come back to town with me and lunch. I do not expect, of course, to take up your day for nothing," he continued. "You will understand, as a professional man, that when your services are required by the authorities, they expect and are willing to pay for them."

"But what use can I be to you?" the doctor asked. "You know all about the man whom I fixed up on the night of the murder. There's nothing more to tell you about that. I'd as soon go up to town and lunch with you as not, but if you think that I've anything more to tell you, you'll only be disappointed."

The Inspector nodded.

"I'm quite content to run the risk of that," he said. "Of course," he continued, "it does not follow in the least that this person was in any way connected with the murder. In fact, so far as I can tell at present, the chances are very much against it. But at the same time it would interest my chief if you were able to identify him."

The doctor nodded.

"I begin to understand," he said.

"If you will consider a day spent up in town equivalent to the treatment of twenty-five patients at your ordinary scale," Inspector Jacks said, "I shall be glad if you would accompany me there by the next train. We will lunch together first, and look for our friend later in the afternoon."

The doctor did not attempt to conceal the fact that he found this suggestion entirely satisfactory. In less than half an hour, the two men were on their way to town.

Curiously enough, Penelope and Prince Maiyo met that morning for the first time in several days. They were both guests of the Duchess of Devenham at a large luncheon party at the Savoy Restaurant. Penelope felt a little shiver when she saw him coming down the stairs. Somehow or other, she had dreaded this meeting, yet when it came, she knew that it was a relief. There was no change in his manner, no trace of anxiety in his smooth, unruffled face. He seemed, if possible, to have grown younger, to walk more buoyantly. His eyes met hers frankly, his smile was wholly unembarrassed. It was not possible for a man to bear himself thus who stood beneath the great shadow!

So far from avoiding her, he came over to her side directly he had greeted his hostess.

"This morning," he said, "I heard some good news. You are to be a fellow guest at Devenham."

"I am afraid," she admitted, "that of my two aunts I impose most frequently upon the one where my claims are the slightest. The Duchess is so good-natured."

"She is charming," the Prince declared. "I am looking forward to my visit immensely. I think I am a little weary of London. A visit to the country seems to me most delightful. They tell me, too, that your spring gardens are wonderful. What London suffers from, I think, at this time of the year, is a lack of flowers. We want something to remind us that the spring is coming, besides these occasional gleams of blue sky and very occasional bursts of sunshine."

"You are a sentimentalist, Prince," she declared, smiling.

"No, I think not," he answered seriously. "I love all beautiful things. I think that there are many men as well as women who are like that. Shall I be very rude and say that in the matter of climate and flowers one grows, perhaps, to expect a little more in my own country."

An uncontrollable impulse moved her. She leaned a little towards him.

"Climate and flowers only?" she murmured. "What about the third essential?"

"Miss Penelope," he said under his breath, "I have to admit that one must travel further afield for Heaven's greatest gift. Even then one can only worship. The stars are denied to us."

The Duchess came sailing over to them.

"Every one is here," she said. "I hope that you are all hungry. After lunch, Prince, I want you to speak to General Sherrif. He has been dying to meet you, to talk over your campaign together in Manchuria. There's another man who is anxious to meet you, too,— Professor Spenlove. He has been to Japan for a month, and thinks about writing a book on your customs. I believe he looks to you to correct his impressions."

"So long as he does not ask me to correct his proofs!" the Prince murmured.

"That is positively the most unkind thing I have ever heard you say," the Duchess declared. "Come along, you good people. Jules has promised me a new omelet, on condition that we sit down at precisely half-past one. If we are five minutes late, he declines to send it up."

They took their places at the round table which had been reserved for the Duchess of Devenham,—not very far, Penelope remembered, from the table at which they had sat for dinner a little more than a fortnight ago. The recollection of that evening brought her a sudden realization of the tragedy which seemed to have taken her life into its grip. Again the Prince sat by her side. She watched him with eyes in which there was a gleam sometimes almost of horror. Easy and natural as usual, with his pleasant smile and simple speech, he was making himself agreeable to one of the older ladies of the party, to whom, by chance, no one had addressed more than a word or so. It was always the same—always like this, she realized, with a sudden keen apprehension of this part of the man's nature. If there was a kindness to be done, a thoughtful action, it was not only he who did it but it was he who first thought of it. The papers during the last few days had been making public an incident which he had done his best to keep secret. He had signalized his arrival in London, some months ago, by going overboard from a police boat into the Thames to rescue a half-drunken lighterman, and when the Humane Society had voted him their medal, he had accepted it only on condition that the presentation was private and kept out of the papers. It was not one but fifty kindly deeds which stood to his credit. Always with the manners of a Prince—gracious, courteous, and genial—never a word had passed his lips of evil towards any human being. The barriers today between the smoking room and the drawing room are shadowy things, and she knew very well that he was held in a somewhat curious respect by men, as a person to whom it was impossible to tell a story in which there was any shadow of indelicacy. The ways of the so-called man of world seemed in his presence as though they must be the ways of some creature of a different and a lower stage of existence. A young man whom he had once corrected had christened him, half jestingly, Sir Galahad, and certainly his life in London, a life which had to bear all the while the test of the limelight, had appeared to merit some such title. These thoughts chased one another through her mind as she looked at him and marvelled. Surely those other things must be part of a bad nightmare! It was not possible that such a man could be associated with wrong-doing—such manner of wrong-doing!

Even while these thoughts passed through her brain, he turned to talk to her, and she felt at once that little glow of pleasure which the sound of his voice nearly always evoked.

"I am looking forward so much," he said, "to my stay at Devenham. You know, it will not be very much longer that I shall have the opportunity of accepting such invitations."

"You mean that the time is really coming when we shall lose you?" she asked suddenly.

"When my work is finished, I return home," he answered. "I fancy that it will not be very long now."

"When you do leave England," she asked after a moment's pause, "do you go straight to Japan?"

He bowed.

"With the Continent I have finished," he said. "The cruiser which His Majesty has sent to fetch me waits even now at Southampton."

"You speak of your work," she remarked, "as though you had been collecting material for a book."

He smiled.

"I have been busy collecting information in many ways," he said,—"trying to live your life and feel as you feel, trying to understand those things in your country, and in other countries too, which seem at first so strange to us who come from the other side of the East."

"And the end of it all?" she asked.

His eyes gleamed for a moment with a light which she did not understand. His smile was tolerant, even genial, but his face remained like the face of a sphinx.

"It is for the good of Japan I came," he said, "for her good that I have stayed here so long. At the same time it has been very pleasant. I have met with great kindness."

She leaned a little forward so as to look into his face. The impassivity of his features was like a wall before her.

"After all," she said, "I suppose it is a period of probation. You are like a schoolboy already who is looking forward to his holidays. You will be very happy when you return."

"I shall be very happy indeed," he admitted simply. "Why not? I am a true son of Japan, and, for every true son of his country, absence from her is as hard a thing to be borne as absence from one's own family."

Somerfield, who was sitting on her other side, insisted at last upon diverting her attention.

"Penelope," he declared, lowering his voice a little, "it isn't fair. You never have a word to say to me when the Prince is here."

She smiled.

"You must remember that he is going away very soon, Charlie," she reminded him.

"Good job, too!" Somerfield muttered, sotto voce.

"And then," Penelope continued, with the air of not having heard her companion's last remark, "he possesses also a very great attraction. He is absolutely unlike any other human being I ever met or heard of."

Somerfield glanced across at his rival with lowering brows.

"I've nothing to say against the fellow," he remarked, "except that it seems queer nowadays to run up against a man of his birth who is not a sportsman,—in the sense of being fond of sport, I mean," he corrected himself quickly.

"Sometimes I wonder," Penelope said thoughtfully, "whether such speeches as the one which you have just made do not indicate something totally wrong in our modern life. You, for instance, have no profession, Charlie, and you devote your life to a systematic course of what is nothing more or less than pleasure-seeking. You hunt or you shoot, you play polo or golf, you come to town or you live in the country, entirely according to the seasons. If any one asked you why you had not chosen a profession, you would as good as tell them that it was because you were a rich man and had no need to work for your living. That is practically what it comes to. You Englishmen work only if you need money. If you do not need money, you play. The Prince is wealthy, but his profession was ordained for him from the moment when he left the cradle. The end and aim of his life is to serve his country, and I believe that he would consider it sacrilege if he allowed any slighter things to divert at any time his mind from its main purpose. He would feel like a priest who has broken his ordination vows."

"That's all very well," Somerfield said coolly, "but there's nothing in life nowadays to make us quite so strenuous as that."

"Isn't there?" Penelope answered. "You are an Englishman, and you should know. Are you convinced, then, that your country today is at the height of her prosperity, safe and sound, bound to go on triumphant, prosperous, without the constant care of her men?"

Somerfield looked up at her in growing amazement.

"What on earth's got hold of you, Penelope?" he asked. "Have you been reading the sensational papers, or stuffing yourself up with jingoism, or what?"

She laughed.

"None of those things, I can assure you," she said. "A man like the Prince makes one think, because, you see, every standard of life we have is a standard of comparison. When one sees the sort of man he is, one wonders. When one sees how far apart he is from you Englishmen in his ideals and the way he spends his life, one wonders again."

Somerfield shrugged his shoulders.

"We do well enough," he said. "Japan is the youngest of the nations. She has a long way to go to catch us up."

"We do well enough!" she repeated under her breath. "There was a great city once which adopted that as her motto,—people dig up mementoes of her sometimes from under the sands."

Somerfield looked at her in an aggrieved fashion.

"Well," he said, "I thought that this was to be an amusing luncheon party."

"You should have talked more to Lady Grace," she answered. "I am sure that she is quite ready to believe that you are perfection, and the English army the one invincible institution in the world. You mustn't take me too seriously today, Charlie. I have a headache, and I think that it has made me dull."...

They trooped out into the foyer in irregular fashion to take their coffee. The Prince and Penelope were side by side.

"What I like about your restaurant life," the Prince said, "is the strange mixture of classes which it everywhere reveals."

"Those two, for instance," Penelope said, and then stopped short.

The Prince followed her slight gesture. Inspector Jacks and Dr. Spencer Whiles were certainly just a little out of accord with their surroundings. The detective's clothes were too new and his companion's too old. The doctor's clothes indeed were as shabby as his waiting room, and he sat where the sunlight was merciless.

"How singular," the Prince remarked with a smile, "that you should have pointed those two men out! One of them I know, and, if you will excuse me for a moment, I should like to speak to him."

Penelope was not capable of any immediate answer. The Prince, with a kindly and yet gracious smile, walked over to Inspector Jacks, who rose at once to his feet.

"I hope you have quite recovered, Mr. Inspector," the Prince said, holding out his hand in friendly fashion. "I have felt very guilty over your indisposition. I am sure that I keep my rooms too close for English people."

"Thank you, Prince," the Inspector answered, "I am perfectly well again. In fact, I have not felt anything of my little attack since."

The Prince smiled.

"I am glad," he said. "Next time you are good enough to pay me a visit, I will see that you do not suffer in the same way."

He nodded kindly and rejoined his friends. The Inspector resumed his seat and busied himself with relighting his cigar. He purposely did not even glance at his companion.

"Who was that?" the doctor asked curiously. "Did you call him Prince?"

Inspector Jacks sighed. This was a disappointment to him!

"His name is Prince Maiyo," he said slowly. "He is a Japanese."

The doctor looked across the restaurant with puzzled face.

"It's queer," he said, "how all these Japanese seem to one to look so much alike, and yet—"

He broke off in the middle of his sentence.

"You are thinking of your friend of the other night?" the Inspector remarked.

"I was," the doctor admitted. "For a moment it seemed to me like the same man with a different manner."

Inspector Jacks was silent. He puffed steadily at his cigar.

"You don't suppose," he asked quietly, "that it could have been the same man?"

The doctor was still looking across the room.

"I could not tell," he said. "I should like to see him again. I wasn't prepared, and there was something so altered in his tone and the way he carried himself. And yet—"

The pause was expressive. Inspector Jacks' eyes brightened. He hated to feel that his day had been altogether wasted.

CHAPTER XXIV.
PRINCE MAIYO BIDS HIGH

Inspector Jacks was in luck at last. Eleven times he had called at St. Thomas's Hospital and received the same reply. Today he was asked to wait. The patient was better—would be able to see him. Soon a nurse in neat uniform came quietly down the corridor and took charge of him.

"Ten minutes, no more," she insisted good-humoredly.

The Inspector nodded.

"One question, if you please, nurse," he asked. "Is the man going to live?"

"Not a doubt about it," she declared. "Why?"

"A matter of depositions," the Inspector exclaimed. "I'd rather let it go, though, if he's sure to recover."

"It's a simple case," she answered, "and his constitution is excellent. There isn't the least need for your to think about depositions. Here he is. Don't talk too long."

The Inspector sat down by the bedside. The patient, a young man, welcomed him a little shyly.

"You have come to ask me about what I saw in Pall Mall and opposite the Hyde Park Hotel?" he said, speaking slowly and in a voice scarcely raised above a whisper. "I told them all before the operation, but they couldn't send for you then. There wasn't time."

The Inspector nodded.

"Tell me your own way," he said. "Don't hurry. We can get the particulars later on. Glad you're going to be mended."

"It was touch and go," the young man declared with a note of awe in his tone. "If the omnibus wheel had turned a foot more, I should have lost both my legs. It was all through watching that chap hop out of the taxicab, too."

The Inspector inclined his head gravely.

"You saw him get in, didn't you?" he asked.

"That's so," the patient admitted. "I was on my way—Charing Cross to the Kensington Palace Hotel, on a bicycle. There was a block—corner of Pall Mall and Haymarket. I caught hold—taxi in front—to steady me."

The nurse bent over him with a glass in her hand. She raised him a little with the other arm.

"Not too much of this, you know, young man," she said with a pleasant smile. "Here's something to make you strong."

"Right you are!"

He drained the contents of the glass and smacked his lips.

"Jolly good stuff," he declared. "Where was I, Mr. Inspector?"

"Holding the back of a taxicab, corner of Regent Street and Haymarket," Inspector Jacks reminded him.

The patient nodded.

"There was an electric brougham," he continued, "drawn up alongside the taxi. While we were there, waiting, I saw a chap get out, speak to some one through the window of the taxi, open the door, and step in. When we moved on, he stayed in the taxi. Dark, slim chap he was," the patient continued, "a regular howling swell,—silk hat, white muffler, white kid gloves,—all the rest of it."

"And afterwards?" the Inspector asked.

"I kept behind the taxi," the youth continued. "We got blocked again at Hyde Park Corner. I saw him step out of the taxi and disappear amongst the vehicles. A moment or two later, I passed the taxi and looked in—saw something had happened—the fellow was lying side-ways. It gave me a bit of a start. I skidded, and over I went. Sort of had an idea that every one in the world had started shouting to me, and felt that I was half underneath an omnibus. Woke up to find myself here."

"Should you know the man again?" the Inspector asked. "I mean the man whom you saw enter and leave the taxi?"

"I think so—pretty sure!"

The nurse came up, shaking her head. Inspector Jacks rose from his seat.

"Right, nurse," he said. "I'm off. Take care of our young friend. He is going to be very useful to us as soon as he can use his feet and get about. I'll come and sit with you for half an hour next visiting day, if I may?" he added, turning to the patient.

"Glad to see you," the youth answered. "My people live down in the country, and I haven't many pals."

Inspector Jacks left the hospital thoughtfully. The smell of anaesthetics somehow reminded him of the library in the house at the corner of St. James' Square. It was not altogether by chance, perhaps, that he found himself walking in that direction. He was in Pall Mall, in fact, before he realized where he was, and at the corner of St. James' Square and Pall Mall he came face to face with Prince Maiyo, walking slowly westwards.

The meeting between the two men was a characteristic one. The Inspector suffered no signs of surprise or even interest to creep into his expressionless face. The Prince, on the other hand, did not attempt to conceal his pleasure at this unexpected encounter. His lips parted in a delightful smile. He ignored the Inspector's somewhat stiff salute, and insisted upon shaking him cordially by the hand.

"Mr. Inspector Jacks," he said, "you are the one person whom I desired to see. You are not busy, I hope? You can talk with me for five minutes?"

The Inspector hesitated for a moment. He was versed in every form of duplicity, and yet he felt that in the presence of this young aristocrat, who was smiling upon him so delightfully, he was little more than a babe in wisdom, an amateur pure and simple. He was conscious, too, of a sentiment which rarely intruded itself into his affairs. He was conscious of a strong liking for this debonair, pleasant-faced young man, who treated him not only as an equal, but as an equal in whose society he found an especial pleasure.

"I have the time to spare, sir, certainly," he admitted.

The Prince smiled gayly.

"Inspector Jacks," he said, "you are a wonderful man. Even now you are asking yourself, 'What does he want to say to me—Prince Maiyo? Is he going to ask me questions, or will he tell me things which I should like to hear?' You know, Mr. Inspector Jacks, between ourselves, you are just a little interested in me, is it not so?"

The detective was dumb. He stood there patiently waiting. He had the air of a man who declines to commit himself.

"Just a little interested in me, I think," the Prince murmured, smiling at his companion. "Ah, well, many of the things I do over here, perhaps, must seem very strange. And that reminds me. Only a short time ago you were asking questions about the man who travelled from Liverpool to London and reached his destination with a dagger through his heart. Tell me, Mr. Inspector Jacks, have you discovered the murderer yet?"

"Not yet," the detective answered.

"I have heard you speak of this affair," the Prince continued, "and before now I expected to read in the papers that you had put your hand upon the guilty one. If you have not done so, I am very sure that there is some explanation."

"It is better sometimes to wait," the detective said quietly.

The Prince bowed as one who understands.

"I think so," he assented, "I think I follow you. On the very next day there was another tragedy which seemed to me even more terrible. I mean the murder of that young fellow Vanderpole, of the American Embassy. Mr. Inspector Jacks, has it ever occurred to you, I wonder, that it might be as well to let the solution of one await the solution of the other?"

Inspector Jacks shrugged his shoulders.

"Occasionally," he admitted reluctantly, "when one is following up a clue, one discovers things."

"You are wonderful!" the Prince declared. "You are, indeed! I know what is in your mind. You have said to yourself, 'Between these two murders there is some connection. They were both done by the hand of a master criminal. The victims in both cases were Americans.' You said to yourself, 'First of all, I will discover the motive; then, perhaps, a clue which seems to belong to the one will lead me to the other, or both?' You are not sure which way to turn. There is nothing there upon which you can lay your hand. You say to yourself, 'I will make a bluff.' That is the word, is it not? You come to me. You tell me gravely that you have reason to suspect some one in my household. That is because you believe that the crimes were perpetrated by some one of my country. You do not ask for information. You think, perhaps, that I would not give it. You confront me with a statement. It was very clever of you, Mr. Inspector Jacks."

"I had reason for what I did, sir," the detective said.

"No doubt," the Prince agreed. "And now, tell me, when are you going to electrify us all? When is the great arrest to take place?"

The detective coughed discreetly.

"I am not yet in a position, sir," he said, "to make any definite announcement."

"Cautious, Mr. Jacks, cautious!" the Prince remarked smilingly. "It is a great quality,—a quality which I, too, have learned how to appreciate. And now for our five minutes' talk. If I say to you, 'Return home with me,' I think you will remember that unpleasant room of mine, and you will recollect an important engagement at Scotland Yard. In the clubs one is always overheard. Walk with me a little way, Mr. Jacks, in St. James' Park. We can speak there without fear of interruption. Come!"

He thrust his arm through the detective's and led him across the street. Mr. Inspector Jacks was only human, and he yielded without protest. They passed St. James' Palace and on to the broad promenade, where there were few passers-by and no listeners.

"You see, my dear Inspector," the Prince said, "I am really a sojourner in your marvellous city not altogether for pleasure. My stay over here is more in the light of a mission. I have certain arrangements which I wish to effect for the good of my country. Amongst them is one concerning which I should like to speak to you."

"To me, sir?" Inspector Jacks repeated.

The Prince twirled his cane and nodded his head.

"It is a very important matter, Mr. Jacks," he said. "It is nothing less than a desire on the part of the city government of Tokio to perfect thoroughly their police system on the model of yours over here. We are a progressive nation, you know, Mr. Jacks, but we are also a young nation, and though I think that we advance all the time, we are still in many respects a long way behind you. We have no Scotland Yard in

Tokio. To be frank with you, the necessity for such an institution has become a real thing with us only during the last few years. Do you read history, Mr. Jacks?"

The Inspector was doubtful.

"I can't say, sir," he admitted, "that I have done much reading since I left school, and that was many years ago."

"Well," the Prince said, "it is one of the axioms of history, Mr. Jacks, that as a country becomes civilized and consequently more prosperous, there is a corresponding growth in her criminal classes, a corresponding need for a different state of laws by which to judge them, a different machinery for checking their growth. We have arrived at that position in Japan, and in my latest despatches from home comes to me a request that I send them out a man who shall reorganize our entire police system. I am a judge of character, Mr. Jacks, and if I can get the man I want, I do not need to ask my friends at Downing Street to help me. I should like you to accept that post."

The Inspector was scarcely prepared for this. He allowed himself to show some surprise.

"I am very much obliged to you, Prince, for the offer," he said. "I am afraid, however, that I should not be competent."

"That," the Prince reminded him, "is a risk which we are willing to take."

"I do not think, either," the detective continued, "that at my time of life I should care to go so far from home to settle down in an altogether strange country."

"It must be as you will, of course," the Prince declared. "Only remember, Mr. Jacks, that a great nation like mine which wants a particular man for a particular purpose is not afraid to pay for him. Your work out there would certainly take you no more than three years. For that three years' work you would receive the sum of thirty thousand pounds."

The detective gasped.

"It is a great sum," he said.

The Prince shrugged his shoulders.

"You could hardly call it that," he said. "Still, it would enable you to live in comfort for the rest of your life."

"And when should I be required to start, sir?" the Inspector asked.

"That, perhaps," the Prince replied, "would seem the hardest part of all. You would be required to start tomorrow afternoon from Southampton at four o'clock."

The Inspector started. Then a new light dawned suddenly in his face.

"Tomorrow afternoon," he murmured.

The Prince assented.

"So far as regards your position at Scotland Yard," he said, "I have influential friends in your Government who will put that right for you. You need not be afraid of any unpleasantness in that direction. Remember, Mr. Inspector, thirty thousand pounds, and a free hand while you are in my country. You are a man, I should judge, of fifty-two or fifty-three years of age. You can spend your fifty-sixth birthday in England, then, and be a man of means for the remainder of your days."

"And this sum of money," the detective said, "is for my services in building up the police force of Tokio?"

"Broadly speaking, yes!" the Prince answered.

"And incidentally," the detective continued, glancing cautiously at his companion, "it is the price of my leaving unsuspected the murderer of two innocent men!"

The Prince walked on in silence. Every line in his face seemed slowly to have hardened. His brows had contracted. He was looking steadfastly forward at the great front of Buckingham Palace.

"I am disappointed in you, Mr. Jacks," he said a little stiffly. "I do not understand your allusion. The money I have mentioned is to be paid to you for certain well-defined services. The other matter you speak of does not interest me. It is no concern of mine whether this man of whom you are in search is brought to justice or not. All that I wish to hear from you is whether or not you accept my offer."

The Inspector shook his head.

"Prince," he said, "there can be no question about that. I thank you very much for it, but I must decline."

"Your mind is quite made up?" the Prince asked regretfully.

"Quite," the Inspector said firmly.

"Japan," the Prince said thoughtfully, "is a pleasant country."

"London suits me moderately well," Inspector Jacks declared.

"Under certain conditions," the Prince continued, "I should have imagined that the climate here might prove most unhealthy for you. You must remember that I was a witness of your slight indisposition the other day."

"In my profession, sir," the detective said, "we must take our risks."

The Prince came to a standstill. They were at the parting of the ways.

"I am very sorry," he said simply. "It was a great post, and it was one which you would have filled well. It is not for me, however, to press the matter."

"It would make no difference, sir," the detective answered.

The Prince was on the point of moving away.

"I shall not seek in any case to persuade you," he said. "My offer remains open if you should change your mind. Think, too, over what I have said about our climate. At your time of life, Mr. Inspector Jacks, and particularly at this season of the year, one should be careful. A sea voyage now would, I am convinced, be the very thing for you. Good day, Mr. Jacks!"

The Prince turned towards Buckingham Palace, and the Inspector slowly retraced his steps.

"It is a bribe!" he muttered to himself slowly, — "a cleverly offered bribe! Thirty thousand pounds to forget the little I have learned! Thirty thousand pounds for silence!"

CHAPTER XXV.
HOBSON'S CHOICE

There were some days when the absence of patients seemed to Dr. Spencer Whiles a thing almost insupportable. Too late he began to realize that he had set up in the wrong neighborhood. In years to come, he reflected gloomily, when the great building estate which was to have been developed more than a year ago was really opened up, there might be an opportunity where he was, a very excellent opportunity, too, for a young doctor of ability. Just now, however, the outlook was almost hopeless. He found himself even looking eagerly forward every day for another visit from Mr. Inspector Jacks. Another trip to town would mean a peep into the world of luxury, whose doors were so closely barred against him, and, what was more important still, it would mean a fee which would keep the wolf from the door for another week. It had come to that with Dr. Whiles. His little stock of savings was exhausted. Unless something turned up within the course of the next few weeks, he knew very well that there was nothing left for him to do but to slip away quietly into the embrace of the more shady parts of the great city, to find a situation somewhere, somehow, beyond the ken of the disappointed creditors whom he would leave behind.

Mr. Inspector Jacks, however, had apparently no further use, for the present at any rate, for his medical friend. On the other hand, Dr. Spencer Whiles was not left wholly to himself. On the fourth day after his visit to London a motor car drew up outside his modest surgery door, and with an excitement which he found it almost impossible to conceal, he saw a plainly dressed young man, evidently a foreigner and, he believed, a Japanese, descend and ring the patients' bell. The doctor had dismissed his boy a week ago, from sheer inability to pay his modest wages, and he did not hesitate for a moment about opening the door himself. The man outside raised his hat and made him a sweeping bow.

"It is Dr. Spencer Whiles?" he asked.

The doctor admitted the fact and invited his visitor to enter.

"It is here, perhaps," the latter continued, "that a gentleman who was riding a bicycle and was run into by a motor car, was brought after the accident and treated so skilfully?"

"That is so," Dr. Whiles admitted. "There was nothing much the matter with him. He had rather a narrow escape."

"I am that gentleman's servant," the visitor continued with a bland smile. "He has sent me down here to see you. The leg which was injured is perfectly well, but there was a pain in the side of which he spoke to you, which has not disappeared. This morning, in fact, it is worse,—much worse. My master, therefore, has sent me to you. He begs that if it is not inconvenient you will return with me at once and examine him."

The doctor drew a little breath. This might mean another week or so of respite!

"Where does your master live?" he asked the man.

"In the West end of London, sir," was the reply. "The Square of St. James it is called."

Dr. Whiles glanced at his watch.

"It will take me some time to go there with you," he said, "and I shall have to arrange with a friend to treat any other patients. Do you think your master will understand that I shall need an increased fee?"

"My master desired me to say," the other answered, "that he would be prepared to pay any fee you cared to mention. Money is not of account with him. He has not had occasion to seek medical advice in London, and as he is leaving very soon, he did not wish to send for a strange physician. He remembered with gratitude your care of him, and he sends for you."

"That's all right," Dr. Whiles declared, "so long as it's understood. You'll excuse me for a moment while I write a note, and I'll come along."

Dr. Whiles had no note to write, but he made a few changes in his toilet which somewhat improved his appearance. In due course he reappeared and was rapidly whirled up to London, the sole passenger in the magnificent car. The man who had brought him the message from his quondam patient was sitting in front, next the chauffeur, so Dr. Whiles had no opportunity of asking him for any information concerning his master. Nor did the car itself slacken speed until it drew up before the door of the large corner house in St. James' Square. A footman in dark livery came running out; a butler bowed upon the steps. Dr. Spencer Whiles was immensely impressed. The servants were all Japanese, but their livery and manners were faultless. He made his way into the hall and followed the butler up the broad stairs.

"My master," the latter explained, "will receive you very shortly. He is but partly dressed at present."

Dr. Spencer Whiles came of a family of successful tradespeople, and he was not used to such quiet magnificence as was everywhere displayed. Yet, with it all, there seemed to him to be an air of gloom about the place, something almost mysterious in the silence of the thick carpets, the subdued voices, and the absence of maidservants. The house itself was apparently an old one. He noticed that the doors were very heavy and thick, the corridors roomy, the absence of light almost remarkable. The apartment into which he was shown, however, came as a pleasant surprise. It was small, but delightfully furnished in the most modern fashion. Its only drawback was that it looked out upon a blank wall.

"My master will come to you in a few minutes," the butler announced. "What refreshments may I have the honor of serving?"

Dr. Whiles waved aside the invitation,—he would at any rate remain professional. The man withdrew, and almost immediately afterwards Prince Maiyo entered the room. The doctor rose to his feet with a little thrill of excitement. The Prince held out his hand.

"I am very pleased to see you again, doctor," he said. "You looked after me so well last time that I was afraid I should have no excuse for sending for you."

"I am glad to find that you are not suffering," the doctor answered. "I understood from your servant that you were feeling a good deal of pain in the side."

"It troubles me at times," the Prince admitted, drawing a chair up towards his visitor, — "just sufficiently, perhaps, to give me the excuse of seeking a little conversation with you. You must let me offer you something after your ride."

"You are very good," the doctor answered. "Perhaps I had better examine you first."

The Prince rang the bell and waved aside the suggestion.

"That," he said, "can wait. In my country, you know, we do not consider that a guest is properly treated unless he partakes of our hospitality the moment he crosses the threshold. The whiskey and soda water," he ordered of the butler who appeared at the door. "We will talk of my ailments," the Prince continued, "in a moment or two. Tell me what you thought of that marvellous restaurant where I saw you the other morning?"

The doctor drew a little breath.

"It was you, then!" he exclaimed.

"But naturally," the Prince murmured. "I took it for granted that you would recognize me."

The doctor found some difficulty in proceeding. He was trying to imagine the cousin of an Emperor riding a bicycle along a country road, staggering into his surgery at midnight, covered with dust, inarticulate, pointing only to the wounds beneath his cheap clothes!

"Nothing," the Prince continued easily, "has impressed me more in your country than the splendor of your restaurants. You see, that side of your life represents something we are altogether ignorant of in Japan."

"It is a very wonderful place," the doctor admitted. "We had luncheon, my friend and I, in the grillroom, but we came for a few minutes into the foyer to watch the people from the restaurant."

The Prince nodded genially.

"By the bye," he remarked, "it is strange that my very good friend—Mr. Inspector Jacks—should also be a friend of yours."

"He is scarcely that," the doctor objected. "I have known him for a very short time."

The Prince raised his eyebrows. The whiskey and soda were brought, and the doctor helped himself. How curiously deficient these Westerners were, the Prince thought, in every instinct of duplicity! As clearly as possible the doctor had revealed the fact that his acquaintance with Inspector Jacks was of precisely that nature which might have been expected.

The Prince sighed. There was but one course open to him.

"Now, Dr. Whiles," he said, "I will tell you something. You must listen to me very carefully, please. I sent for you not so much on account of any immediate pain but because my general health has been giving me a little trouble lately. I have come to the conclusion that I require the services of a medical attendant always at hand."

The doctor looked at his prospective patient skeptically.

"You have not the appearance," he remarked, "of being in ill health."

"Perhaps not," the Prince answered. "Perhaps even, there is not for the moment very much the matter with me. One has humors, you know, my dear doctor. I have a somewhat large suite here with me in England, but I do not number amongst them a physician. I wanted to ask you to accept that position in my household for two months."

"Do you mean come and live here?" the doctor asked.

"That is exactly what I do mean," the Prince answered. "I am thankful to observe that your apprehensions are so acute. I warn you that I am going to make some very curious conditions. I do not know whether money is an object to you. If not, I am powerless. If it is, I propose to make it worth your while."

The doctor did not hesitate.

"Money," he said, "is the greatest object in life to me. I have none, and I want some very badly."

The Prince smiled.

"I find your candor delightful," he declared. "Now tell me, Dr. Whiles, how many patients have you in your neighborhood absolutely dependent upon your services?"

The doctor hesitated, opened his mouth and closed it again.

"Not one!" he declared.

Once more the Prince's lips parted. His smile this time was definite, transfiguring.

"I find you, Dr. Whiles," he announced, "a most charmingly reasonable person. I make you my offer, then, with every confidence, although I warn you that there will be some strange conditions attached to it. I ask you to accept the post of private physician to this household for the space of one—it may be two months, and I offer you also, as an honorarium, the fee of one thousand guineas."

The doctor sat quite still for a moment. He was in a condition when speech was difficult. Then his eyes fell upon his tumbler of whiskey and soda still half filled. He emptied it at a draught.

"A thousand guineas!" he repeated hoarsely.

"I trust that you will find the sum attractive," the Prince said smoothly, "because, as I have warned you before, there are one or two curious conditions coupled with the post."

"I don't care what the conditions are," the doctor said slowly. "I accept!"

The Prince nodded.

"You are the man I thought you were, doctor," he said. "The first condition, then, is this. You see the sitting room we are now in—a pleasant little apartment, I think,—books, you see, papers, a smoking cabinet in which I can assure you that you will find the finest Havana cigars and the best cigarettes to be procured in London. Through here"—the Prince threw open an inner door—"is a small sleeping apartment. It has, as you see, the same outlook. It is comfortable if not luxurious."

The doctor sighed.

"I am not used to luxury," he said.

"These two rooms will be yours," the Prince announced, "and the first condition of our arrangement is that until two months are up, or our engagement is finished, you do not leave them."

The doctor stared at him blankly.

"Are you in earnest, sir?" he asked.

"In absolute earnest," the Prince assured him. "Not only that, but I require you to keep your whereabouts, until after the period of time I have mentioned, an entire secret from every one. I gather that you are not married, and that there is no one living in your house to whom it would seem necessary to disclose your movements. In any case, this is another of my conditions. You are neither to write nor receive any letters whilst here. You are to figure in the neighborhood from which you came as a man who has disappeared,—as a man, in short, who has found it impossible to pay his way and has preferred simply to slip out of his place. At the end of two months you can reappear or not, as you choose. That rests with yourself."

The doctor smiled faintly. To make some sort of disappearance had been his precise intention, but to disappear in this fashion and make his return to the world with a thousand guineas in his pocket, had not exactly come within the scope of his imagination. It was a situation full of allurements. Nevertheless he was bewildered.

"I am to live in these two rooms?" he demanded. "I am to let no one know where I am, to write no letters, to receive none? My duties are to be simply to treat you?"

"When required," the Prince remarked dryly.

"I suppose," the doctor asked, "my friend Mr. Jacks was speaking the truth when he told me your name?"

"My name is Prince Maiyo," the Prince said.

Mechanically the doctor helped himself to another whiskey and soda.

"You are to be my only patient," he said thoughtfully. "May I take the liberty of feeling your pulse, Prince?"

The Prince extended his hand. The doctor felt it and resumed his seat.

"There is, of course, nothing whatever the matter with you," he declared. "You are, I should say, in absolutely perfect health. You have no need of a physician."

"On the contrary," the Prince protested, smiling, "I need you, Dr. Whiles, so much that I am paying you a thousand guineas—"

"To remain in these two rooms," the doctor remarked quietly.

"It is not your business to think that or to know that," the Prince said. "Do you accept my offer?"

"If I should refuse?" the doctor asked.

The Prince hesitated.

"Do not let us suppose that," he said. "It is not a pleasant suggestion. I do not think that you mean to refuse."

"Frankly, I do not," the doctor answered. "And yet treat it as a whim of mine and answer my question. Supposing I should?"

"The matter would arrange itself in precisely the same way," the Prince answered. "You would not leave these rooms for two months."

The doctor leaned back in his chair and laughed shortly.

"This is rather hard luck on Inspector Jacks," he said. "He paid me ten guineas the other day to lunch with him."

"Mr. Inspector Jacks," the Prince remarked, "is scarcely in a position to bid you an adequate sum for your services."

"It appears to me," the doctor continued, "that I am kidnapped."

"An admirable word," the Prince declared. "At what time do you usually lunch?"

The doctor smiled.

"I am not used to motoring," he said, "or interviews of this exciting character. I lunch, as a rule, when I can get anything to eat. The present seems to me to be a most suitable hour."

The Prince nodded, and rose to his feet.

"I will send my servant," he said, "to take your orders. My cook is very highly esteemed here, and I can assure you that you will not be starved. Please also make out a list of the newspapers, magazines, and books with which you would like to be supplied. I fear that, for obvious reasons, my people would hardly be able to anticipate your wants."

"And about that examination?" the doctor remarked.

"I shall do myself the pleasure of seeing you every day," the Prince answered. "There will be time enough for that."

With an amiable word of farewell the Prince departed. The doctor threw himself into an easy chair. His single exclamation was laconic but forcible.

CHAPTER XXVI.
SOME FAREWELLS

Never did Prince Maiyo show fewer signs of his Japanese origin than when in the company of other men of his own race. Side by side with His Excellency the Baron Hesho, the contrasts in feature and expression were so marked as to make it hard, indeed, to believe that these two men could belong to the same nation. The Baron Hesho had high cheekbones, a yellow skin, close-cropped black hair, and wore gold-rimmed spectacles through which he beamed upon the whole world. The Prince, as he lounged in his wicker chair and watched the blue smoke of his cigarette curl upwards, looked more like an Italian—perhaps a Spaniard. The shape of his head was perfectly Western, perfectly and typically Romanesque. The carriage of his body must have been inherited from his mother, of whom it was said that no more graceful woman ever walked. Yet between these two men, so different in all externals, there was the strongest sympathy, although they met but seldom.

"So we are to lose you soon, Prince," the Baron was saying.

"Very soon indeed," Prince Maiyo answered. "Next week I go down to Devenham. I understand that the Prime Minister and Sir Edward Bransome will be there. If so, that, I think, will be practically my leave-taking. There is no object in my staying any longer over here."

The Baron blinked his eyes meditatively.

"I have seen very little of you, Maiyo," he said, "since your last visit to the Continent. I take it that your views are unchanged?"

The Prince assented.

"Unchanged indeed," he answered,—"unchangeable, I think almost that I might now say. They have been wonderful months, these last months, Baron," he continued. "I have seen some of those things which we in Japan have heard about and wondered about all our lives.

I have seen the German army at manoeuvres. I have talked to their officers. Where I could, I have talked to the men. I have been to some of their great socialist meetings. I have heard them talk about their country and their Emperor, and what would happen to their officers if war should come. I have seen the French artillery. I have been the guest of the President. I have tried to understand the peculiar attitude which that country has always adopted toward us. I have been, unrecognized, in St. Petersburg. I have tried to understand a little the resources of that marvellous country. I came back here in time for the great review in the Solent. I have seen the most magnificent ships and the most splendid naval discipline the world has ever known. Then I have explored the interior of this island as few of our race have explored it before, not for the purpose of studying the manufactures, the trades, the immense shipbuilding industries,—simply to study the people themselves."

The Baron nodded gravely.

"I ask no questions," he said. "It is the Emperor's desire, I know, that you go straight to him. I take it that your mind is made up,—you have arrived at definite conclusions?"

"Absolutely." Prince Maiyo answered. "I shall make no great secret of them. You already, my dear Baron, know, I think, whither they lead. I shall be unpopular for a time, I suppose, and your own position may be made a little difficult. After that, things will go on pretty much the same. Of one thing, though, I am assured. I see it as clearly as the shepherd who has lain the night upon the hillside sees the coming day. It may be twelve months, it may be two years, it may even be three, but before that time has passed the clouds will have gathered, the storm will have burst. Then, I think, Hesho, our master will be glad that we are free."

The Baron agreed.

"Only a few nights ago," he said, "Captain Koki and the other attaches spent an evening with me. We have charts and pieces, and with locked doors we played a war game of our own invention. It should all be over in three weeks."

Prince Maiyo laughed softly.

"You are right," he said. "I have gone over the ground myself. It could be done in even less time. You should ask a few of our friends to that war game, Baron. How they would smile! You read the newspapers of the country?"

"Invariably," the Ambassador answered.

"There is an undercurrent of feeling somewhere," the Prince continued,—"one of the cheaper organs is shrieking all the time a brazen warning. Patriotism, as you and I understand it, dear friend, is long since dead, but if one strikes hard enough at the flint, some fire may come. Hesho, how short our life is! How little we can understand! We have only the written words of those who have gone before, to show us the cities and the empires that have been, to teach us the reasons why they decayed and crumbled away. We have only our own imagination to help us to look forward into the future and see the empires that may rise, the kingdoms that shall stand, the kingdoms that shall fall. Amongst them all, Hesho, there is but this much of truth. It is our own dear country and our one great rival across the Pacific who, in the years to come, must fight for the supremacy of the world."

"It will be no fight, that," the Ambassador answered slowly,— "no fight unless a new prophet is born to them. The money-poison is sucking the very blood from their body. The country is slowly but surely becoming honey-combed with corruption. The voices of its children are like the voices from the tower of Babel. If their strong man should arise, then the fight will be the fiercest the world has ever known. Even then the end is not doubtful. The victory will be ours. When the universe is left for them and for us, it will be our sons who shall rule. Listen, Maiyo."

"I listen," the Prince answered.

The Baron Hesho had laid aside his spectacles. He leaned a little towards his companion. His voice had fallen to a whisper, his hand fell almost caressingly upon his friend's shoulder.

"I would speak of something else," he continued. "Soon you go to the Duke's house. You will meet there the people who are in authority over this country. When you leave it, everything is finished. Tell me, is the way homeward safe for you?"

"Wonderful person!" Prince Maiyo said, smiling.

"No, I am not wonderful," the Ambassador declared. "All the time I have had my fears. Why not? A month ago I sought your aid.

I knew from our friends in New York that a man was on his way to England with letters which made clear, beyond a doubt, the purpose of this world journey of the American fleet. I sent for you. We both agreed that it was an absolute necessity for us to know the contents of those letters."

"We discovered them," the Prince answered. "It was well that we did."

"You discovered them," the Ambassador interrupted. "I have taken no credit for it. The credit is yours. But in this land there are so many things which one may not do. The bowstring and the knife are unrecognized. Civilization has set an unwholesome value upon human life. It is the maudlin sentiment which creeps like corruption through the body of a dying country."

"I know it," the Prince declared, sighing. "I know it very well indeed."

"Dear Maiyo," the Ambassador asked, "how well do you know it?"

"My friend," the Prince answered, "it were better for you not to ask that question."

"Here under this roof," the Baron continued, "is sanctuary, but in the streets and squares beyond, it seems to me—and I have thought this over many times,—it seems to me that even the person of the great Prince, cousin of the Emperor, holy son of Japan, would not be safe."

Prince Maiyo shrugged his shoulders. There was gravity in his face, but it was the gravity of a man who has learnt to look upon serious things with a light heart.

"I, also," he said, "have weighed this matter very carefully in my mind. What I did was well done, and if the bill is thrust into my face, I must pay. First of all, Baron, I promise you that I shall finish my work. After that, what does it matter? You and I know better than this nation of life-loving shopkeepers. A week, a year, a span of years,—of what account are they to us who have sipped ever so lightly at the great cup? If we died tomorrow for the glory of our country, should we not say to one another, you and I, that it was well?"

The Baron rose to his feet and bowed. Into his voice there had crept a note almost of reverence.

"Prince," he said, "almost you take me back to the one mother country. Almost your words persuade me that the strangeness of these Western lands is a passing thing. We wonder, and as we wonder they shall crumble away. The sun rises in the East."

The Prince also rose. Servants came silently forward, bearing his hat and gloves.

"Perhaps," the Prince smiled, as he made his adieux—

"Perhaps," the Ambassador echoed. "Who can tell?"

The Prince sent away his carriage and walked homeward, greeting every now and then an acquaintance. He walked cheerfully and with a smile upon his face. There was nothing in his appearance which could possibly have indicated to the closest observer that this was a man who had taken death by the hand. At the corner of Regent Street and Pall Mall he overtook Inspector Jacks. He leaned forward at once and touched the detective on the shoulder.

"Mr. Jacks," he said, "it is pleasant to see you once more. I was afraid that I should have to leave without bidding you farewell."

The Inspector started. The Prince laughed to himself as he watched that gesture. Indeed, a man who showed his feelings so easily would be very much at a loss in Tokio!

"You are going away, Prince?" the Inspector asked quickly. "When?"

"The exact day is not fixed," the Prince replied, "but it is true that I am going home. I have finished my work, and, you see, there is nothing to keep me over here any longer. Tell me, have you had any fortune yet? I read the papers every day, hoping to see that you have cleared up those two terrible affairs."

Inspector Jacks shook his head.

"Not yet, Prince," he said.

"Not yet," the Prince echoed. "Dear me, that is very unfortunate!"

Inspector Jacks watched the people who were passing, for a moment, with a fixed, unseeing gaze.

"I am afraid," he said, "that we must seem to you very slow and very stupid. Very likely we are. And yet, yet in time we generally reach our goal. Sometimes we go a long way round. Sometimes we wait almost over long, but sooner or later we strike."

The Prince nodded sympathetically.

"The best of fortune to you, Mr. Jacks!" he said. "I wish you could have cleared these matters up before I left for home. It is pure selfishness, of course, but I have always felt a great interest in your work."

"If we do not clear them up before you leave the country, Prince," the Inspector answered, "I fear that we shall never clear them up at all."

The Prince passed on smiling. A conversation with Inspector Jacks seemed always to inspire him. It was a fine afternoon and Pall Mall was crowded. In a few moments he came face to face with Somerfield, who greeted him a little gloomily.

"Sir Charles," the Prince said, "I hope that I shall have the pleasure of meeting you at Devenham?"

"I am not sure," Somerfield answered. "I have been asked, but I promised some time ago to go up to Scotland. I have a third share in a river there, and the season for salmon is getting on."

"I am sorry," the Prince declared. "I have no doubt, however, but that Miss Morse will induce you to change your mind. I should regret your absence the more," he continued, "because this, I fear, is the last visit which I shall be paying in this country."

Somerfield was genuinely interested.

"You are really going home?" he asked eagerly.

"Almost at once," the Prince answered.

"Only for a time, I suppose?" Somerfield continued.

The Prince shook his head.

"On the contrary," he said, "I imagine that this will be a long goodbye. I think I can promise you that if ever I reach Japan I shall remain there. My work in this hemisphere will be accomplished."

Somerfield looked at him with the puzzled air of a man who is face to face with a problem which he cannot solve.

"You'll forgive my putting it so plainly, Prince," he remarked, "but do you mean to say that after having lived over here you could possibly settle down again in Japan?"

The Prince returned for a moment his companion's perplexed gaze. Then his lips parted, his eyes shone. He laughed softly, gracefully, with genuine mirth.

"Sir Charles," he said, "I shall not forget that question. I think that of all the Englishmen whom I have met you are the most English of all. When I think of your great country, as I often shall do, of her sons and her daughters, I will promise you that to me you shall always represent the typical man of your race and fortune."

The Prince left his companion loitering along Pall Mall, still a little puzzled. He called a taxi and drove to Devenham House. The great drawing rooms were almost empty. Lady Grace was just saying goodbye to some parting guests. She welcomed the Prince with a little flush of pleasure.

"I find you alone?" he remarked.

"My mother is opening a bazaar somewhere," Lady Grace said. "She will be home very soon. Do let me give you some tea."

"It is my excuse for coming," the Prince admitted.

She called back the footman who had shown him in.

"China tea, very weak, in a china teapot with lemon and no sugar. Isn't that it?" she asked, smiling.

"Lady Grace," he declared, "you spoil me. Perhaps it is because I am going away. Every one is kind to the people who go away."

She looked at him anxiously.

"Going away!" she exclaimed. "When? Do you mean back to Japan?"

"Back to my own country," he answered. "Perhaps in two weeks, perhaps three—who can tell?"

"But you are coming to Devenham first?" she asked eagerly.

"I am coming to Devenham first," he assented. "I called this afternoon to let your father know the date on which I could come. I promised that he should hear from me today. He was good enough to say either Thursday or Friday. Thursday, I find, will suit me admirably."

She drew a little sigh.

"So you are going back," she said softly. "I wonder why so many people seem to have taken it for granted that you would settle down here. Even I had begun to hope so."

He smiled.

"Lady Grace," he said, "I am not what you call a cosmopolitan. To live over here in any of these Western countries would seem to denote that one may change one's dwelling place as easily as one changes one's clothes. The further east you go, the more reluctant one is, I think, to leave the shadow of one's own trees. The man who leaves my country leaves it to go into exile. The man who returns, returns home."

She was a little perplexed.

"I should have imagined," she said, "that the people who leave your country as emigrants to settle in American or even over here might have felt like that. But you of the educated classes I should have thought would have found more over here to attract you, more to induce you to choose a new home."

He shook his head.

"Lady Grace," he said, "believe me that is not so. The traditions of our race—the call of the blood, as you put it over here—is as powerful a thing with our aristocratics as with our peasants. We find much here to wonder at and admire, much that, however unwillingly, we are forced to take back and adopt in our own country, but it is a strange atmosphere for us, this. For my country-people there is but one real home, but one motherland."

"Yet you have seemed so contented over here," she remarked. "You have entered so easily into all our ways."

He set down his teacup and smiled at her for a moment gravely.

"I came with a purpose," he said. "I came in order to observe and to study certain features of your life, but, believe me, I have felt the strain—I have felt it sometimes very badly. These countries, yours especially, are like what one of your great poets called the Lotus-Lands for us. Much of your life here is given to pursuits which we do not understand, to sports and games, to various forms of what we should call idleness. In my country we know little of that. In one way or another, from the Emperor to the poor runner in the streets, we work."

"Is there nothing which you will regret?" she asked.

"I shall regret the friends I have made,—the very dear friends," he repeated, "who have been so very much kinder to me than I have deserved. Life is a sad pilgrimage sometimes, because one may not linger for a moment at any one spot, nor may one ever look back. But I know quite well that when I leave here there will be many whom I would gladly see again."

"There will be many, Prince," she said softly, "who will be sorry to see you go."

The Prince rose to his feet. Another little stream of callers had come into the room. Presently he drank his tea and departed. When he reached St. James' Square, his majordomo came hurrying up and whispered something in his own language.

The Prince smiled.

"I go to see him," he said. "I will go at once."

CHAPTER XXVII.
A PRISONER

Dr. Spencer Whiles was sitting in a very comfortable easy chair, smoking a particularly good cigar, with a pile of newspapers by his side. His appearance certainly showed no signs of hardship. His linen, and the details of his toilet generally, supplied from some mysterious source into which he had not inquired, were much improved. Notwithstanding his increased comfort, however, he was looking perplexed, even a little worried, and the cause of it was there in front of him, in the advertisement sheets of the various newspapers which had been duly laid upon his table.

The Prince came in quietly and closed the door behind him.

"Good afternoon, my friend!" he said. "I understood that you wished to see me."

The doctor had made up his mind to adopt a firm attitude. Nevertheless the genial courtesy of the Prince's tone and manner had the same effect upon him as it had upon most people. He half rose to his feet and became at once apologetic.

"I hope that I have not disturbed you, Prince," he said. "I thought that I should like to have a word or two with you concerning something which I have come across in these journals."

He tapped them with his forefinger, and the Prince nodded thoughtfully.

"Your wonderful Press!" he exclaimed. "How much it is responsible for! Well, Dr. Whiles, what have the newspapers to say to you?"

The doctor handed across a carefully folded journal and pointed to a certain paragraph.

"Will you kindly read this?" he begged.

The Prince accepted the sheet and read the paragraph aloud:

"FIFTY POUNDS REWARD! Disappeared from his home in Long Whatton on Wednesday morning last, Herbert Spencer Whiles, Surgeon. The above reward will be paid to any one giving information which will lead to the discovery of his present whereabouts. Was last seen in a motor car, Limousine body, painted dark green, leaving Long Whatton in the direction of London."

The Prince laid down the paper, smiling.

"Well?" he asked. "That seems clear enough. Some one is willing to give fifty pounds to know where you are."

The doctor tapped the advertisement with his forefinger impressively.

"Fifty pounds!" he repeated. "There isn't a person in the world to whom the knowledge of my movements is worth fifty pounds—except—"

"Except?" the Prince murmured.

"Except Mr. Inspector Jacks," Dr. Whiles said slowly.

The Prince seemed scarcely to grasp the situation.

"Well," he said, "fifty pounds is not a great deal of money. Some unknown person—possibly, as you suggest, Mr. Jacks—is willing to give fifty pounds to discover your whereabouts. I, on the other hand, am giving a thousand guineas to keep you here as my guest. The odds do not seem even, do they?"

"Put in that way," Dr. Whiles admitted, "they certainly do not. But there is another thing which has come into my mind."

The Prince smiled and helped himself to one of the very excellent cigarettes which had been provided for the delectation of his visitor.

"Pray treat me with every confidence, Dr. Whiles," he said. "Tell me exactly what is in your thoughts."

"Well, then, I will," the doctor answered. "Sitting here with nothing particular to do, one has plenty of leisure to think. For the first time, I have seriously tried to puzzle out what Mr. Inspector Jacks really wanted with me, why he came down to ask me about the person whom I treated for injuries resulting from a bicycle accident one Wednesday evening not long ago, why he took me up to London to see if I could identify that person in a very different guise. I have tried to put the pieces together and to ask myself what he meant by it all."

"With so much time upon your hands, Dr. Whiles," the Prince remarked, "you can scarcely fail to have arrived at some reasonable explanation."

"I don't know whether it is reasonable or not," the doctor answered, "but the obvious explanation is getting on my nerves. There are two things which I cannot get away from. One is that I cannot for the life of me imagine your riding a bicycle twelve or fifteen miles north of London between eleven o'clock and midnight; and the other—"

"Come, the other?" the Prince remarked encouragingly.

"The other," the doctor continued, "is the fact that within half a mile of my house runs the main London and North Western line."

"The London and North Western Railway line," the Prince repeated, "and what has that to do with it?"

"This much," the doctor answered, "that on that very night, about half an hour before your—shall we call it bicycle accident?—the special train from Liverpool to London passed along that line. You will remember the tragic occurrence which took place before she reached London, the murder of the man Hamilton Fynes. If you read the report of the evidence at the inquest, you will notice the engine driver's declaration that the only time on the whole journey when he travelled at less than forty miles an hour was when passing over the viaduct and before entering the tunnel which is plainly visible from my house."

"This is very interesting," the Prince remarked, "but it is not new. We have known all this before. Perhaps, though, some fresh thing has come into your mind connected with these happenings. If so, please do not hesitate. Let me hear it."

"It is a fresh thing to me," the doctor said,—"fresh, in a sense, though all the time I have had an uneasy feeling at the back of my head. I know now what it was which brought Inspector Jacks to see me. I know now what it was he had at the back of his head concerning the man who met with a bicycle accident at this psychological moment."

"Inspector Jacks is a very shrewd fellow," the Prince said. "I should not be in the least surprised if you were entirely right."

The doctor moved restlessly in his chair. His eyes remained on his companion's face, as though fascinated.

"Can't you understand," he said, "that Inspector Jacks is on your track? Rightly or wrongly, he believes that you had something to do with the murder on the train that night."

The Prince nodded amiably. He seemed in no way discomposed.

"I feel convinced," he said, "that you are right. I agree with you. I believe that Inspector Jacks has had that idea for some little time now."

The doctor gripped the sides of his chair and stared at this man who discussed a matter so terrible with calm and perfect ease.

"Yes, I have felt that more than once," the Prince continued. "My presence upon the spot at that precise moment with injuries which had to be explained somehow or other, was, without doubt, unfortunate."

The two men sat for several moments without further speech. The doctor's features seemed to reflect something of the horror which he undoubtedly felt. The Prince appeared only a trifle bored.

"So that is why," the former exclaimed hoarsely, "I have been appointed your physician in chief!"

"I had given you the credit, my dear doctor," the Prince said smoothly, "of having arrived at that decision some time ago. To a man of your perceptions there can scarcely have been any question about it at all. Besides, even Princes, you know, do not give fees of a thousand guineas for nothing."

Dr. Whiles rose slowly to his feet.

"You know the secret of that murder!" he declared.

"Why ask me?" the Prince answered. "If I tell you that I do, you may find conscientious scruples about remaining here. A man is not bound, you know, to give himself away. Make the best of things, and do not try to see too far."

The doctor was looking a little shaken.

"If you were mixed up in that affair," he said, "and if I remain here when my evidence is needed, I become an accomplice."

"Only if you remain here voluntarily," the Prince reminded him cheerfully. "Remember that and be comforted. No effort that you could make now would bring you into touch with Mr. Inspector Jacks until I am quite prepared. So you see, my dear doctor, that you have nothing with which to reproach yourself. I will not insult you," he continued, "by suggesting that a reward of fifty pounds could possibly have influenced your attitude. If you have suffered your mind to dwell upon it for a single moment, try and remember the relative unimportance of such an amount when compared with a thousand guineas."

The doctor moved to the window and back again.

"Supposing," he said, "I decline to remain here? Supposing I say that, believing you now to have a guilty knowledge of this murder, I repudiate our bargain? Supposing I say that I will have nothing more to do with your thousand guineas,—that I will leave this house?"

"Then we come to close quarters," the Prince answered, "and you force me to tell you in plain words that, until I am ready for you to leave it, you are as much a prisoner in this room as though the keys of the strongest fortress in Europe were turned upon you. I have told you this before. I thought that we perfectly understood one another."

"I did not understand," the doctor protested. "I knew that there was trouble, but I did not know that it was this!"

"The fact of your knowing or not knowing makes no difference," the Prince answered. "You are no longer a free agent. The only question for you to decide is whether you remain here willingly or whether you will force me to remind you of our bargain."

The doctor was sitting down again now. All the time he watched the Prince with a gleam in his eyes, partly of horror, partly of fear. He no longer doubted but that he was in the presence of a criminal.

"I am sorry," the Prince continued, "that you have allowed this little matter to disturb you. I thought that we had arranged it all at our last interview. If you did not surmise my reasons for keeping you here, then I am afraid I gave you credit for more intelligence than you possess. You will excuse me now, I am sure," he added, rising. "I have some letters to send off before I change. By the bye, do you care to give me your parole? It might, perhaps, lessen the inconvenience to which you are unfortunately subject."

The doctor shook his head.

"No," he said, "I will not give my parole!"

Late that night, he tried the handle of his door and found it open. The corridor outside was in thick darkness. He felt his way along by the wall. Suddenly, from behind, a pair of large soft hands gripped him by the throat. Slowly he was drawn back—almost strangled.

"Let me go!" he called out, struggling in vain to find a body upon which he could gain a grip.

The grasp only tightened.

"Back to your rooms!" came a whisper through the darkness.

The doctor returned. When he staggered into his sitting room, he turned up the electric light. There were red marks upon his throat and perspiration upon his forehead. He opened the door once more and looked out upon the landing, striking a match and holding it over his head. There was no one in sight, yet all the time he had the uncomfortable feeling that he was being watched. For the first time in his life he wondered whether a thousand guineas was, after all, such a magnificent fee!

Almost at the same time the Prince sat back in the shadows of the Duchess of Devenham's box at the Opera and talked quietly to Lady Grace.

"But tell me, Prince," she begged, "I know that you are glad to go home, but won't you really miss this a little,—the music, the life, all these things that make up existence here? Your own country is wonderful, I know, but it has not progressed so far, has it?"

He shook his head.

"I think," he said, "that the portion of our education which we have most grievously neglected is the development of our recreations. But then you must remember that we are to a certain extent without that craving for amusement which makes these things necessary for you others. We are perhaps too serious in my country, Lady Grace. We lack altogether that delightful air of irresponsibility with which you Londoners seem to make your effortless way through life."

She was a little perplexed.

"I don't believe," she said, "that in your heart you approve of us at all."

"Do not say that, Lady Grace," he begged. "It is simply that I have been brought up in so different a school. This sort of thing is very wonderful, and I shall surely miss it. Yet nowadays the world is being linked together in marvellous fashion. Tokio and London are closer today than ever they have been in the world's history."

"And our people?" she asked. "Do you really think that our people are so far apart? Between you and me, for instance," she added, meaning to ask the question naturally enough, but suddenly losing confidence and looking away from him,—"between you and me there seems no radical difference of race. You might almost be an Englishman—not one of these men of fashion, of course, but a statesman or a man of letters, some one who had taken hold of the serious side of life."

"You pay me a very delightful compliment," he murmured.

"Please repay me, then, by being candid," she answered. "Consider for a moment that I am a typical English girl, and tell me whether I am so very different from the Japanese women of your own class?"

He hesitated for a moment. The question was not without its embarrassments.

"Men," he said, "are very much the same, all the world over. They are like the coarse grass which grows everywhere. But the flowers, you know, are different in every country."

Lady Grace sighed. Perhaps she had been a trifle too daring! She was willing enough, at any rate, to let the subject drift away.

"Soon the curtain will go up," she said, "and we can talk no longer. I should like to tell you, though, how glad I am—how glad we all are—that you can come to us next week."

"I can assure you that I am looking forward to it," he answered a little gravely. "It is my farewell to all of you, you know, and it seems to me that those who will be your father's guests are just those with whom I have been on the most intimate terms since I came to England."

She nodded.

"Penelope is coming," she said quickly,—"you know that?—Penelope and Sir Charles Somerfield."

"Yes," he answered, "I heard so."

The curtain went up. The faint murmur of the violins was suddenly caught up and absorbed in the thunderous music of a march. Lady Grace moved nearer to the front. Prince Maiyo remained where he was among the shadows. The music was in his ears, but his eyes were half closed.

CHAPTER XXVIII.
PATRIOTISM

The Duke's chef had served an Emperor with honor—the billiard room at Devenham Castle was the most comfortable room upon earth. The three men who sat together upon a huge divan, the three men most powerful in directing the councils of their country, felt a gentle wave of optimism stealing through their quickened blood. Nevertheless this was a serious matter which occupied their thoughts.

"We are becoming," the Prime Minister said, "much too modern. We are becoming over-civilized out of any similitude to a nation of men of blood and brawn."

"You are quoting some impossible person," Sir Edward Bransome declared.

"One is always quoting unconsciously," the Prime Minister admitted with a sigh. "What I mean is that five hundred years ago we should have locked this young man up in a room hung with black crape, and with a pleasant array of unfortunately extinct instruments we should have succeeded, beyond a doubt, in extorting the truth from him."

"And if the truth were not satisfactory?" the Duke asked, lighting a cigar.

"We should have endeavored to change his point of view," the Prime Minister continued, "even if we had to change at the same time the outline of his particularly graceful figure. The age of thumbscrews and the rack was, after all, a very virile age. Just consider for a moment our positions—three of the greatest and most brilliant statesmen of our day—and we can do very little save wait for this young man to declare himself. We are the puppets with whom he plays. It rests with him whether our names are written upon the scroll of fame or whether our administration is dismissed in half a dozen contemptuous words by the coming historian. It rests with him whether our friend

Bransome here shall be proclaimed the greatest Foreign Minister that ever breathed, and whether I myself have a statue erected to me in Westminster Yard, which shall be crowned with a laurel wreath by patriotic young ladies on the morning of my anniversary."

The Duke stretched himself out with a sigh of content. His cigar was burning well, and the flavor of old Armignac lingered still upon his palate.

"Come," he protested, "I think you exaggerate Maiyo's importance just a little, Haviland. Hesho seems excellently disposed towards us, and, after all, I should have thought his word would have had more weight in Tokio than the word of a young man who is new to diplomacy, and whose claims to distinction seem to rest rather upon his soldiering and the fact that he is a cousin of the Emperor."

The Prime Minister sighed.

"Dear Duke," he said, "no one of us, not even myself, has ever done that young man justice. To me he represents everything that is most strenuous and intellectual in Japanese manhood. The spirit of that wonderful country runs like the elixir of life itself through his veins. Since the day he brought me his letter from the Emperor, I have watched him carefully, and I believe I can honestly declare that not once in these eighteen months has he looked away from his task, nor has he given to one single person even an inkling of the thoughts which have passed through his mind. He came back from the Continent, from Berlin, from Paris, from Petersburg, with a mass of acquired information which would have made some of our blue-books read like Hans Andersen's Fairy Tales. He had made up his mind exactly what he thought of each country, of their political systems, of their social life, of their military importance. He had them all weighed up in the hollow of his hand. He was willing to talk as long as I, for instance, was willing to listen. He spoke of everybody whom he had met and every place which he had visited without reserve, and yet I guarantee that there is no person in England today, however much he may have talked with him, who knows in the least what his true impressions are."

"Haviland is right," Bransome agreed. "Many a time I have caught myself wondering, when he talks so easily about his travels, what the real thoughts are which lie at the back of his brain. We know, of course, what the object of those travels was. He went as no tourist. He went with a deep and solemn purpose always before him. He went to find out whether there was any other European Power whose alliance would be a more advantageous thing for Japan than a continuation of their alliance with us. Such a thing has never been mentioned or hinted at between us, but we know it all the same."

"I wonder," the Duke remarked, "whether we shall really get the truth out of him before he goes."

The Prime Minister shook his head.

"Look at him now teaching old Lady Saunderson how to hold her cue. He singled her out because she was the least attractive person playing, because no one took any particular notice of her, and every one seemed disposed to let her go her own way! Those girls were all buzzing around him as though he were something holy, but you see how gently he eluded them! Watch what an interest she is taking in the game now. He has been encouraging the poor old lady until her last few shots have been quite good. That is Maiyo all the world over. I will wager that he is thinking of nothing on earth at this moment but of making that poor old lady feel at her ease and enjoy her game. A stranger, looking on, would imagine him to be just a kind-hearted, simple-minded fellow. Yet there is not one of us three who has wit enough to get a single word from him against his will. You shall see. There is an excellent opportunity here. I suppose both of you read his speech at the Herrick Club last night?"

"I did," the Duke answered.

"And I," Bransome echoed. "It seemed to me that he spoke a little more freely than usual."

"He went as near to censure as I have ever heard him when speaking of any of the institutions of our country," the Prime Minister declared. "I will ask him about it directly we get the chance. You shall see how he will evade the point."

"You will have to be quick if you mean to get hold of him," the Duke remarked. "See, the game is over and there he goes with Penelope."

The Prime Minister rose to his feet and intercepted them on their way to the door.

"Miss Morse," he said, "may we ransom the Prince? We want to talk to him."

"Do you insinuate," she laughed, "that he is a captive of mine?"

"We are all captives of Miss Morse's," Bransome said with a bow, "and all enemies of Somerfield's."

Somerfield, hearing his name, came up to them. The Duchess, too, strolled over to the fire. The Prime Minister and Bransome returned with Maiyo towards the corner of the room where they had been sitting.

"Prince," the Prime Minister said, "we have been talking about your speech at the Herrick Club last night."

The Prince smiled a little gravely.

"Did I say too much?" he asked. "It all came as a surprise to me — the toast and everything connected with it. I saw my name down to reply, and it seemed discourteous of me not to speak. But, as yet, I do not altogether understand these functions. I did not altogether understand, for instance, how much I might say and how much I ought to leave unsaid."

"We have read what you said," Bransome remarked. "What we should like to hear, if I may venture to say so, is what you left unsaid."

The Prince for a moment was thoughtful. Perhaps he remembered that the days had passed when it was necessary for him to keep so jealously his own counsel. Perhaps his natural love of the truth triumphed. He felt a sudden longing to tell these people who had been kind to him the things which he had seen amongst them, the things which only a stranger coming fresh to the country could perhaps fully comprehend.

"What I said was of little importance," the Prince remarked, "but I felt myself placed in a very difficult position. Before I knew what to expect, I was listening to a glorification of the arms of my country at the expense of Russia. I was being hailed as one of a nation who possess military genius which had not been equalled since the days of Hannibal and Caesar. Many things of that sort were said, many things much too kind, many things which somehow it grieved me to listen to. And when I stood up to reply, I felt that the few words which I must say would sound, perhaps, ungracious, but they must be said. It was one of those occasions which seemed to call for the naked truth."

Penelope and the Duchess had joined the little group.

"May we stay?" the former asked. "I read every word of your speech," she added, turning to the Prince. "Do tell us why you spoke so severely, what it was that you objected to so strongly in General Ennison's remarks?"

The Prince turned earnestly towards her.

"My dear young lady," he said, "all that I objected to was this over-glorification of the feats of arms accomplished by us. People over here did not understand. On the one side were the great armies of Russia,—men drawn, all of them, from the ranks of the peasant, men of low nerve force, men who were not many degrees better than animals. They came to fight against us because it was their business to fight, because for fighting they drew their scanty pay, their food, and their drink, and the clothes they wore. They fought because if they refused they faced the revolver bullets of their officers,—men like themselves, who also fought because it was their profession, because it was in the traditions of their family, but who would, I think, have very much preferred disporting themselves in the dancing halls of their cities, drinking champagne with the ladies of their choice, or gambling with cards. I do not say that these were not brave men, all of them. I myself saw them face death by the hundreds, but the lust of battle was in their veins then, the taste of blood upon their palates. We do not claim to be called world conquerors because we overcame these men. If one could have seen into the hearts of our own soldiers as they marched into battle, and seen also into the hearts of those others who lay there sullenly waiting, one would not have wondered then. There was, indeed, nothing to wonder at. What we cannot make you understand over here is that every Japanese soldier who crept across the bare plains or lay stretched in the trenches, who loaded his rifle and shot and killed and waited for death,—every man felt something beating in his heart which those others did not feel. We have no great army, Mr. Haviland, but what we have is a great nation who have things beating in their heart the knowledge of which seems somehow to have grown cold amongst you Western people. The boy is born with it; it is there in his very soul, as dear to him as the little home where he lives, the blossoming trees under which he plays. It leads him to the rifle and the drill ground as naturally as the boys of your country turn to the cricket fields and the football ground. Over here you call that spirit patriotism. It was something which beat in the heart of every one of those hundreds of thousands of men, something which kept their eyes clear and bright as they marched into battle, which made them look Death itself in the face, and fight even while the blackness crept over them. You see, your own people have so many interests, so many excitements, so much to distract. With us it is not so. In the heart of the Japanese comes the love of his parents, the love of his wife and children, and, deepest, perhaps, of all the emotions he knows, the strong magnificent background to his life, the love of the country which bore him, which shelters them. It is for his home he fights, for his simple joys amongst those who are dear to him, for the great mysterious love of the Motherland. Forgive me if I have expressed myself badly, have repeated myself often. It is a matter which I find it so hard to talk about, so hard here to make you understand."

"But you must not think, Prince, that we over here are wholly lacking in that same instinct," the Duke said. "Remember our South African war, and the men who came to arms and rallied round the flag when their services were needed."

"I do remember that," the Prince answered. "I wish that I could speak of it in other terms. Yet it seems to me that I must speak as I find things. You say that the men came to arms. They did, but how? Untrained, unskilled in carrying weapons, they rushed across the seas to be the sport of the farmers who cut them off or shot them down, to be a hindrance in the way of the mercenaries who fought for you. Yes, you say they rallied to the call! What brought them? Excitement, necessity, necessities of their social standing, bravado, cheap heroism—any one of these. But I tell you that patriotism as we understand it is a deeper thing. In the land where it flourishes there is no great pre-eminence in what you call sports or games. It does not come like a whirlwind on the wings of disaster. It grows with the limbs and the heart of the boy, grows with his muscles and his brawn. It is part of his conscience, part of his religion. As he realizes that he has a country of his own to protect, a dear, precious heritage come down to him through countless ages, so he learns that it is his sacred duty to know how to do his share in defending it. The spare time of our youth, Mr. Haviland, is spent learning to shoot, to scout, to bear hardships, to acquire the arts of war. I tell you that there was not one general who went with our troops to Manchuria, but a hundred thousand. We have no great army. We are a nation of men whose religion it is to fight when their country's welfare is threatened."

There was a short silence. The Prime Minister and Bransome exchanged rapid glances.

"These, then," Penelope said slowly, "were the things you left unsaid."

The Prince raised his hand a little—a deprecatory gesture.

"Perhaps even now," he said, "it was scarcely courteous of me to say them, only I know that they come to you as no new thing. There are many of your countrymen who are speaking to you now in the Press as I, a stranger, have spoken. Sometimes it is harder to believe one of your own family. That is why I have dared to say so much,—I, a foreigner, eager and anxious only to observe and to learn. I think, perhaps, that it is to such that the truth comes easiest."

Of a purpose, the three men who were there said nothing. The Prince offered Penelope his arm.

"I will not be disappointed," he said. "You promised that you would show me the palm garden. I have talked too much."

CHAPTER XXIX.

A RACE

The Prince, on his way back from his usual before-breakfast stroll, lingered for a short time amongst the beds of hyacinths and yellow crocuses. Somehow or other, these spring flowers, stiffly set out and with shrivelled edges—a little reminiscent of the last east wind—still seemed to him, in their perfume at any rate, to being him memories of his own country. Pink and blue and yellow, in all manner of sizes and shapes, the beds spread away along the great front below the terrace of the castle. This morning the wind was coming from the west. The sun, indeed, seemed already to have gained some strength. The Prince sat for a moment or two upon the gray stone balustrade, looking to where the level country took a sudden ascent and ended in a thick belt of pine trees. Beyond lay the sea. As he sat there with folded arms, he was surely a fatalist. The question as to whether or not he should ever reach it, should ever find himself really bound for home, was one which seemed to trouble him slightly enough. He thought with a faint, wistful interest of the various ports of call, of the days which might pass, each one bringing him nearer the end. He suffered himself, even, to think of that faint blur upon the horizon, the breath of the spicy winds, the strange home perfumes of the bay, as he drew nearer and nearer to the outstretched arms of his country. Well, if not he, another! It was something to have done one's best.

The rustle of a woman's garment disturbed him, and he turned his head. Penelope stood there in her trim riding habit,—a garb in which he had never seen her. She held her skirts in her hand and looked at him with a curious little smile.

"It is too early in the morning, Prince," she said, "for you to sit there dreaming so long and so earnestly. Come in to breakfast. Every one is down, for a wonder."

"Breakfast, by all means," he answered, coming blithely up the broad steps. "You are going to ride this morning?"

"I suppose we all are, more or less," she answered. "It is our hunt steeplechases, you know. Poor Grace is in there nearly sobbing her eyes out. Captain Chalmers has thrown her over. Lady Barbarity—that's Grace's favorite mare, and her entry for the cup—turned awkward with him yesterday, and he won't have anything more to do with her."

"From your tone," he remarked, pushing open the French windows, "I gather that this is a tragedy. I, unfortunately, do not understand."

"You should ask Grace herself," Penelope said. "There she is."

Lady Grace looked round from her place at the head of the breakfast table.

"Come and sympathize with me, Prince," she cried. "For weeks I have been fancying myself the proud possessor of the hunt cup. Now that horrid man, Captain Chalmers, has thrown me over at the last moment. He refuses to ride my mare because she was a little fractious yesterday."

"It is a great misfortune," the Prince said in a tone of polite regret, "but surely it is not irreparable? There must be others—why not your own groom?"

A smile went round the table. The Duke hastened to explain.

"The race is for gentlemen riders only," he said. "The horses have to be the property of members of the hunt. There would be no difficulty, of course, in finding a substitute for Captain Chalmers, but the race takes place this morning, and I am afraid, with all due respect to my daughter, that her mare hasn't the best of reputations."

"I won't have a word said against Lady Barbarity," Lady Grace declared. "Captain Chalmers is a good horseman, of course but for a lightweight he has the worst hands I ever knew."

"But surely amongst your immediate friends there must be many others," the Prince said. "Sir Charles, for instance?"

"Charlie is riding his own horse," Lady Grace answered. "He hasn't the ghost of a chance, but, of course, he won't give it up."

"Not I!" Somerfield answered, gorgeous in pink coat and riding breeches. "My old horse may not be fast, but he can go the course, and I'm none too certain of the others. Some of those hurdles'll take a bit of doing."

"It is a shame," the Prince remarked, "that you should be disappointed, Lady Grace. Would they let me ride for you?"

Nothing the Prince could have said would have astonished the little company more. Somerfield came to a standstill in the middle of the room, with a cup of tea in one hand and a plate of ham in the other.

"You!" Lady Grace exclaimed.

"Do you really mean it, Prince?" Penelope cried.

"Well, why not?" he asked, himself, in turn, somewhat surprised. "If I am eligible, and Lady Grace chooses, it seems to me very simple."

"But," the Duke intervened, "I did not know—we did not know that you were a sportsman, Prince."

"A sportsman?" the Prince repeated a little doubtfully. "Perhaps I am not that according to your point of view, but when it comes to a question of riding, why, that is easy enough."

"Have you ever ridden in a steeplechase?" Somerfield asked him.

"Never in my life," the Prince declared. "Frankly, I do not know what it is."

"There are jumps, for one thing," Somerfield continued,—"pretty stiff affairs, too."

"If Lady Grace's mare is a hunter," the Prince remarked, "she can probably jump them."

"The question is whether—" Somerfield began, and stopped short.

The Prince looked up.

"Yes?" he asked.

Somerfield hesitated to complete his sentence, and the Duke once more intervened.

"What Somerfield was thinking, my dear Prince," he said, "was that a steeplechase course, as they ride in this country, needs some knowing. You have never been on my daughter's mare before."

The Prince smiled.

"So far as I am concerned," he said, "that is of no account. There was a day at Mukden—I do not like to talk of it, but it comes back to me—when I rode twelve different horses in twenty-four hours, but perhaps," he added, turning to Lady Grace, "you would not care to trust your horse with one who is a stranger to your—what is it you call them?—steeplechases."

"On the contrary, Prince," Lady Grace exclaimed, "you shall ride her, and I am going to back you for all I am worth."

Bransome, who was also in riding clothes, although he was not taking part in the steeplechases himself, glanced at the clock.

"You are running it rather fine," he said. "You'll scarcely have time to hack round the course."

"Some one must explain it to me," the Prince said. "I need only to be told where to go. If there is no time for that, I must stay with the other horses until the finish. There is a flat finish perhaps?"

"About three hundred yards," the Duke answered.

"Have you any riding clothes?" Penelope whispered to him.

"Without a doubt," he answered. "I will go and change in a few minutes."

"We start in half an hour," Somerfield remarked. "Even that allows us none too much time."

"Perhaps," the Duke suggested diffidently, "you would like to ride over, Prince? It is a good eleven miles, and you would have a chance of getting into your stride."

The Prince shook his head.

"No," he said, "I should like to motor with you others, if I may."

"Just as you like, of course," the Duke agreed. "Grace's mare is over there now. We shall be able to have a look at her before the race, at any rate."

The opinions, after the Prince had left the table, were a little divided as to what was likely to happen.

"For a man who has never even hunted and knows nothing whatever about the country," Somerfield declared, "to attempt to ride in a steeplechase of this sort is sheer folly. If you take my advice, Lady Grace, you will get out of it. Lady Barbarity is far too good a mare to have her knees broken."

"I am perfectly content to take my risks," Lady Grace answered confidently. "If the Prince had never ridden before in his life, I would trust him."

Somerfield turned away, frowning.

"What do you think about it, Penelope?" he asked.

"I am afraid," she answered, "that I agree with Grace."

Two punctures and a leaking valve delayed them over an hour on the road. When they reached their destination, the first race was already over.

"It's shocking bad luck," the Duke declared, "but there's no earthly chance of your seeing the course, Prince. Come on the top of the stand with me, and bring your glasses. I think I can point out the way for you."

"That will do excellently," the Prince answered. "There is no need to go and look at every jump. Show me where we start and as near as possible the way we have to go, and tell me where we finish."

The course was a natural one, and the stand itself on a hill. The greater part of it was clearly visible from where they stood. The Duke pointed out the water jump with some trepidation, but the Prince's glasses rested on it only for a moment. He pointed to a clump of trees.

"Which side there?" he asked.

"To the left," the Duke answered. "Remember to keep inside the red flags."

The Prince nodded.

"Where do we finish?" he asked.

The Duke showed him.

"That is all right," he said. "I need not look any more."

In the paddock some of the horses were being led around. The Prince noted them approvingly.

"Very nice horses," he said, — "light, but very nice. That one I like best," he added, pointing to a dark bay mare, who was already giving her boy some trouble.

"That's lucky," the Duke answered, "for she's your mount. I must go and talk to the clerk about your entry. It is a little late, but I think that it will be all right."

The Prince glanced over Lady Grace's mare and turned aside to join Penelope and Somerfield.

"I like the look of my horse, Sir Charles," he said. "I think that I shall beat you today."

"We both start at five to one," Somerfield answered. "Shall we have a bet?"

"With pleasure," the Prince agreed. "Will you name the amount? I do not know what is usual."

"Anything you like," Somerfield answered, "from ten pounds to a hundred."

"One hundred,—we will say one hundred, then," the Prince declared. "My mount against yours. So!"

He threw off his overcoat, and they saw for the first time that he was dressed in English riding clothes of dark material, but absolutely correct cut.

"I must go now and be introduced to the Clerk of the Course," he said. "Ah, here is Lady Grace!" he added. "Come with me, Lady Grace. Your father is seeing about my entry. I think that in five minutes the bell will ring."

Everything was in order, and a few minutes later the Prince came out. The mare was stripped, and the whole party gathered round to watch him mount. He swung himself into the saddle without hesitation. The mare suddenly reared. Prince Maiyo only smiled, and with loose reins stooped and patted her neck. He seemed to whisper something in her ear, and she stood for a moment afterwards quite still. Lady Grace drew a quick breath.

"What did you say to her, Prince?" she asked. "She is behaving beautifully except for that first start."

"Your mare understands Japanese, Lady Grace," the Prince answered, smiling. "She and I are going to be great friends. Show me the way, please. Ah, I follow that other horse! I see. Lady Grace, au revoir. You shall have your cup."

"Gad, I believe she will!" the Duke exclaimed. "Look at the fellow ride. His body is like whalebone."

The parade in front of the stand was a short one. The Prince rode by in the merest canter. The mare made one wild plunge which would have unseated any ordinary person, but her rider never even moved in his saddle.

"I never saw a fellow sit so close in my life," the Duke declared. "Do you know, Grace, I believe, I really believe he'll ride her!"

Lady Grace laughed scornfully.

"I have a year's allowance on already," she said, "so you had better pray that he does. I think it is very absurd of you all," she added, "because the Prince cares nothing for games, to conclude that he is any the less likely to be able to do the things that a man should do. He perhaps cannot ride about on a trained pony with a long stick and knock a small ball between two posts, but I think that if he had to ride for his own life or the life of others he would show you all something."

"They're off!" the Duke exclaimed.

They watched the first jump breathlessly. The Prince, riding a little apart, simply ignored the hurdle, and the mare took it in her stride. They turned the corner and faced an awkward post and rails. The leading horse took off too late and fell. The Prince, who was close behind, steered his mare on one side like lightning. She jumped like a cat,—the Prince never moved in his seat.

"He rides like an Italian," Bransome declared, shutting up his glasses. "There's never a thing in this race to touch him. I am going to see if I can get any money on."

Another set of hurdles and then the field were out of sight. Soon they were visible again in the valley. The Prince was riding second now. Somerfield was leading, and there were only three other horses left. They cleared a hedge and two ditches. At the second one Somerfield's horse stumbled, and there was a suppressed cry. He righted himself almost at once, however, and came on. Then they reached the water jump. There was a sudden silence on the stand and the hillside. Somerfield took off first, the Prince lying well away from him. Both cleared it, but whereas Lady Grace's mare jumped wide and clear, and her rider never even faltered in his saddle, Somerfield lost all his lead and only just kept his seat. They were on the homeward way now, with only one more jump, a double set of hurdles. Suddenly, in the flat, the Prince seemed to stagger in his saddle. Lady Grace cried out.

"He's over, by Jove!" the Duke exclaimed. "No, he's righted himself!"

The Prince had lost ground, but he came on toward the last jump, gaining with every stride. Somerfield was already riding his mount for all he was worth, but the Prince as yet had not touched his whip. They drew closer and closer to the jump. Once more the silence came. Then there was a little cry,—both were over. They were turning the corner coming into the straight. Somerfield was leaning forward now, using his whip freely, but it was clear that his big chestnut was beaten. The Prince, with merely a touch of the whip and riding absolutely upright, passed him with ease, and rode in a winner by a dozen lengths. As he cantered by the stand, they all saw the cause of his momentary stagger. One stirrup had gone, and he was riding with his leg quite stiff.

"You've won your money, Grace," the Duke declared, shutting up his glass. "A finely ridden race, too. Did you see he'd lost his stirrup? He must have taken the last jump without it. I'll go and fetch him up."

The Duke hurried down. The Prince was already in the weighing room smoking a cigarette.

"It is all right," he said smiling. "They have passed me. I have won. I hope that Lady Grace will be pleased."

"She is delighted!" the Duke exclaimed, shaking him by the hand. "We all are. What happened to your stirrup?"

"You must ask your groom," the Prince answered. "The leather snapped right in the flat, but it made no difference. We have to ride like that half the time. It is quite pleasant exercise," he continued, "but I am very dirty and very thirsty. I am sorry for Sir Charles, but his horse was not nearly so good as your daughter's mare."

They made their way toward the stand, but met the rest of the party in the paddock. Lady Grace went up to the Prince with outstretched hands.

"Prince," she declared, "you rode superbly. It was a wonderful race. I have never felt so grateful to any one in my life."

The Prince smiled in a puzzled way.

"My dear young lady," he said, "it was a great pleasure and a very pleasant ride. You have nothing to thank me for because your horse is a little better than those others."

"It was not my mare alone," she answered,—"it was your riding."

The Prince laughed as one who does not understand.

"You make me ashamed, Lady Grace," he declared. "Why, there is only one way to ride. You did not think that because I was not English I should fall off a horse?"

"I am afraid," the Duke remarked smiling, "that several Englishmen have fallen off!"

"It is a matter of the horse," the Prince said. "Some are not trained for jumping. What would you have, then? In my battalion we have nine hundred horsemen. If I found one who did not ride so well as I do, he would go back to the ranks. We would make an infantryman of him. Miss Morse," he added, turning suddenly to where Penelope was standing a little apart. "I am so sorry that Sir Charles' horse was not quite so good as Lady Grace's. You will not blame me?"

She looked at him curiously. She did not answer immediately. Somerfield was coming towards them, his pink coat splashed with mud, his face scratched, and a very distinct frown upon his forehead. She looked away from him to the Prince. Their eyes met for a moment.

"No!" she said. "I do not blame you!"

CHAPTER XXX.
INSPECTOR JACKS IMPORTUNATE

They were talking of the Prince during those few minutes before they separated to dress for dinner. The whole of the house-party, with the exception of the Prince himself, were gathered around the great open fireplace at the north end of the hall. The weather had changed during the afternoon, and a cold wind had blown in their faces on the homeward drive. Every one had found comfortable seats here, watching the huge logs burn, and there seemed to be a general indisposition to move. A couple of young men from the neighborhood had joined the house-party, and the conversation, naturally enough, was chiefly concerned with the day's sport. The young men, Somerfield especially, were inclined to regard the Prince's achievement from a somewhat critical standpoint.

"He rode the race well enough," Somerfield admitted, "but the mare is a topper, and no mistake. He had nothing to do but to sit tight and let her do the work."

"Of course, he hadn't to finish either," one of the newcomers, a Captain Everard Wilmot, remarked. "That's where you can tell if a fellow really can ride or not. Anyhow, his style was rotten. To me he seemed to sit his horse exactly like a groom."

"You will, perhaps, not deny him," the Duke remarked mildly, "a certain amount of courage in riding a strange horse of uncertain temper, over a strange country, in an enterprise which was entirely new to him."

"I call it one of the most sporting things I ever heard of in my life," Lady Grace declared warmly.

Somerfield shrugged his shoulders.

"One must admit that he has pluck," he remarked critically. "At the same time I cannot see that a single effort of this sort entitles a man to be considered a sportsman. He doesn't shoot, nor does he ever ride except when he is on military service. He neither plays games nor has he the instinct for them. A man without the instinct for games is a fellow I cannot understand. He'd never get along in this country, would he, Wilmot?"

"No, I'm shot if he would!" that young man replied. "There must be something wrong about a man who hasn't any taste whatever for sport."

Penelope suddenly intervened—intervened, too, in somewhat startling fashion.

"Charlie," she said, "you are talking like a baby! I am ashamed of you! I am ashamed of you all! You are talking like narrow-minded, ignorant little squireens."

Somerfield went slowly white. He looked across at Penelope, but the angry flash in his eyes was met by an even brighter light in her own.

"I will tell you what I think!" she exclaimed. "I think that you are all guilty of the most ridiculous presumption in criticising such a man as the Prince. You would dare—you, Captain Wilmot, and you, Charlie, and you, Mr. Hannaway," she added, turning to the third young man, "to stand there and tell us all in a lordly way that the Prince is no sportsman, as though that mysterious phrase disposed of him altogether as a creature inferior to you and your kind! If only you could realize the absolute absurdity of any of you attempting to depreciate a person so immeasurably above you! Prince Maiyo is a man, not an overgrown boy to go through life shooting birds, playing games which belong properly to your schooldays, and hanging round the stage doors of half the theatres in London. You are satisfied with your lives and the Prince is satisfied with his. He belongs to a race whom you do not understand. Let him alone. Don't presume to imagine yourselves his superior because he does not conform to your pygmy standard of life."

Penelope was standing now, her slim, elegant form throbbing with the earnestness of her words, a spot of angry color burning in her cheeks. During the moment's silence which followed, Lady Grace too rose to her feet and came to her friend's side.

"I agree with every word Penelope has said," she declared.

The Duchess smiled.

"Come," she said soothingly, "we mustn't take this little affair too seriously. You are all right, all of you. Every one must live according to his bringing up. The Prince, no doubt, is as faithful to his training and instincts as the young men of our own country. It is more interesting to compare than to criticise."

Somerfield, who for a moment had been too angry to speak, had now recovered himself.

"I think," he said stiffly, "that we had better drop the subject. I had no idea that Miss Morse felt so strongly about it or I should not have presumed, even here and amongst ourselves, to criticise a person who holds such a high place in her esteem. Everard, I'll play you a game of billiards before we go upstairs. There's just time."

Captain Wilmot hesitated. He was a peace-loving man, and, after all, Penelope and his friend were engaged.

"Perhaps Miss Morse—" he began.

Penelope turned upon him.

"I should like you all to understand," she declared, "that every word I said came from my heart, and that I would say it again, and more, with the same provocation."

There was a finality about Penelope's words which left no room for further discussion. The little group was broken up. She and Lady Grace went to their rooms together.

"Penelope, you're a dear!" the latter said, as they mounted the stairs. "I am afraid you've made Charlie very angry, though."

"I hope I have," Penelope answered. "I meant to make him angry. I think that such self-sufficiency is absolutely stifling. It makes me sometimes almost loathe young Englishmen of his class."

"And you don't dislike the Prince so much nowadays?" Lady Grace remarked with transparent indifference.

"No!" Penelope answered. "That is finished. I misunderstood him at first. It was entirely my own fault. I was prejudiced, and I hated to feel that I was in the wrong. I do not see how any one could dislike him unless they were enemies of his country. Then I fancy that they might have cause."

Lady Grace sighed.

"To tell you the truth, Penelope," she said, "I almost wish that he were not quite so devotedly attached to his country."

Penelope was silent. They had reached Lady Grace's room now, and were standing together on the hearthrug in front of the fire.

"I am afraid he is like that," Penelope said gently. "He seems to have none of the ordinary weaknesses of men. I, too, wish sometimes that he were a little different. One would like to think of him, for his own sake, as being happy some day. He reminds me somehow of the men who build and build, toiling always through youth unto old age. There seems no limit to their strength, nor any respite. They build a palace which those who come after them must inhabit."

Once more Lady Grace sighed. She was looking into the heart of the fire. Penelope took her hands.

"It is hard sometimes, dear," she said, "to realize that a thing is impossible, that it is absolutely out of our reach. Yet it is better to bring one's mind to it than to suffer all the days."

Lady Grace looked up. At that moment she was more than pretty. Her eyes were soft and bright, the color had flooded her cheeks.

"But I don't see *why* it should be impossible, Penelope," she protested. "We are equals in every way. Alliances between our two countries are greatly to be desired. I have heard my father say so, and Mr. Haviland. The trouble is, Pen," she added with trembling lips, "that he does not care for me."

"You cannot tell," Penelope answered. "He has never shown any signs of caring for any woman. Remember, though, that he would want you to live in Japan."

"I'd live in Thibet if he asked me to," Lady Grace declared, raising her handkerchief to her eyes, "but he never will. He doesn't care. He doesn't understand. I am very foolish, Penelope."

Penelope kissed her gently.

"Dear," she said, "you are not the only foolish woman in the world."...

Conversation amongst the younger members of the house-party at Devenham Castle was a little disjointed that evening. Perhaps Penelope, who came down in a wonderful black velveteen gown, with a bunch of scarlet roses in her corsage, was the only one who seemed successfully to ignore the passage of arms which had taken place so short a while ago. She talked pleasantly to Somerfield, who tried to be dignified and succeeded only in remaining sulky. Chance had placed her at some distance from the Prince, to whom Lady Grace was talking with a subdued softness in her manner which puzzled Captain Wilmot, her neighbor on the other side.

"I saw you with all the evening papers as usual, Bransome," the Prime Minister remarked during the service of dinner. "Was there any news?"

"Nothing much," the Foreign Secretary replied. "Consuls are down another point and the Daily Comet says that you are like a drowning man clinging to the raft of your majority. Excellent cartoon of you, by the bye. You shall see it after dinner."

"Thank you," the Prime Minister said. "Was there anything about you in the same paper by any chance?"

"Nothing particularly abusive," Sir Edward answered blandly. "By the bye, the police declare that they have a definite clue this time, and are going to arrest the murderer of Hamilton Fynes and poor dicky Vanderpole tonight or tomorrow."

"Excellent!" the Duke declared. "It would have been a perfect disgrace to our police system to have left two such crimes undetected. Our respected friend at the Home Office will have a little peace now."

"How about me?" Bransome grumbled. "Haven't I been worried to death, too?"

The Prince, who had just finished describing to Lady Grace a typical landscape of his country, turned toward Bransome.

"I think that I heard you say something about a discovery in connection with those wonderful murder cases," he said. "Has any one actually been arrested?"

"My paper was an early edition," Bransome answered, "but it spoke of a sensational denouement within the next few hours. I should imagine that it is all over by now. At the same time it's absurd how the Press give these things away. It seems that some fellow who was bicycling saw a man get in and out of poor Dicky's taxi and is quite prepared to swear to him."

"Has he not been rather a long time in coming forward with his evidence?" the Prince remarked. "I do not remember to have seen any mention of such a person in the papers before."

"He watched so well," Bransome answered, "and was so startled that he was knocked down and run over. The detective in charge of the case found him in a hospital."

"These things always come out sooner or later," the Prime Minister remarked. "As a matter of fact, I am inclined to think that our police wait too long before they make an arrest. They play with their victim so deliberately that sometimes he slips through their fingers. Very often, too, they let a man go who would give himself away from sheer fright if he felt the touch of a policeman upon his shoulder."

"As a nation," Bransome remarked, helping himself to the entree, "we handle life amongst ourselves with perpetual kid gloves. We are always afraid of molesting the liberty of the subject. A trifle more brutality sometimes would make for strength. We are like a dentist whose work suffers because he is afraid of hurting his patient."

Somerfield was watching his fiancee curiously.

"Are you really very pale tonight, Penelope," he asked, "or is it those red flowers which have drawn all the color from your cheeks?"

"I believe that I am pale," Penelope answered. "I am always pale when I wear black and when people have disagreed with me. As a matter of fact, I am trying to make the Prince feel homesick. Tell me," she asked him across the round table, "don't you think that I remind you a little tonight of the women of your country?"

The Prince returned her gaze as though, indeed, something were passing between them of greater significance than that half-bantering question.

"Indeed," he said, "I think that you do. You remind me of my country itself—of the things that wait for me across the ocean."

The Prince's servant had entered the dining room and whispered in the ear of the butler who was superintending the service of dinner. The latter came over at once to the Prince.

"Your Highness," he said, "some one is on the telephone, speaking from London. They ask if you could spare half a minute."

The Prince rose with an interrogative glance at his hostess, and the Duchess smilingly motioned him to go. Even after he had left the room, when he was altogether unobserved, his composed demeanor showed no signs of any change. He took up the receiver almost blithely. It was Soto, his secretary, who spoke to him.

"Highness," he said, "the man Jacks with a policeman is here in the hall at the present moment. He asks permission to search this house."

"For what purpose?" the Prince asked.

"To discover some person whom he believes to be in hiding here," the secretary answered. "He explains that in any ordinary case he would have applied for what they call a search warrant. Owing to your Highness' position, however, he has attended here, hoping for your gracious consent without having made any formal application."

"I must think!" the Prince answered. "Tell me, Soto. You are sure that the English doctor has had no opportunity of communicating with any one?"

"He has had no opportunity," was the firm reply. "If your Highness says the word, he shall pass."

"Let him alone," the Prince answered. "Refuse this man Jacks permission to search my house during my absence. Tell him that I shall be there at three o'clock tomorrow afternoon and that at that hour he is welcome to return."

"It shall be done, Highness," was the answer.

The Prince set down the receiver upon the instrument and stood for a moment deep in thought. It was a strange country, this,—a strange end which it seemed that he must prepare to face. He felt like the man who had gone out to shoot lions and returning with great spoil had died of the bite of a poisonous ant!

CHAPTER XXXI.
GOODBYE!

The Prince on his return from the library intercepted Penelope on her way across the hall.

"Forgive me," he said, "but I could not help overhearing some sentences of your conversation with Sir Charles Somerfield as we sat at dinner. You are going to talk with him now, is it not so?"

"As soon as he comes out from the dining room."

He saw the hardening of her lips, the flash in her eyes at the mention of Somerfield's name.

"Yes!" she continued, "Sir Charles and I are going to have a little understanding."

"Are you sure," he asked softly, "that it will not be a misunderstanding?"

She looked into his face.

"What does it matter to you?" she asked. "What do you care?"

"Come into the conservatory for a few minutes," he begged. "You know that I take no wine and I prefer not to return into the dining room. I would like so much instead to talk to you before you see Sir Charles."

She hesitated. He stood by her side patiently waiting.

"Remember," he said, "that I am a somewhat privileged person just now. My days here are numbered, you see."

She turned toward the conservatories.

"Very well," she said, "I must be like every one else, I suppose, and spoil you. How dare you come and make us all so fond of you that we look upon your departure almost as a tragedy!"

He smiled.

"Indeed," he declared, "there is a note of tragedy even in these simplest accidents of life. I have been very happy amongst you all, Miss Penelope. You have been so much kinder to me than I have deserved. You have thrown a bridge across the gulf which separates us people of alien tongues and alien manners. Life has been a pleasant thing for me here."

"Why do you go so soon?" she whispered.

"Miss Penelope," he answered, "to those others who ask me that question, I shall say that my mission is over, that my report has been sent to my Emperor, and that there is nothing left for me to do but to follow it home. I could add, and it would be true, that there is very much work for me still to accomplish in my own country. To you alone I am going to say something else."

She was no longer pale. Her eyes were filled with an exceedingly soft light. She leaned towards him, and her face shone as the face of a woman who prays that she may hear the one thing in life a woman craves to hear from the lips she loves best.

"Go on," she murmured.

"I want to ask you, Miss Penelope," he continued, "whether you remember the day when you paid a visit to my house?"

"Very well," she answered.

"I was showing you a casket," he went on.

She gripped his arm.

"Don't!" she begged. "Don't, I can't bear any more of that. You don't know how horrible it seems to me! You don't know—what fears I have had!"

He looked away from her.

"I have sometimes wondered," he said, "what your thoughts were at that moment, what you have thought of me since."

She shivered a little, but did not answer him.

"Very soon," he reminded her, "I shall have passed out of your life."

He heard the sudden, half-stifled exclamation. He felt rather than saw the eyes which pleaded with him, and he hastened on.

"You understand what is meant by the inevitable," he continued. "Whatever has happened in the matters with which I have been concerned has been inevitable. I have had no choice—sometimes no choice in such events is possible. Do not think," he went on, "that I tell you this to beg for your sympathy. I would not have a thing other than as it is. But when we have said goodbye, I want you to believe the best of me, to think as kindly as you can of the things which you may not be able to comprehend. Remember that we are not so emotional a nation as that to which you belong. Our affections are but seldom touched. We live without feeling for many days, sometimes for longer, even, than many days. It has not been so altogether with me. I have felt more than I dare, at this moment, to speak of."

"Yet you go," she murmured.

"Yet I go," he assented. "Nothing in the world is more certain than that I must say farewell to you and all of my good friends here. In a sense I want this to be our farewell. Leaving out of the question just now the more serious dangers which threaten me, the result of my mission here alone will make me unpopular in this country. As the years pass, I fear that nothing can draw your own land and mine into any sort of accord. That is why I asked you to come here with me and listen while I said these few words to you, why I ask you now that, whatever the future may bring, you will sometimes spare me a kindly thought."

"I think you know," she answered, "that you need not ask that."

"You will marry Sir Charles Somerfield," he continued, "and you will be happy. In this country men develop late. Somerfield, too, will develop, I am sure. He will become worthy even, I trust, to be your husband, Miss Penelope. Something was said of his going into Parliament. When he is Foreign Minister and I am the Counsellor of the Emperor, we may perhaps send messages to one another, if not across the seas, through the clouds."

A man's footstep approached them. Somerfield himself drew near and hesitated. The Prince rose at once.

"Sir Charles," he said, "I have been bidding farewell to Miss Penelope. I have had news tonight over the telephone and I find that I must curtail my visit."

"The Duke will be disappointed," Somerfield said. "Are you off at once?"

"Probably tomorrow," the Prince answered. "May I leave Miss Penelope in your charge?" he added with a little bow. "The Duke, I believe, is awaiting me."

He passed out of the conservatory. Penelope sat quite still.

"Well," Somerfield said, "if he is really going—"

"Charlie," she interrupted, "if ever you expect me to marry you, I make one condition, and that is that you never say a single word against Prince Maiyo."

"The man whom a month ago," he remarked curiously, "you hated!"

She shook her head.

"I was an idiot," she said. "I did not understand him and I was prejudiced against his country."

"Well, as he actually is going away," Sir Charles remarked with a sigh of content, "I suppose it's no use being jealous."

"You haven't any reason to be," Penelope answered just a little wistfully. "Prince Maiyo has no room in his life for such frivolous creatures as women."

The Prince found the rest of the party dispersed in various directions. Lady Grace was playing billiards with Captain Wilmot. She showed every disposition to lay down her cue when he entered the room.

"Do come and talk to us, Prince," she begged. "I am so tired of this stupid game, and I am sure Captain Wilmot is bored to tears."

The Prince shook his head.

"Thank you," he said, "but I must find the Duke. I have just received a telephone message and I fear that I may have to leave tomorrow."

"Tomorrow!" she cried in dismay.

The Prince sighed.

"If not tomorrow, the next day," he answered. "I have had a summons—a summons which I cannot disobey. Shall I find your father in the library, Lady Grace?"

"Yes!" she answered. "He is there with Mr. Haviland and Sir Edward. Are you really going to waste your last evening in talking about treaties and such trifles?"

"I am afraid I must," he answered regretfully.

"You are a hopelessly disappointing person," she declared a little pitifully.

"It is because you are all much too kind to me that you think so," he answered. "You make me welcome amongst you even as one of yourselves. You forget—you would almost teach me to forget that I am only a wayfarer here."

"That is your own choice," she said, coming a little nearer to him.

"Ah, no," he answered. "There is no choice! I serve a great mistress, and when she calls I come. There are no other voices in the world for one of my race and faith. The library you said, Lady Grace? I must go and find your father."

He passed out, closing the door behind him. Captain Wilmot chalked his cue carefully.

"That's the queerest fellow I ever knew in my life," he said. "He seems all the time as though his head were in the clouds."

Lady Grace sighed. She too was chalking her cue.

"I wonder," she said, "what it would be like to live in the clouds."

CHAPTER XXXII.
PRINCE MAIYO SPEAKS

The library at Devenham Castle was a large and sombre apartment, with high oriel windows and bookcases reaching to the ceiling. It had an unused and somewhat austere air. Tonight especially an atmosphere of gloom seemed to pervade it. The Prince, when he opened the door, found the three men who were awaiting him seated at an oval table at the further end of the room.

"I do not intrude, I trust?" the Prince said. "I understood that you wished me to come here."

"Certainly," the Duke answered, "we were sitting here awaiting your arrival. Will you take this easy chair? The cigarettes are at your elbow."

The Prince declined the easy chair and leaned for a moment against the table.

"Perhaps later," he said. "Just now I feel that you have something to say to me. Is it not so? I talk better when I am standing."

It was the Prime Minister who made the first plunge. He spoke without circumlocution, and his tone was graver than usual.

"Prince," he said, "this is perhaps the last time that we shall all meet together in this way. You go from us direct to the seat of your Government. So far there has been very little plain speaking between us. It would perhaps be more in accord with etiquette if we let you go without a word, and waited for a formal interchange of communications between your Ambassador and ourselves. But we have a feeling, Sir Edward and I, that we should like to talk to you directly. Before we go any further, however, let me ask you this question. Have you any objection, Prince, to discussing a certain matter here with us?"

The Prince for several moments made no reply. He was still standing facing the fireplace, leaning slightly against the table behind him. On his right was the Duke, seated in a library chair. On his left the Prime Minister and Sir Edward Bransome. The Prince seemed somehow to have become the central figure of the little group.

"Perhaps," he said, "if you had asked me that question a month ago, Mr. Haviland, I might have replied to you differently. Circumstances, however, since then have changed. My departure will take place so soon, and the kindness I have met here from all of you has been so overwhelming, that if you will let me I should like to speak of certain things concerning which no written communication could ever pass between our two countries."

"I can assure you, my dear Prince, that we shall very much appreciate your doing so," Mr. Haviland declared.

"I think," the Prince continued, "that the greatest and the most subtle of all policies is the policy of perfect truthfulness. Listen to me, then. The thing which you have in your mind concerning me is true. Two years I have spent in this country and in other countries of Europe. These two years have not been spent in purposeless travel. On the contrary, I have carried with me always a definite and very fixed purpose."

The Prime Minister and Bransome exchanged rapid glances.

"That has been our belief from the first," Bransome remarked.

"I came to Europe," the Prince continued gravely, "to make a report to my cousin the Emperor of Japan as to whether I believed that a renewal of our alliance with you would be advantageous to my country. I need not shrink from discussing this matter with you now, for my report is made. It is, even now, on its way to the Emperor."

There was a moment's silence, a silence which in this corner of the great room seemed marked with a certain poignancy. It was the Prime Minister who broke it.

"The report," he said, "is out of your hands. The official decision of your Government will reach us before long. Is there any reason why you should not anticipate that decision, why you should not tell us frankly what your advice was?"

"There is no reason," the Prince answered. "I will tell you. I owe that to you at least. I have advised the Emperor not to renew the treaty."

"Not to renew," the Prime Minister echoed.

This time the silence was portentous. It was a blow, and there was not one of the three men who attempted to hide his dismay.

"I am afraid," the Prince continued earnestly, "that to you I must seem something of an ingrate. I have been treated by every one in this country as the son of a dear friend. The way has been made smooth for me everywhere. Nothing has been hidden. From all quarters I have received hospitality which I shall never forget. But you are three just men. I know you will realize that my duty was to my country and to my country alone. No one else has any claims upon me. What I have seen I have written of. What I believe I have spoken."

"Prince," Mr. Haviland said, "there is no one here who will gainsay your honesty. You came to judge us as a nation and you have found us wanting. At least we can ask you why?"

The Prince sighed.

"It is hard," he said. "It is very hard. When I tell you of the things which I have seen, remember, if you please, that I have seen them with other eyes than yours. The conditions which you have grown up amongst and lived amongst all your days pass almost outside the possibility of your impartial judgment. You have lived with them too long. They have become a part of you. Then, too, your national weakness bids your eyes see what you would have them see."

"Go on," Mr. Haviland said, drumming idly with his fingers upon the table.

"I have had to ask myself," the Prince continued,—"it has been my business to ask myself what is your position as a great military power, and the answer I have found is that as a great military power it does not exist. I have had to ask myself what would happen to your country in the case of a European war, where your fleet was distributed to guard your vast possessions in every quarter of the world, and the answer to that is that you are, to all practical purposes, defenceless. In almost any combination which could arrange itself, your country is at the mercy of the invader."

Bransome leaned forward in his chair.

"I can disprove it," he declared firmly. "Come with me to Aldershot next week, and I will show you that those who say that we have no army are ignorant alarmists. The Secretary for War shall show you our new scheme for defensive forces. You have gone to the wrong authorities for information on these matters, Prince. You have been entirely and totally misled."

The Prince drew a little breath.

"Sir Edward," he said, "I do not speak to you rashly. I have not looked into these affairs as an amateur. You forget that I have spent a week at Aldershot, that your Secretary for War gave me two days of his valuable time. Every figure with which you could furnish me I am already possessed of. I will be frank with you. What I saw at Aldershot counted for nothing with me in my decision. Your standing army is good, beyond a doubt,—a well-trained machine, an excellent plaything for a General to move across the chessboard. It might even win battles, and yet your standing army are mercenaries, and no great nation, from the days of Babylon, has resisted invasion or held an empire by her mercenaries."

"They are English soldiers," Mr. Haviland declared. "I do not recognize your use of the word."

"They are paid soldiers," the Prince said, "men who have adopted soldiering as a profession. Come, I will not pause half-way. I will tell you what is wrong with your country. You will not believe it. Some day you will see the truth, and you will remember my words. It may be that you will realize it a little sooner, or I would not have dared to speak as I am speaking. This, then, is the curse which is eating the heart out of your very existence. The love of his Motherland is no longer a religion with your young man. Let me repeat that,—I will alter one word only. The love of his Motherland is no longer *the* religion or even part of the religion of your young man. Soldiering is a profession for those who embrace it. It is so that mercenaries are made. I have been to every one of your great cities in the North. I have been there on a Saturday afternoon, the national holiday. That is the day in Japan on which our young men march and learn to shoot, form companies and attend their drill. Feast days and holidays it is always the same. They do what tradition has made a necessity for them. They do it without grumbling, whole-heartedly, with an enthusiasm which has in it something almost of passion. How do I find the youth of your country engaged? I have discovered. It is for that purpose that I have toured through England. They go to see a game played called football. They sit on seats and smoke and shout. They watch a score of performers—one score, mind—and the numbers who watch them are millions. From town to town I went, and it was always the same. I see their white faces in a huge amphitheatre, fifteen thousand here, twenty thousand there, thirty thousand at another place. They watch and they shout while these men in the arena play with great skill this wonderful game. When the match is over, they stream into public houses. Their afternoon has been spent. They talk it over. Again they smoke and drink. So it is in one town and another,—so it is everywhere,—the strangest sight of all that I have seen in Europe. These are your young men, the material out of which the coming generation must be fashioned? How many of them can shoot? How many of them can ride? How many of them have any sort of uniform in which they could prepare to meet the enemy of their country? What do they know or care for anything outside their little lives and what they call their love of sport,—they who spend five days in your grim factories toiling before machines,—their one afternoon, content to sit and watch the prowess of others! I speak to these footballers themselves. They are strong men and swift. They are paid to play this game. I do not find that even one of them is competent to strike a blow for his country if she needs him. It is because of your young men, then, Mr. Haviland, that I cannot advise Japan to form a new alliance with you. It is because you are not a serious people. It is because the units of your nation have ceased to understand that behind the life of every great nation stands the love of God, whatever god it may be, and the love of Motherland. These things may not be your fault. They may, indeed, be the terrible penalty of success. But no one who lives for ever so short a time amongst you can fail to see the truth. You are commercialized out of all the greatness of life. Forgive me, all of you, that I say it so plainly, but you are a race who are on the downward grade, and Japan seeks for no alliance save with those whose faces are lifted to the skies."

The pause which followed was in itself significant. The Duke alone remained impassive. Bransome's face was dark with anger. Even the Prime Minister was annoyed. Bransome would have spoken, but the former held out his hand to check him.

"If that is really your opinion of us, Prince," he said, "it is useless to enter into argument with you, especially as you have already acted upon your convictions. I should like to ask you this question, though.

A few weeks ago an appeal was made to our young men to bring up to its full strength certain forces which have been organized for the defence of the country. Do you know how many recruits we obtained in less than a month?"

"Fourteen thousand four hundred and seventy-five," the Prince answered promptly, "out of nearly seven millions who were eligible. This pitiful result of itself might have been included amongst my arguments if I had felt that arguments were necessary. Mr. Haviland, you may drive some of these young men to arms by persuasion, by appealing to them through their womankind or their employers, but you cannot create a national spirit. And I tell you, and I have proved it, that the national spirit is not there. I will go further," the Prince continued with increased earnestness, "if you still are not weary of the subject. I will point out to you how little encouragement the youth of this country receive from those who are above them in social station. In every one of your counties there is a hunt, cricket clubs, golf clubs in such numbers that their statistics absolutely overwhelm me. Everywhere one meets young men of leisure, well off, calmly proposing to settle down and spend the best part of their lives in what they call country life. They will look after their estates; they will hunt a little, shoot a little, go abroad for two months in the winter, play golf a little, lawn tennis, perhaps, or cricket. I tell you that there are hundreds and thousands of these young men, with money to spare, who have no uniform which they could wear,—no, I want to change that!" the Prince cried with an impressive gesture,—"who have no uniform which they will be able to wear when the evil time comes! How will they feel then, these young men of family, whose life has been given to sports and to idle amusements, when their womankind come shrieking to them for protection and they dare not even handle a gun or strike a blow! They must stand by and see their lands laid waste, their womankind insulted. They must see the land run red with the blood of those who offer a futile resistance, but they themselves must stand by inactive. They are not trained to fight as soldiers,—they cannot fight as civilians."

"The Prince forgets," Bransome remarked dryly, "that an invasion of this country—a practical invasion—is very nearly an impossible thing."

The Prince laughed softly.

"My friend," he said, "if I thought that you believed that, although you are a Cabinet Minister of England I should think that you were the biggest fool who ever breathed. Today, in warfare, nothing is impossible. I will guarantee, I who have had only ten years of soldiering, that if Japan were where Holland is today, I would halve my strength in ships and I would halve my strength in men, and I would overrun your country with ease at any time I chose. You need not agree with me, of course. It is not a subject which we need discuss. It is, perhaps, out of my province to allude to it. The feeling which I have in my heart is this. The laws of history are incontrovertible. So surely as a great nation has weakened with prosperity, so that her limbs have lost their suppleness and her finger joints have stiffened, so surely does the plunderer come in good time. The nation which loses its citizen army drives the first nail into its own coffin. I do not say who will invade you, or when, although, to my thinking, any one could do it. I simply say that in your present state invasion from some one or other is a sure thing."

"Without admitting the truth of a single word you have said, my dear Prince," the Prime Minister remarked, "there is another aspect of the whole subject which I think that you should consider. If you find us in so parlous a state, it is surely scarcely dignified or gracious, on the part of a great nation like yours, to leave us so abruptly to our fate. Supposing it were true that we were suffering a little from a period of too lengthened prosperity, from an attack of over-confidence. Still think of the part we have played in the past. We kept the world at bay while you fought with Russia."

"That," the Prince replied, "was one of the conditions of a treaty which has expired. If by that treaty our country profited more than yours, that is still no reason why we should renew it under altered conditions. Gratitude is an admirable sentiment, but it has nothing to do with the making of treaties."

"We are, nevertheless," Bransome declared, "justified in pointing out to you some of the advantages which you have gained from your alliance with us. You realize, I suppose, that save for our intervention the United States would have declared war against you four months ago?"

"Your good offices were duly acknowledged by my Government," the Prince admitted. "Yet what you did was in itself of no consequence.

It is as sure as north is north and south is south that you and America would never quarrel for the sake of Japan. That is another reason, if another reason is needed, why a treaty between us would be valueless. You and I—the whole world knows that before a cycle of years have passed Japan and America must fight. When that time comes, it will not be you who will help us."

"An alliance duly concluded between this country—"

The Prince held out both his hands.

"Listen," he said. "A fortnight ago a certain person in America wrote and asked you in plain terms what your position would be if war between Japan and America were declared. What was your reply?"

Bransome was on the point of exclaiming, but the Prime Minister intervened.

"You appear to be a perfect Secret Service to yourself, Prince," he said smoothly. "Perhaps you can also tell us our reply?"

"I can tell you this much," the Prince answered. "You did not send word back to Washington that your alliance was a sacred charge upon your honor and that its terms must be fulfilled to the uttermost letter. Your reply, I fancy, was more in the nature of a compromise."

"How do you know what our reply was?" Mr. Haviland asked.

"To tell you the truth, I do not," the Prince answered, smiling. "I have simply told you what I am assured that your answer must have been. Let us leave this matter. We gain nothing by discussing it."

"You have been very candid with us, Prince," Mr. Haviland remarked. "We gather that you are opposed to a renewal of our alliance chiefly for two reasons,—first, that you have formed an unfavorable opinion of our resources and capacity as a nation; and secondly, because you are seeking an ally who would be of service to you in one particular eventuality, namely, a war with the United States. You have spent some time upon the Continent. May we inquire whether your present attitude is the result of advances made to you by any other Power? If I am asking too much, leave my question unanswered."

The Prince shook his head slowly.

"Tonight," he said, "I am speaking to you as one who is willing to show everything that is in his heart. I will tell you, then. I have been to Germany, and I can assure you of my own knowledge that Germany possesses the mightiest fighting machine ever known in the world's history. That I do truthfully and honestly believe. Yet listen to me. I have talked to the men and I have talked to the officers. I have seen them in barracks and on the parade ground, and I tell you this. When the time arrives for that machine to be set in motion, it is my profound conviction that the result will be one of the greatest surprises of modern times. I say no more, nor must you ask me any questions, but I tell you that we do not need Germany as an ally. I have been to Russia, and although our hands have crossed, there can be no real friendship between our countries till time has wiped out the memory of our recent conflict. France hates us because it does not understand us. The future of Japan is just as clear as the disaster which hangs over Great Britain. There is only one possible ally for us, only one possible combination. That is what I have written home to my cousin the Emperor. That is what I pray that our young professors will teach throughout Japan.. That is what it will be my mission to teach my country people if the Fates will that I return safely home. East and West are too far apart. We are well outside the coming European struggle. Our strength will come to us from nearer home."

"China!" the Prime Minister exclaimed.

"The China of our own making," the Prince declared, a note of tense enthusiasm creeping into his tone,—"China recreated after its great lapse of a thousand years. You and I in our lifetime shall not see it, but there will come a day when the ancient conquests of Persia and Greece and Rome will seem as nothing before the all-conquering armies of China and Japan. Until those days we need no allies. We will have none. We must accept the insults of America and the rough hand of Germany. We must be strong enough to wait!"

A footman entered the room and made his way to the Duke's chair.

"Your Grace," he said, "a gentleman is ringing up from Downing Street who says he is speaking from the Home Office."

"Whom does he want?" the Duke asked.

"Both Your Grace and Mr. Haviland," the man replied. "He wished me to say that the matter was of the utmost importance."

The Duke rose at once and glanced at the clock.

"It is an extraordinary hour," he remarked, "for Heseltine to be wanting us. Shall we go and see what it means, Haviland? You will excuse us, Prince?"

The Prince bowed.

"I think that we have talked enough of serious affairs tonight," he said. "I shall challenge Sir Edward to a game of billiards."

CHAPTER XXXIII.
UNAFRAID

The Prince, still fully attired, save that in place of his dress coat he wore a loose smoking jacket, stood at the windows of his sitting room at Devenham Castle, looking across the park. In the somewhat fitful moonlight the trees had taken to themselves grotesque shapes. Away in the distance the glimmer of the sea shone like a thin belt of quicksilver. The stable clock had struck two. The whole place seemed at rest. Only one light was gleaming from a long low building which had been added to the coach houses of recent years for a motor garage. That one light, the Prince knew, was on his account. There his chauffeur waited, untiring and sleepless, with his car always ready for that last rush to the coast, the advisability of which the Prince had considered more than once during the last twenty-four hours. The excitement of the evening, the excitement of his unwonted outburst, was still troubling him. It was not often that he had so far overstepped the bounds which his natural caution, his ever-present self-restraint, imposed upon him. He paced restlessly to and fro from the sitting room to the bedroom and back again. He had told the truth,—the bare, simple truth. He had seen the letters of fire in the sky, and he had read them to these people because of their kindness, because of a certain affection which he bore them. To them it must have sounded like a man speaking in a strange tongue. They had not understood. Perhaps, even, they would not believe in the absolute sincerity of his motives. Again he paused at the window and looked over the park to that narrow, glittering stretch of sea. Why should he not for once forget the traditions of his race, the pride which kept him there to face the end! There was still time. The cruiser which the Emperor had sent was waiting for him in Southampton Harbor. In twenty-four hours he would be in foreign waters. He thought of these things earnestly, even wistfully, and yet he knew that he could not go. Perhaps they would be glad of an opportunity of getting rid of him now that he had spoken his mind. In any case, right was on their side. The end, if it must come, was simple enough!

He turned away from the window with a little shrug of the shoulders. Even as he did so, there came a faint knocking at the door. His servant had already retired. For a moment it seemed to him that it could mean but one thing. While he hesitated, the handle was softly turned and the door opened. To his amazement, it was Penelope who stood upon the threshold.

"Miss Morse!" he exclaimed breathlessly.

She held out her hand as though to bid him remain silent. For several seconds she seemed to be listening. Then very softly she closed the door behind her.

"Miss Penelope," he cried softly, "you must not come in here! Please!"

She ignored his outstretched hand, advancing a little further into the room. There was tragedy in her white face. She seemed to be shaking in every limb, but not with nervousness. Directly he looked into her eyes, he knew very well that the thing was close at hand!

"Listen!" she whispered. "I had to come! You don't know what is going on! For the last half hour the telephone has been ringing continuously. It is about you! The Home Office has been ringing up to speak to the Prime Minister. The Chief Inspector of Scotland Yard has been to see them. One of their detectives has collected evidence which justifies them in issuing a warrant for your arrest."

"For my arrest," the Prince repeated.

"Don't you understand?" she continued breathlessly. "Don't you see how horrible it is? They mean to arrest you for the murder of Hamilton Fynes and Dicky Vanderpole!"

"If this must be so," the Prince answered, "why do they not come? I am here."

"But you must not stay here!" she exclaimed. "You must escape! It is too terrible to think that you should—oh, I can't say it!—that you should have to face these charges. If you are guilty, well, Heaven help you!—If you are guilty, I want you to escape all the same!"

He looked at her with the puzzled air of one who tries to reason with a child.

"Dear Miss Penelope," he said, "this is kind of you, but, after all, remember that I am a man, and I must not run away."

"But you cannot meet these charges!" she interrupted. "You cannot meet them! You know it! Oh, don't think I can't appreciate your point of view! If you killed those men, you killed them to obtain papers which you believed were necessary for the welfare of your country. Oh, it is not I who judge you! You did not do it, I know, for your own gain. You did it because you are, heart and soul, a patriot. But here, alas! they do not understand. Their whole standpoint is different. They will judge you as they would a common criminal. You must fly,—you must, indeed!"

"Dear Miss Penelope," he said, "I cannot do that! I cannot run away like a thief in the dark. If this thing is to come, it must come."

"But you don't understand!" she continued, wringing her hands. "You think because you are a great prince and a prince of a friendly nation that the law will treat you differently. It will not! They have talked of it downstairs. You are not formally attached to any one in this country. You are not even upon the staff of the Embassy. You are here on a private mission as a private person, and there is no way in which the Government can intervene, even if it would. You are subject to its laws and you have broken them. For Heaven's sake, fly! You have your motor car here. Let your man drive you to Southampton and get on board the Japanese cruiser. You mustn't wait a single moment. I believe that tomorrow morning will be too late!"

He took her hands in his very tenderly and yet with something of reverence in his gesture. He looked into her eyes and he spoke very earnestly. Every word seemed to come from his heart.

"Dear Miss Penelope," he said, "it is very, very kind of you to have come here and warned me. Only you cannot quite understand what this thing means to me. Remember what I told you once. Life and death to your people in this country seem to be the greatest things which the mind of man can hold. It is not so with us. We are brought up differently. In a worthy cause a true Japanese is ready to take death by the hand at any moment. So it is with me now. I have no regret. Even if I had, even if life were a garden of roses for me, what is ordained must come. A little sooner or a little later, it makes no matter."

She sank on her knees before him.

"Can't you understand why I am here?" she cried passionately. "It was I who told of the silken cord and knife!"

He was wholly unmoved. He even smiled, as though the thing were of no moment.

"It was right that you should do so," he declared. "You must not reproach yourself with that."

"But I do! I do!" she cried again. "I always shall! Don't you understand that if you stay here they will treat you—"

He interrupted, laying his hand gently upon her shoulder.

"Dear young lady," he said, "you need never fear that I shall wait for the touch of your men of law. Death is too easily won for that. If the end which you have spoken of comes, there is another way—another house of rest which I can reach."

She rose slowly to her feet. The absolute serenity of his manner bespoke an impregnability of purpose before which the words died away on her lips. She realized that she might as well plead with the dead!

"You do not mind," he whispered, "if I tell you that you must not stay here any longer?"

He led her toward the door. Upon the threshold he took her cold fingers into his hand and kissed them reverently.

"Do not be too despondent," he said. "I have a star somewhere which burns for me. Tonight I have been looking for it. It is there still," he added, pointing to the wide open window. "It is there, undimmed, clearer and brighter than ever. I have no fear."

She passed away without looking up again. The Prince listened to her footsteps dying away in the corridor. Then he closed the door, and, entering his bedroom, undressed himself and slept...

When Prince Maiyo awoke on the following morning, the sunshine was streaming into the room, and his grave-faced valet was standing over his bed.

"His Highness' bath is ready," he announced.

The Prince dressed quickly and was first in the pleasant morning room, with its open windows leading on to the terrace. He strolled outside and wandered amongst the flower beds. Here he was found, soon afterwards, by the Duke's valet.

"Your Highness," the latter said, "His Grace has sent me to look for you. He would be glad if you could spare him a moment or two in the library."

The Prince followed the man to the room where his host was waiting for him. The Duke, with his hands behind his back, was pacing restlessly up and down the apartment.

"Good morning, Duke," the Prince said cheerfully. "Another of your wonderful spring mornings. Upon the terrace the sun is almost hot. Soon I shall begin to fancy that the perfume of your spring flowers is the perfume of almond and cherry blossom."

"Prince," the Duke said quietly, "I have sent for you as your host. I speak to you now unofficially, as an Englishman to his guest. I have been besieged through the night, and even this morning, with incomprehensible messages which come to me from those who administer the law in this country. Prince, I want you to remember that however effete you may find us as a nation from your somewhat romantic point of view, we have at least realized the highest ideals any nation has ever conceived in the administration of the law. Nobleman and pauper here are judged alike. If their crime is the same, their punishment is the same. There is no man in this country who is strong enough to arrest the hand of justice."

The Prince bowed.

"My dear Duke," he said, "it has given me very much pleasure, in the course of my investigations, to realize the truth of what you have just said. I agree with you entirely. You could teach us in Japan a great lesson on the fearless administration of the law. Now in some other countries—"

"Never mind those other countries," the Duke interrupted gravely. "I did not send for you to enter into an academic discussion. I want you clearly to understand how I am placed, supposing a distinguished member of my household—supposing even you, Prince Maiyo—were to come within the arm of the law. Even the great claims of hospitality would leave me powerless."

"This," the Prince admitted, "I fully apprehend. It is surely reasonable that the stranger in your country should be subject to your laws."

"Very well, then," the Duke continued. "Listen to me, Prince. This morning a London magistrate will grant what is called a search warrant which will enable the police to search, from attic to cellar, your house in St. James' Square. An Inspector from Scotland Yard will be there this afternoon awaiting your return, and he believes that he has witnesses who will be able to identify you as one who has broken the laws of this country. I ask you no questions. There is the telephone on the table. My eighty-horse-power Daimler is at the door and at your service. I understand that your cruiser in Southampton Harbor is always under steam. If there is anything more, in reason, that I can do, you have only to speak." The Prince shook his head slowly.

"Duke," he said, "please send away your car, unless it will take me to London quicker than my own. What I have done I have done, and for what I have done I will pay."

The Duke laid his hands upon the young man's shoulders and looked down into his face. The Duke was over six feet high, and broad in proportion. Before him the Prince seemed almost like a boy.

"Maiyo," he said, "we have grown fond of you,—my wife, my daughter, all of us. We don't want harm to come to you, but there is the American Ambassador watching all the time. Already he more than half suspects. For our sakes, Prince,—come, I will say for the sake of those who are grateful to you for your candor and truthfulness, for the lessons you have tried to teach us,—make use of my car. You will reach Southampton in half an hour."

The Prince shook his head. His lips had parted in what was certainly a smile. At the corners they quivered, a little tremulous.

"My dear friend," he said, and his voice had softened almost to affection, "you do not quite understand. You look upon the things which may come from your point of view and not from mine. Remember that, to your philosophy, life itself is the greatest thing born into the world. To us it is the least. If you would do me a service, please see that I am able to start for London in half an hour."

CHAPTER XXXIV.
BANZAI!

It was curious how the Prince's sudden departure seemed to affect almost every member of the little house party. At first it had been arranged that the Duke, Mr. Haviland, Sir Edward Bransome, and the Prince should leave in the former's car, the Prince's following later with the luggage. Then the Duchess, whose eyes had filled with tears more than once after her whispered conversation with her husband, announced that she, too, must go to town. Lady Grace insisted upon accompanying her, and Penelope reminded them that she was already dressed for travelling and that, in any case, she meant to be one of the party. Before ten o'clock they were all on their way to London.

The Prince sat side by side with Lady Grace, the other two occupants of the car being the Duke himself and Mr. Haviland. No one seemed in the least inclined for conversation. The Duke and Mr. Haviland exchanged a few remarks, but Lady Grace, leaning back in her seat, her features completely obscured by a thick veil, declined to talk to any one. The Prince seemed to be the only one who made any pretence at enjoying the beauty of the spring morning, who seemed even to be aware of the warm west wind, the occasional perfume of the hedgeside violets, and the bluebells which stretched like a carpet in and out of the belts of wood. Lady Grace's eyes, from beneath her veil, scarcely once left his face. Perhaps, she thought, these things were merely allegorical to him. Perhaps his eyes, fixed so steadfastly upon the distant horizon, were not, as it seemed, following the graceful outline of that grove of dark green pine trees, but were indeed searching back into the corners of his life, measuring up the good and evil of it, asking the eternal question—was it worth while?

In the other car, too, silence reigned. Somerfield was the only one who struggled against the general air of depression.

"After all," he remarked to Bransome, "I don't see what we're all so blue about. If Scotland Yard are right, and the Prince is really the guilty person they imagine him, I cannot see what sympathy he deserves. Of course, they look upon this sort of thing more lightly in his own country, but, after all, he was no fool. He knew his risks."

Penelope spoke for the first time since they had left Devenham.

"If you begin to talk like that, Charlie," she said, "I shall ask the Duchess to stop the car and put you down here in the road."

Somerfield laughed, not altogether pleasantly.

"Seven miles from any railway station," he remarked.

Penelope shrugged her shoulders.

"I should not care in the least what happened to you, today or at any other time," she declared.

After that, Somerfield held his peace, and a somewhat strained silence followed. Soon they reached the outskirts of London. Long before midday they slackened speed, after crossing Battersea Bridge, and the two cars drew alongside. They had arranged to separate here, but, curiously enough, no one seemed to care to start the leave taking.

"You see the time!" the Prince exclaimed. "It is barely eleven o'clock. I want you all, if you will, to come with me for ten minutes only to my house. Tomorrow it will be dismantled. Today I want you each to choose a keepsake from amongst my treasures. There are so many ornaments over here, engravings and bronzes which are called Japanese and which are really only imitations. I want you to have something, if you will, to remember me by, all of you, something which is really the handicraft of my country people."

The Duke looked for a moment doubtful.

"It wants an hour to midday," the Prince said, softly. "There is time."

They reached St. James' Square in a few minutes. There were no signs of disturbance. The door flew open at their approach. The same solemn-faced, quietly moving butler admitted them. The Prince led the way into the room upon the ground floor which he called his library.

"It is a fancy of mine," he said, smiling, "to say goodbye to you all here. You see that there is nothing in this room which is not really the product of Japan. Here I feel, indeed, as though I had crossed the seas and were back under the shadow of my own mountains. Here

I feel, indeed, your host, especially as I am going to distribute my treasures."

He took a picture from the wall and turned with it to the Duke.

"Duke," he said, "this engraving is a rude thing, but the hand which guided the steel has been withered for two hundred years, and no other example remains of its cunning. Mr. Haviland," he added, stepping to his writing table, "this lacquered shrine, with its pagoda roof, has been attributed to Kobo-Daishi, and has stood upon the writing table of seven emperors. Sir Edward, this sword, notwithstanding its strange shape and gilded chasing, was wielded with marvellous effect, if history tells the truth, a hundred and thirty years ago by my great-grandfather when he fought his way to the throne. Sir Charles, you are to go into Parliament. Some day you will become a diplomat. Some day, perhaps, you will understand our language. Just now I am afraid," he concluded, "this will seem to you but a bundle of purple velvet and vellum, but it is really a manuscript of great curiosity which comes from the oldest monastery in Asia, the Monastery of Koya-San."

He turned to the Duchess.

"Duchess," he said, "you see that my tapestries have already gone. They left yesterday for Devenham Castle. I hope that you will find a place there where you may hang them. They are a little older than your French ones, and time, as you may remember, has been kind to them. It may interest you to know that they were executed some thirteen hundred and fifty years ago, and are of a design which, alas, we borrowed from the Chinese."

The Prince paused for a moment. All were trying to express their thanks, but no one was wholly successful. He waved their words gently aside.

"Lady Grace," he said, turning to the statuette of Buddha in a corner of the room and taking from its neck a string of strange blue stones, "I will not ask you to wear these, for they have adorned the necks of idols for many centuries, but if you will keep them for my sake, they may remind you sometimes of the color of our skies."

Once more he went to his writing table. From it he lifted, almost reverently, a small bronze figure,—the figure of a woman, strongly built, almost squat, without grace, whose eyes and head and arms reached upwards.

"Miss Penelope," he said, "to you I make my one worthless offering. This statuette has no grace, no shapeliness, according to the canons of your wonderful Western art. Yet for five generations of my family it has been the symbol of our lives. We are not idol worshippers in Japan, yet one by one the men of my race have bent their knee before this figure and have left their homes to fight for the thing which she represents. She is not beautiful, she does not stand for the joys and the great gifts of life, but she represents the country which to us stands side by side with our God, our parents, and our Emperor. Nothing in life has been dearer to me than this, Miss Penelope. To no other person would I part with it."

She took it with a sudden hysterical sob, which seemed to ring out like a strange note upon the unnatural stillness of the room. And then there came a thing which happened before its time. The door was opened. Inspector Jacks came in. With him were Dr. Spencer Whiles and the man who a few days ago had been discharged from St. Thomas' Hospital. Of the very distinguished company who were gathered there, Inspector Jacks took little notice. His eyes lit upon the form of the Prince, and he drew a sigh of relief. The door was closed behind him, and he saw no way by which he could be cheated of his victory. He took a step forward, and the Prince advanced courteously, as though to meet him. The others, for those few seconds, seemed as though they had lost the power of speech or movement. Then before a word could be uttered by either the Inspector or the Prince, the door was opened from the outside, and a man came running in,—a man dressed in a shabby blue serge suit, dark and thin. He ran past the Inspector and his companions, and he fell on his knees before his master.

"I confess!" he cried. "It was I who climbed on to the railway car! It was I who stabbed the American man in the tunnel and robbed him of his papers! The others are innocent. Marki, who brought the car for me, knew nothing. Those who saw me return to this house knew nothing. No man was my confidant. I alone am guilty! I thought they could not discover the truth, but they have hunted me down. He is there—the doctor who bandaged my knee. I told him that it was a bicycle accident. Listen! It was I who killed the young American Vanderpole. I followed him from the Savoy Hotel. I dressed myself in the likeness of my master, and I entered his taxi as a pleasant jest.

Then I strangled him and I robbed him too! He saw me—that man!" Soto cried, pointing to the youth who stood at the Inspector's left hand. "He was on his bicycle. He skidded and fell through watching me. I told my master that I was in trouble, and he has tried to shield me, but he did not know the truth. If he had, he would have given me over as I give myself now. What I did I did because I love Japan and because I hate America!"

His speech ended in a fit of breathlessness. He lay there, gasping. The doctor bent forward, looking at him first in perplexity and afterwards in amazement. Then very slowly, and with the remnants of doubt still in his tone, he answered Inspector Jacks' unspoken question.

"He is the image of the man who came to me that night," he declared. "He is wearing the same clothes, too."

"What do you say?" the Inspector whispered hoarsely to the youth on his other side. "Don't hurry. Look at him carefully."

The young man hesitated.

"He is the same height and figure as the man I saw enter the taxi," he said. "I believe that it is he."

Inspector Jacks stepped forward, but the Prince held out his hand.

"Wait!" he ordered, and his voice was sterner than any there had ever heard him use. There was a fire in his eyes from which the man at his feet appeared to shrink.

"Soto," the Prince said, and he spoke in his own language, so that no person in that room understood him save the one whom he addressed,—"why have you done this?"

The man lay there, resting now upon his side, and supporting himself by the palm of his right hand. His upturned face seemed to have in it all the passionate pleading of a dumb animal.

"Illustrious Prince," he answered, speaking also in his own tongue, "I did it for Japan! Who are you to blame me, who have offered his own life so freely? I have no weight in the world. For you the future is big. You will go back to Japan, you will sit at the right hand of the Emperor. You will tell him of the follies and the wisdom of these strange countries. You will guide him in difficulties. Your hand will be upon his as he writes across the sheets of time, for the glory of the Motherland. Banzai, illustrious Prince! I, too, am of the immortals!"

He suddenly collapsed. The doctor bent over him, but the Prince shook his head slowly.

"It is useless," he said. "The man has confessed his crime. He has told me the whole truth. He has taken poison."

Lady Grace began to cry softly. The air of the room seemed heavy with pent-up emotions. The Prince moved slowly toward the door and threw it open. He turned towards them all.

"Will you leave me?" he asked. "I wish to be alone."

His eyes were like the eyes of a blind man.

One by one they left the room, Inspector Jacks amongst them. The only person who spoke, even in the hall, was the Inspector.

"It was the Prince who brought the doctor here," he muttered. "He must have known! At least he must have known!"

Mr. Haviland touched him on the arm.

"Inspector Jacks!" he whispered.

Inspector Jacks saluted.

"The murderer is dead," he continued, speaking still under his breath. "Silence is a wonderful gift, Mr. Jacks. Sometimes its reward is greater even than the reward of action."

They passed from the house, and once more its air of deep silence was unbroken. The Prince stood in the middle of that strange room, whose furnishings and atmosphere seemed, indeed, so marvellously reminiscent of some far distant land. He looked down upon the now lifeless figure, raised the still, white fingers in his for a moment, and laid them reverently down. Then his head went upward, and his eyes seemed to be seeking the heavens.

"So do the great die," he murmured. "Already the Gods of our fathers are calling you Soto the Faithful. Banzai!"